THORNS & ROSES

THORNS & ROSES

Isaac Hallenberg

Library of Congress Control Number:		2006909298
ISBN 10:	Hardcover	1-4257-3966-0
	Softcover	1-4257-3965-2
ISBN 13:	Hardcover	978-1-4257-3966-9
	Softcover	978-1-4257-3965-2

This book was printed in the United States of America.

To order additional copies of this book, contact:
Xlibris Corporation
1-888-795-4274
www.Xlibris.com
Orders@Xlibris.com
36129

Dedicated to my wife, who has shared many of my
adventures and misadventures.

STORIES FROM UNCENSORED SEASONS

Good stories are patch-up jobs,
like sixties' blue-jeans, like life.
Old pants and true tales
are a personal archeology,
digs down to dancing or dangerous memories;
a piece from your first son's shirt,
a bit from your brother's slacks,
a snatch from your wife's red blouse,
a scrap from that ratty old jacket,
things long loved and time-lost,
faded fabric fantasies.
Every sewn-in something
was cut from the gut.
The best is worn from wear,
becoming more meaningful than material.

Such stories are not silk underwear.
They are not fit for fine, fat, Victorian butts.
They wear well on blues singers,
brick layers, bong bringers,
bar tenders, back-door men.
They are stories kids chase,
bright as the patch on Johnny Nolan's ass,
rough patches on knees not made for kneeling,
crotch patches cut from
Joseph's coat of many colors,
stories you read with coffee in the kitchen,
stories good for Irish oration,
beer-stained stories from the people's pub,
good-by harder tales,
race track recitations
where stumblebums bet in the boiler room,
stories for smiling poker players
and old jakes with jaundiced eyes.
Here is knuckle truth.
Sometimes the magic happens.

Sometimes the guru is found
in a back alley with broken bottles.
Forget the fireside chat,
all politic and spit polish.
Angels could come dressed in drag.
Thorns are a rose's closest lover.
Zen heaven is an uncensored season.
Time goes midnight creeping
while sacred sleaze
mixes with sentimental suchness.

Real stories only the heart remembers.

Lasse Hallenberg (Steve Hanson)

PART ONE

THE PAST AS PROLOGUE

He who kisses the joy as it flies
Lives in eternity's sunrise.
William Blake

"Giddup Bob—c'mawn Joe, giddup Bob—c'mawn Joe." I must have been about eight years old at the time, looking out from the second-story window of the bedroom that I shared with my brother, and watching as our neighbor, Sampson Sims, plowed his field with a team of horses. Calling their names over and over, the big black man snapped the reins and urged them on. The field was across from the rutted gravel road that ran by our place. I should have taken a picture or got a longer look, because in an instant, or so it seems now, Sampson's plow and horses disappeared from the Midwest farm landscape. One holdout, a Redlsheimer who farmed to the south of us, was still plowing with horses, but with the coming of the Second World War technology and tractors had replaced even his team. The iron-wheeled tractors were forbidden use of the roads by the many signs that read "Use No Lugs." Neither reading nor heeding, some of the farmers drove on, leaving slashes in the tar of Newell Avenue where their iron wheels had gone. And the horses, where had they gone? We joked about aged horses and aged relatives going to the glue factory, but in our little neighborhood they probably ended up at Stuyvesant's farm where, when the wind was right, the neighborhood was reminded that Mr. Stuyvesant kept minks. Once while I was visiting there, a gaggle of young Stuyvesants led me to the plow horse repository, and I was stunned to see hideless horses, pink and glistening, hanging from a rafter in the barn. The immense animals had been gutted, skinned, and hung upside down using a block and tackle, awaiting their fate as Mister Stuyvesant's mink food. The mink skins were stored in a trunk like the steamer trunks hauled by immigrants to the promised land. The pelts were stiff after being scraped of fat and then dried on metal stretchers. Before the mice and rats could get to them, the pelts were sold to a buyer, eventually finding their way into coats for the lady friends of well-heeled gentlemen. Missus Styvesant labored on in a faded cotton housedress, Oshkoshes, and an old cloth coat for the cold weather, never to have so much as a mink shawl draped around her bent shoulders. The Stuyvesants had nine children and lived on eighty acres, which probably helped shape Mary's attitude. She was the oldest, and when I was sitting with her one day, by a pond in the newly developed subdivision next to their farm, a carful of young girls went speeding past. She called them "rich bitches" and it wasn't so much the term she used as the edge in her voice that startled me.

Anyway, Sampson Sims encouraged his horses until they passed out of sight, shielded from view by our apple trees, heading up toward Sederholm's house on the corner of our gravel road and Newell Avenue, the paved road that was our artery to greater horizons. As Sampson and his team left, purple grackles and blackbirds showed up to breakfast on the exposed worms. The stubble of last year's corn was turned under and the soil was dark and shiny as crow's wings. The birds arrived without bidding, as by some process still unknown to humans, they knew when a meal was ready. My mother, hoping for a similar response, called me to breakfast with a "Hurry up. You'll be late for school if you don't hurry."

The land across the gravel road belonged to the Sederholms, and was farmed on shares, with Pa, Mister Sims and Mister Mirando all wanting the use of it. Mister Sederholm had no equipment to plant his acreage, and not much interest in working. He was rumored to have witnessed a terrible accident at a long forgotten job, and spent his days in a haze of alcohol-fueled forgetfulness. At one time he almost finished a wooden sauna east of the house, with plans to charge admission to anyone wanting a sauna bath and a cedar whacking. The project was never completed, and the building stood there unused, yellowed and in increasing disrepair. I don't think that anyone ever took a sauna in his building. Finally, and inevitably, the Sederholms died and the house was sold, but before all this happened, Pa had had the use of the land for a year. After the tenancies of Pa and Sampson Sims, the Mirandos took over and raised corn and soybeans on the acreage. They planted tomatoes on their own property, and sold bushels of them through an ad in the local paper. Pa still coveted the use of that land and would stand by the parlor window, watching them. "Lookit," he said, "Missus Mirando is out picking tomatoes. In those floppy old rags she looks like a scarecrow." Her husband putted around the field so slowly that it looked as if he might plow up a sleeping ground hog. "Hhmmph," my father snorted, looking out at the Ford 9N, certain that he could have done a better job with his Allis Chalmers. "He's goin' so slow that he'll never get it done before fall."

Sampson Sims lived with his wife and his animals down a lane on the other side of the gravel road. The couple had probably raised children, long since dispersed to town, and by the early 1940's he seemed one of the ancients to me. As time passed, Sampson and his wife moved into the Cannondale subdivision, closer to town. I heard the rumor that he lived to be over 100 years old. The weathered two-track lane was later covered with asphalt and a new brick house built on the property. We knew that the family living there was in for a surprise. Every few years or so came a big rain, and running through our pasture was a ditch we called the gully. Normally dry, when we first moved out there it was deep enough that a child standing in the ditch couldn't be seen from our house. During a big rain the gully became a fast-moving muddy river, aimed directly down a slight decline toward Sampson's house. He and his wife took to sleeping on their kitchen table when the spring rains came, the torrent rolling past them on the kitchen floor. A bane to the Sims, the rain was a blessing to me and my little brother, exposing the glittery pieces of quartz that hid in the gully bank. We pored over the sparkly beauties for hours, picking, choosing, then carrying our treasures back up to the house, where we stored them in old Maxwell House cans. The greatest find one summer was an orange rock, smaller than a basketball, bigger than a baseball, and big enough to require some planning to get it back home. With the help of my red wagon and a great sense of purpose, I brought back the rock and placed it by the front porch, where it became a feature in Ma's flower garden. Pa's plan was to fill in the gully by throwing garbage, old bottles, busted concrete blocks and the like at twenty foot intervals. As time passed, and as the rains came, the gully started to fill with good, black dirt from the farm in back of ours.

Sampson Sims and his wife lived in a shack made of cast-off material he'd picked up here and there and put to good use, long before anyone had heard the word "recycling". My brother and I liked to race down the lane toward his house, slamming on our coaster brakes at the last possible moment. The prospect of peeking in on a life so different from our own held both fright and fascination. "Hey! What you kids doin' here?" was a standard greeting from the shack at the end of the lane. We did get close enough to see his pet raccoon, kept in a cage filled so high with turds that the poor 'coon could only pace back and forth, scraping his head on the cage ceiling. Another way to the shack was by going down the end of our street to the railroad tracks, swinging open the iron gate, and heading toward town on the tracks. We'd always feel a shiver of excitement when we were on foot, since we knew he kept a pack of dogs. We'd sneak up close enough to watch as Sampson fed them. "Heaahh Lobo, Heaahh One-Eye," he'd call, and as he bent over to give them their food, another three or four scruffy mutts would come running. I've long since forgotten their names, but Sampson knew each dog as well as Santa Claus knew his reindeer. No doubt the old man chuckled and shook his head at the little white boys peeking through the weeds, but he paid us no mind.

One time, when I was walking down toward Sampson's, my nose led me to the remains of a large black animal decomposing in the summer heat. Fueled by reading old issues of The National Geographic, my imagination informed me that this was the carcass of a large black bear. There was no denying it, and no sense in getting too close, either, as more might be lurking close by. I turned and ran back to the farm, where an eternity passed before Pa came home from work, to hear about my discovery. After I told him, Pa walked me down the road to the railroad tracks and up to the carcass. He saw right away that this was the body of a large black dog. I should have known, since bear sightings in our area of Illinois were a thing of the remote past. Although my brother and I continued our secret shack-watching, we never heard Mr. Sims call Lobo's name again.

To feed his pigs, Sampson Sims collected lettuce leaves and rotting fruit from local produce markets. There were several produce stands and truck gardens around town, owned by Greek families who made daily runs to Market Street in Chicago for fresh produce. Except for the A&P grocery stores, there were no supermarkets near us, and the produce stands were our main source of potatoes and fresh fruit. Mister Sims transported the garbage back to his pigs in an old truck missing so many wooden stakes that fallout was inevitable. Piles of fermenting fruit and slimy lettuce used to litter the road in front of our drive, rekindling the simmering feud between the intractable African and the implacable Scandinavian, with us kids sent out to shovel the mess into the ditch. Things usually heated up even more in spring when the rains turned our gravel road to quicksand and Sampson's truck, midway between our house and the paved road, would hunker down in the mud. Not able to get around it, Pa and Uncle Julian had to park their cars on Newell Avenue and walk.

Sampson's Hampshire pigs stayed relatively unsatisfied with their diet of slippery lettuce leaves, and often escaped to our place to forage for apples. We didn't spray our trees, and consequently the apples had more than enough wiggly protein, not to mention that we had a lot of drops—apples falling from the tree before their time. The variety was Duchess, an early apple that made a pretty fine pie. All this juicy goodness was more than Sampson's pets could resist, and they came often to feed at our "trough". Hearing them work their way through the orchard usually stirred our dog, Prince, into action, but the Hampshires proved too much for our trusty friend. Ever a fan of apple pie, Pa came up with a solution to the unfettered pig problem. When he was a youngster, Pa's mother had always warned him about playing with "that bad Billy Wilson". As an adult, however, Billy had found the "right" side of the law to be more profitable, so he changed his allegiance, and, on the way, picked up the name of "Lucky". A quick phone call to Lucky Wilson, now an officer in the sheriff's department, and a visit was made to our neighborhood, a rare occurrence for a county official. A shiny black police car drove down the lane to Sampson's shack, and the porcine apple raids were a thing of the past.

On the west side of our house was a vineyard of concord grapes and a wooden shack that Pa built called the "brooder house" where, for the first few weeks of life, the baby chicks lived under a brooder stove to keep warm. It had little cloth curtains on the side so that the chicks could go in and out. On the outside was their feed and water, the water turned purple by the addition of potassium permanganate. My mother always spoke, in hushed tones, of the dreaded coccidiosis which could carry off these little chicks in no time at all. (They would be carried off at some point, without doubt, but at Ma's discretion.) Baby chicks can only be purchased through the mail now, delighting the postal clerks who process them, but on our farm we were still able to buy from a local hatchery on North Illinois Street. After plunking down our money, we carried the chicks home in a cardboard box fitted with circular holes about the size of a quarter. My brother and I saved the boxes and colored the cardboard circles, using them for play money. We would peek into the brooder house often to observe the soft little wonders and listen to them cheeping. When their downy tuft was replaced by discernible feathers, we removed the brooder stove.

Where the grape vines used to grow were rows of blackened fence posts with wires stretched between them. Pa had started a fire to burn out some weeds, but it got out of control and burned up the vineyard. On the other side of the fence was a dwelling converted from a former chicken house, with a few tumbledown outbuildings, all on five or six acres of weeds. The fence line between the properties was full of brambles and cover that proved to be an excellent source of rabbits, when I was old enough to hunt. Unerringly, the rabbits would run onto the neighbor's property, forcing me to shoot from the wrong side of the fence. I had to retrieve my game carefully, fearful that someone might be at home next door, and I learned the "low crawl" early on. Before the rabbit got stiff and cold, I would hurry to the basement where I skinned it after hanging the rabbit on the coal bin door. There were two nails driven into the door, and the game was hung upside down by tying its legs with twine. By supper time we were eating fried rabbit, taking care not to bite down on the scattered lead shot.

When we first moved to the country, an old man and his nephew lived on the place next door. Periodically, the nephew made sabbaticals to the mental institution in Aglin, the so-called "funny farm". Although we never saw him in daylight, we would often find large footprints in our garden, left there as he roamed the fields in darkness. In my mind's eye he was eight feet tall, a gaunt and bony specter, dressed all in black, and wearing a stove pipe hat.

Only once did the nephew appear to us in daylight. My brother and I were out playing on our gravel road, traffic being scarce in those days, and it must been after a recent rain, since we were sailing little wooden boats in a puddle A large man, though not nearly eight feet in height, strode by without acknowledging us. We kept our eyes glued on the boats, not daring to look up until long after he had passed. Only later in the day, when Pa came home from work, did we learn that our next door neighbor had gone to the back of the house, knocked on the screen door, and, when Ma answered, had asked her for the loan of some matches. Ma said that she was all out, and he left. Many nights thereafter I lay awake, picturing the nephew with a handful of matches, and wondering what I would do if the house caught fire. Adding to my worries at the time was the chapter book that Ma was reading to us, that old classic, Black Beauty. The story of a horse, it also included the vivid description of a barn fire from which, luckily, Beauty escapes. This gave me renewed hope, each time my mind revisited the scene, and the long drop from our second story bedroom window seemed not so daunting after all. As with most worries, though, nothing came to pass, and neither our house nor our neighbor's burned. The garden footprints disappeared, the uncle and his nephew moved away, and were never heard from again.

The place went up for sale, and I remember my father saying they wanted too much for it. The price, if I remember correctly, was twenty-five hundred dollars. Whoever owned it said they wanted to give Pa first chance to buy the property, before turning it over to a real estate company. Pa said since it used to be a chicken house, the place wasn't worth what they were asking. As I write this, I remember an old friend recently telling me that the chicken house dwelling is but a memory, replaced with a palatial four hundred thousand dollar house. After the old man and his nephew disappeared, Doctor Stubblefield, who practiced medicine in Chicago, bought the property. A large jovial man, we referred to him, in accordance with the times, as the "Colored Doc". He fixed up the old place, adding a small pond with a weeping willow on its bank, and ducks and geese floating there. Since he lived in Chicago, where he had his practice, Doc Stubblefield was only there on weekends, usually accompanied by one or more of his girlfriends. Sometimes workers showed up with him, probably indentured for payment of medical bills incurred by themselves or some family member. They were put to work painting, planting, doing repairs. We would often sneak up to the fence and observe the hapless workers chopping with their hoes after the Doc had planted a field of corn. He was a large bald-headed man given to wearing a white shirt, even when it wasn't Sunday. He told Ma and Pa if we kids ever needed appendectomies, he would be happy to provide the service. Since Chicago was a long way to travel with a rupturing appendix, we were relieved that ours remained intact. When the Doc wasn't there, we tormented his tom turkey by "gobbling" at him as we walked past the place on our way home from school. The old tom puffed himself up and gobbled right back at us.

In pig-free intervals we had the apple orchard to ourselves. Uncle Julian, Pa's bachelor brother, was full of ideas, and showed us how to dig a hole in the ground, line it and layer the apples in straw. Later we would dig up our stash and bite into the apples, still crisp and fresh. Unbeknownst to our parents, he showed us how to make "apple jack" We fermented apple juice in glass bottles with a balloon placed on top. That way air wouldn't get to the cider and turn it to vinegar. We added yeast and extra sugar just to make sure that the "apple jack" would have plenty of horsepower. The balloons on the top of the bottles gradually expanded from the carbon dioxide produced, and when fermentation had stopped, we took the bottles from their hiding place in the barn out to our hut. The bottles now held a golden liquid hazy with floating sediment and, we assured each other, plenty of kick. In back of the farm, next to the barbed-wire fence and under a large mulberry tree, my brother and I together with some of the neighborhood boys, had built our hut, constructed from whatever we could scrounge up: old gunny sacks, rolled tar paper, scraps of wood. We even incorporated an old window, and through it could see the Doc's field hands out hoeing. In summer, we couldn't be seen or heard from the house, shielded by distance and by Pa's corn field. Made braver by uncorking and drinking the murky nectar of fermented apple juice, we'd crawl out from the hut and sing all the scurrilous songs we could muster. The doc's field hands would stop, look up from their work, and then ignore us. Lacking an attentive audience or an extensive repertoire, we'd soon retreat to the hut and laze away the rest of the afternoon. Not long afterward, Pa burned down the hut, claiming that it was at Mister Clark's insistence. He was our neighbor to the back, with a large dairy farm, and his son was one of our hut-building crew. No doubt he told Will, his son, that the burning was Mr. Hallenberg's idea.

Before we moved to the farm, we lived in a tiny house in the Bedford Park subdivision. The depression of the 1930's was still making gainful employment hard to find, and my father was lucky enough to be working three days a week in the foundry. The basement of the house had been dug, some years before, by using a team of horses, and the house built with the aid of a retired Swedish carpenter and an army of relatives. Many years later Pa would snort in disgust at the thought of people living together in "hippie communes". Although he didn't see it that way, we had had our own little commune, with any number people inhabiting our little bungalow, living together in a scant 900 square feet of space, the only requisite for inclusion being Hallenberg blood. Uncle Julian and Little Grandma, Pa's mother, were a constant, and at other times uncles and aunts came and went, blown about by the changing winds of economic exigency. None of my mother's family members ever stayed with us. Their favored perch was with Ma's folks, because grandpa had a steady job with the railroad. Grandma was called "Big Grandma" out of contrast to my Grandma Hallenberg, who was so much smaller in size that we dubbed her "Little Grandma". Big Grandma may have visited us when we lived in Bedford Park, but I don't remember seeing her until we were living on the farm. There was ill will between my father and his wife's family. Pa said that they didn't like him because he had taken away their only good wage earner. Ma had worked in the foundry with my father, but when she got married, she threw away her work boots. After moving to the farm, she started working harder than ever, but she and Pa saw their labor as meaningful. One of my parent's sayings was "as lazy as sin". Hard work was seen as something ordained by God.

Little Grandma had divorced Grandpa Hallenberg before I was born. Uncle Julian would take us to visit Grandpa at his house, next door to our uncle Ansgar's. Since Pa disdained the company of not only his father-in-law but of his own father as well, it was up to Uncle Julian to keep the lines of communication open. Grandpa Hallenberg had an addiction to strong drink. I had heard many times the stories of grandpa's love of music, inspired and fueled, as is so often the case, by the muse of alcohol. Pa said that Grandpa had bought a pump organ which he tended to play while he was drinking. As the songs grew sadder and more contemplative, his head would nod and sink lower and lower, until they'd find him, in the morning, with his head resting heavily on the keyboard. Grandpa made his own beer, using malt and the wild hops he gathered along the railroad tracks. He had a still where he made hard liquor from a mash of potatoes. Pa said that Grandpa was reported to have seen a *tomptegubbe*, a kind of Swedish leprechaun, and had strolled with him, deep in conversation. Having little use for leprechauns, or *tompte* either, the family assumed it was just another alcohol-charged chimera. Grandpa's house was even smaller than ours, and his water came from a pitcher pump on the drain board of the sink. It had to be primed by pouring in water before each use, then pumping the handle so that water poured into the sink. We were told not to drink the water there because the well point was driven down using only a few sections of pipe, producing only surface water and because, since there was no indoor toilet, the privy was just a stone's throw from the house. The summers were hot and when we went to visit, we'd find Grandpa in the cool dark basement of his little house, listening to old 78 rpm's on his gramophone. After each play it was necessary to rewind the spring, cranking it by hand, a job we loved. The records were in Swedish, no doubt stirring forgotten memories of better days, those memories enriched and bettered by the passage of time. The music was so mournful, sadder even than the choral dirges sung in our church. He had made the case for the records himself, out of old posters from the Washington Park race track, since burned to the ground. I was only four or five at the time, but I wondered why anyone would live in a damp basement. My only real memory of him was when he looked down at my brother and me from an immense height and said, "You kids are sooo entelliyent." And then he died. If only I could have known Grandpa Hallenberg longer. If only I could have known Ma's father better. Now that I am a grandfather, I see that young children need and enjoy the savvy and spark that a grandpa can bring to their lives. Grandpa Hallenberg's funeral was held at Sunbum's Funeral Home instead of Swanson's, from where all the old country Swedes were launched. Sunbum's was cheaper. I was too young to understand what was happening, but the flowers smelled wonderful. Uncle Julian told me later that there was an old man who came to the wake, and when asked how he knew Grandpa Hallenberg, the man replied that he didn't know him at all, he'd just come to smell the flowers.

When my brother was born, I remember my parents standing in the door, looking at a little bundle of blankets with a face peeking out. They were beaming at him, and, leaning over for my inspection, asked what I thought of him. "Take him back where he came from," I said. But they didn't, and instead moved me into a bedroom with Little Grandma. She was stooped over from a disintegrating spine and wore dresses that concealed whatever shape she may have had when young. I never saw her without an apron. She used it for everything: she wiped her hands on it, polished fruit with it, and wrung the daylights out of it when she was worried or upset. I never remember her taking a bath. She didn't smell bad, but had a scent that suggested talcum and old musty paper. Little Grandma and Uncle Julian had lived with us for as long as I could remember, but by the time I was four and my brother was born, I remember other Hallenbergs showing up for intermittent stays. Aunt Virginia, the career woman, had moved to San Francisco, and flew back to Chicago on the big four-engine planes of that era. She came to visit and brought us silver dollars she had won in Las Vegas, having stopped there to gamble before coming on to Chicago. In my world she was a true exotic, with big red painted lips exuding great clouds of smoke from her Lucky Strikes. In San Francisco, she lived with another woman in Chinatown. My parents spoke of how she could have married one of the rich and well connected Allingtons, who owned farms outside of Rustbelt City. He was quite some catch, according to my parents, and they failed to understand the appeal of what they perceived as her dissolute life as an unmarried woman in California, far from home.

Aunt Fanny came back to visit from Kansas City, where she had moved after marrying. She had had bad luck with husbands. Her first died in the Spanish flu epidemic of 1918, while he was in the army. The flu carried off more people than were killed in the war. Subsequent husbands carried themselves off, the most recent one having put on his hat and left, to work construction jobs in Anchorage, Alaska. Every time one of her children came to visit, Little Grandma was overjoyed and, when they took their leave, she would stand at the back door wringing her apron and crying "I'll never see them again." In the ensuing years the scene would be repeated, as each of her far-flung visitors came and left. She lived to be just short of one hundred and three. All six of her children were there for her funeral.

Uncle Ansgar was the most vocal and aggressive member of Pa's family. Around town he was known as Squawk, but the one time I used the nickname, my father angrily corrected me, saying I was never to call Uncle Ansgar by that name. Pa said that's what the Polacks called him when he went to work as a section hand on the local railroad. He was only fourteen and his voice was still changing when he picked up his sledge hammer and left to repair the tracks. The hands were commonly called "gandy dancers." My only run-in with them happened when my brother and I were walking the railroad tracks to the creek, with our poles over our shoulders and our "minnie" bucket in hand. If we caught any fish, we threw them into the minnow bucket, along with some water, to keep them more or less preserved until we got them home and cleaned them for supper. We didn't hear the section hands approaching on the tracks behind us, on their hand-propelled cart, and were startled to hear a large florid-faced man yelling at us. "That's the way ten thousand kids get killed every year" he screamed. Experience having been a better teacher than our mother's admonitions to be careful, we continued to use the tracks to get to the creek but from then on always looked behind us. The train on that line only came by once a day, and one of the engineers was our grandfather. In those days, of course, it was a steam engine, and Uncle Julian called it the "Toonerville Trolley" after a weekly cartoon strip in the newspapers. We called them the funny papers back in those days and they came as part of the Sunday papers.

When World War II began, Uncle Ansgar got a job as a guard at the ammunition plant, thanks to the priority hiring of soldiers who had been in the Great War. The job must have come with fringe benefits, as that year my brother and I wore new black pea jackets to school. In our upstairs closet we had a wooden box labeled as machine gun ammunition, but filled with office supplies to be used for school. The only stipulation for use was to dummy up should any classmates ask where the items were purchased.

Uncle Ansgar showed up at our house on Sundays, spiffed up and wearing a clean white shirt. It was, to our knowledge, used only for Sunday visits to his mother, as the last time that he'd entered a church was on his confirmation day. The same was true for Uncle Julian. but he'd gone one step further and no longer owned a white shirt. Since Rustbelt City in those days was a city of immigrants, most of the church services weren't in English. The children of Grandma and Grandpa Hallenberg were all confirmed at the Swedish Lutheran Church and in the mother tongue. Uncle Ansgar's Sunday visits were preceded by a loud banging and pounding on the door, and announced with a raucous "It's Barnacle Bill from over the hill." Pa usually ignored him. Since our uncle made no pretense of social niceties but came for the sole purpose of seeing his dear little mother (lilla mor), one of us would have to open the door to him. He would breeze in, wrapped in a haze of cheap whiskey and Marvel cigarettes. The stench of a smoldering Marvel, once inhaled, is never to be forgotten; it was, at that time, the cheapest brand of all the tailor made cigarettes. Lacking even enough money for packs of Marvels, there was always a sack of Bull Durham tobacco to be purchased, along with papers, to roll your own smokes. Our uncle was a large red-haired man, with hands so huge that one of them could cover the face of a grown man. He went straight to Little Grandma, who looked so tiny, sitting upright with anticipation in her big yellow rocking chair. Uncle Ansgar would wax maudlin when talking to his mother, holding her bony hands, staring into her face and calling her "*lilla mor*" (little mother). He must have been a favorite of hers, but the kindly young man, when he returned home from his tour of the trenches, trenches filled with cooties and blood, was somewhat unhinged. To protect himself from the soldiers of Kaiser Bill, he slept with his trench knife at the ready, and awoke at attention to stab the wall. Every year, sure as clockwork, Uncle Ansgar would appear on Mother's Day, the largest and gaudiest card that money could buy clutched in his outsize mitts. Adorned with ribbons, dried flowers, satin pillows and wafting a fragrance even the Marvels couldn't conceal, the card would be presented to Lilla Mor. Despite Ma and Pa having dutifully and happily fed and clothed her, which they would continue to do for the better part of 50 years, Little Grandma thought the sun rose and set on her Ansgar. And Uncle Ansgar, though he had long ago unburdened himself from the strictures of organized religion, remembered well the story of Mary and Martha.

As the years went on, my brother and I were to hear all about Uncle Ansgar's many exploits from Bill Harrigan, one of our fellow card players in the back room at Sofie's Club House. Once a week we'd gather to play poker at Sofie's, a restaurant and pizza parlor owned by Sofia and Armando Miglorini. Armando, known to us as Squash, used to work with our uncle at the wallpaper mill when jobs in Rustbelt City were easy to come by. Our uncle was a natural target for torment since he had a short fuse and consistently rose to the bait. Bill and Squash said they used to eat out of Uncle Ansgar's lunch bucket when he wasn't looking. Squash said our uncle would turn around, grab him by the collar and lift him up off the floor. Then he'd ask if Squash was the one who ate half of his sandwich. Not smelling any peanut butter on Squash's breath, Uncle Ansgar considered him to be not guilty. It was a while before Squash realized that he would always be first in the interrogation lineup since he was short and not very heavy. They told us that when the shift was over, Uncle Ansgar elbowed everybody out of the way so that he would be first in line at the time clock, and first to punch out. On a dead run, he'd grab his coat from the hook on the wall and take off. Hoping for disaster, Squash and Bill nailed his coat to the wall one day, and watched as Uncle Ansgar, with a great tearing sound, fell down, clutching pieces of torn coat in his hands. When I told Pa what the old men at Sofie's had related to us, Pa just said that his brother had always been a bully.

Uncle Julian lived with us until our sister was ready for her own room, at which point he moved to the house that used to be Grandpa Hallenberg's. We could usually find Uncle Julian at the end of a smoke curl, as he smoked a pipe and was continually relighting it. Pa thought he smoked matches instead of tobacco. When Uncle Julian laughed, he blew out on the pipe, scattering hot coals down the front of his shirt and pants, with the constant appearance of having been shot at and hit. When he went to town he proudly wore the big and heavy, black, shiny shoes he called police shoes. The rest of us called them clod hoppers. Uncle Julian never married, and his major source of entertainment, as far as I knew, was going downtown on Saturday nights. He took in a movie at one of the many theaters in town, and ate a hot tamale on the way home. At night after work, he'd sit up in his room and listen to his short wave radio, usually a station in Havana, Cuba. He ran a wire out of the second story window, stretching for a hundred feet out to a tree in the apple orchard. On special occasions, he invited us kids in to his room to hear the short wave radio whistle and buzz. His favorite spot on the dial was Radio Cuba. Nailed to the side of the garage next to his car was an auto license plate that read "Cuba", and that was the closest he ever got to the palm trees and sunny beaches of his promised land, the land that he dreamed about. In his entire life he never left the county in which he was born. I was envious of his movie-going. We lived in the country, and since our frugal Pa did not cotton to "foolishness", we could count on one hand the number of movies we had seen. Uncle Julian was fond of cowboy movies and, to satisfy my curiosity and avoid having to escort us to the movies, he said that the cowboys really didn't do too much. "They just ride around on a stage," he told me. Expecting to see live cowboys on real horses galloping across the wooden stage at the front of the theater, I was surprised to find, upon finally going to a movie, that they actually were riding in a Wells Fargo stage coach, six-guns a-blazing, up on a flickering movie screen.

There were two archetypes in our familial gene pool: the short, eccentric folks with dark hair and long noses; and the large, eccentric folks with red-hair and short tempers. Uncle Julian was of the former stock, with dark hair that didn't show gray until almost the end of his life, and a long nose that was bent over and crooked. In fact, his beak was so long that he could swipe the end of it with his tongue, a feat of some distaste to me now, but amazing when we were kids. When I asked him how his nose got that way he told me,"I was running in the dark, and ran into a barbed wire fence." I watched with interest and studied how he put away his pipe, tobacco, and matches into something called a smoking stand. About three feet high, it had a glass ash tray on top of a wooden body. The doors opened easily, and were never locked. The matches fascinated me, hissing and glowing with a yellow flame when struck. Then Uncle Julian would tip them upside down over his pipe and he would make these strange sucking sounds. The tobacco glowed red, the match was tipped up, and my uncle blew hard on the match. Thinking to repeat this performance, but in relatively delicious privacy, I set about to convince my younger brother to give it a try. Instead of lighting just one match, the entire book went up in flames and he let out a terrible wail. The smoking stand disappeared from the parlor. Years later, match companies put the striker on the opposite side of the matchbook, saving the fingers of many a younger brother.

The matchbook episode happened at the Bedford Park house, before we moved to the country. The back yard was a small one, like those of our neighbors, and had a sandbox and swing. In the days of having to push hand mowers, my father thought the yard was just the right size. Billy and Eunice Lawndale lived on the corner, and they were my first playmates. They had me lie down on their back porch where they said they were going to play doctor, and perform an operation on me. Sensibly enough, I got scared and ran home before they could cut off anything essential. To put me at ease, Billy invited me back to his house where he took me to his bedroom. He opened up a dresser drawer where he kept his treasured gum wrappers, and offered me a sniff. The silvery treasures were from packages of Juicy Fruit and Spearmint, from which the gum had long disappeared. But the smell remained.

On the north side of the house lived the Swansons. Bud Swanson was a local amateur athlete, and the first time my young eyes beheld him in his baseball uniform, I thought he was a clown. My parents told me that, no, he was only going to play in a softball game. Pa and Uncle Julian hadn't gotten along with the Swansons ever since our snapping turtle came up missing. One Saturday when the Hallenberg grownups returned from fishing, the catch of the day was a large snapping turtle. Having caught the monster in a muddy river and wrestled it home, they put it into a wash tub of clean water to soak out the silt. Coming out to admire their prize the next morning, they found the tub empty. Naturally, they blamed their next door neighbor and hard feelings ensued, as the thought of turtle soup, especially at the right price, had had their taste buds tingling.

Like most little boys, I couldn't wait to grow up and, sensing I was ready, Ma sent me on my first big errand. I was to go to the grocery store on Beale Street, the next street to the east of us. She gave me a note to present to the butcher, a man named Gus Carlson, for some ground beef for supper. I got to the store alright, but when I walked in, the man with the blood stained white apron looked huge, looming above the counter. He leaned over and said, "So vat can I do for you, sonny?" Speechless with fear, and unable to hold up the crumpled paper in my hand, I panicked and left, squeaking out a quick "Nothing, thank you" as I turned and ran out the door. When my mother arrived, looking for me, I was playing in the dirt alongside the store with a neighborhood kid named Skinny or Stinky or some such nickname I've forgotten. Ma went into the store to get the order, then came out, took my hand and led me home. It was my first big failure in life.

By the back door was a wooden bench with an arbor of climbing roses growing over it. We didn't live very far from the Stoney Island railroad tracks. Down in the ravine by the tracks was a wooded area, known to be a hobo jungle. The common wisdom was that hobos marked the houses where families lived who were generous enough to share food with those who were down and out. I was standing at the back door while Little Grandma was feeding one of these homeless men. He was enjoying a meal of roast beef and potatoes with gravy. In amazement, I watched as he pulled out a large knife, speared a potato on the end of it, and popped the entire potato into his mouth. I was shocked, as my parents would never have allowed me to spear a potato or eat it whole. Grandma stood and watched him while he ate, twisting her apron with pleasure at his joy as he ate on, oblivious to the small boy and the little old lady watching him.

Grandma wanted to feed people. She told me that in Europe, when she was a little girl, she asked her father if there was anything to eat. "Go up in the hills and look for lingonberries," she was told. There was a famine in Scandinavia at the time, and that experience of hunger colored the rest of her long life. Instead of hoarding food, she wanted to see everyone eat. Well into her nineties she baked all the bread for our family, and would cut off slices with a knife while balancing the oval loaf on her hip. Bread had kept her alive, she said, on her long journey from Sweden to America, when she had set out with only a few pieces of meat and two loaves. A family by the name of Wallberg sponsored her, and in return for her passage she worked as a cook. She went on to work for a wealthy old Rustbelt City family until her marriage to Grandpa Hallenberg. The family surname was the name of a color, either brown or white or green. She was proud of her cooking and of the fact. that, while young Irish girls were employed as housemaids, she was commanding the kitchen, preparing the family's favorite dishes and to their obvious satisfaction. As a youngster I was treated to roast beef and suet pudding with a gelatinous sauce, and only later came to realize that these dishes were not the Swedish food of grandma's roots. I never remember Little Grandma having any money, as she worked long before retirements, social security, or IRA's. Somebody must have given her some money though, as she probably was in her eighties when she took a bus and went downtown, returning with a present for me. It was a blue and white ceramic dog with a red tongue, my first bank. In order to get your coins back, you had to break the bank. One of the few treasures from childhood still intact, the bank, with only a few pennies rattling around in its belly, lives on a shelf at the home of one of our daughters.

It was never a problem to find a gift for Little Grandma. We loved to pick out pins for her birthday and Christmas. The array at the nickel and dime store was staggering; flowers, bugs, butterflies, little dogs and cats with beaded eyes, and all in a rainbow of sparkling glass and stone. I favored the larger and showier pins, and the excitement of choosing was only surpassed by anticipation of Grandma's delight on opening her gift. After dutiful expressions of joy and thanks, at the end of the day she would place the pin, still in its box, in a dresser drawer, to be put away for "good". The only other presents that we bought for her were stockings and peppermints. Ma would purchase the heavy brown cotton stockings, worn by Little Grandma and by most of the other immigrant ladies of a certain age and class. The stockings went all the way up her legs, or so I was told, since I can honestly say that I never saw Grandma's legs. For all that I know she may have had two artificial pins beneath the thick brown hose. The soft peppermints that we bought for her were called *polkagrisor*, and she would pop them in her mouth, then suck her coffee through them. Old habits are hard to break, and it hasn't taken long for my visiting grandchildren to find my own stash of soft mints.

Although he hadn't before, Uncle Ansgar started to bring Aunt Eileen with him when he came to visit. She was failing and couldn't be left alone at home. I overheard my parents talking in hushed tones between themselves about how Aunt Eileen had baked a cake for Uncle Ansgar that was full of roofing nails. Aunt Eileen had grown terribly thin, the skin just hanging from her arms so that I could see bones and blood vessels. And when she plucked at my shirt with her long fingers, speaking unintelligible words that sounded like "ibby and jibby ", I couldn't leave the room fast enough. Most of the time, my uncle left her sitting by herself at our dining room table, where she stared at something only she could see. Before Aunt Eileen became sick, Pa said she had been a good sport, going fishing with the guys, and even used to be able to climb a telephone pole. One day our phone rang, and I remember Ma shouting, "My God! She's hit a car in front of Stromboli's tavern." And with that, the adults rushed out of the house to head for the scene. As unbelievable as it now seems, she still had the car keys, and had been driving on the highway into town. Being a child, I figured that someone as smart as my Pa could straighten everything out before the cops got there.

Little Grandma's expression was one of infinite sadness when Uncle Ansgar sat talking with her in a voice so low so that no one else could hear. Her feet dangled about six inches from the floor as she sat in the yellow rocker, listening to her child whose life was so full of pain. But he smelled of whiskey and that infuriated Pa. As a child Pa remembered the family doing without while Grandpa Hallenberg salved his depression in alcohol. Pa said that he had had no shoes to wear to school, and in order to attend school he had to wear a pair of his sister's shoes. No doubt embarrassed beyond belief by the boys at school, Pa never forgave his father and from then on had a lifelong antipathy to alcohol. Uncle Ansgar was visiting, and my uncle made a comment about how he had been in the army. Pa told him "I think that you were with Colonel Barleycorn in the Whiskey Brigade, or maybe, you were in the underground balloon corps." In retrospect, it seemed a harsh thing to say to a war hero, even if he could be more than a little trying.

But Uncle Ansgar got more than a little of his own back. After Aunt Eileen died, my uncle acquired a girlfriend. It really bothered Pa when we'd drive down South Illinois Street, and see Uncle Ansgar's truck by the A & P store. He was parked on the street with his girlfriend, and they were throwing beer cans out the window of a panel truck. There was no mistaking his identity, as his truck bore the A. Hallenberg name, painted on both doors in large, bold letters. My father thought long and hard about how this looked to the people he knew, especially the people at the Lutheran church. I was more interested in seeing what the woman looked like. How could he even get a woman, since he wasn't classically handsome or rich, and wasn't a kid anymore? He liked to say he was enterprising, that's how. He claimed to trade cats, dead and skinned, for bottles of whiskey at the C and M tavern. Bragging that eight cats would get him a fifth of Four Roses, the cats wound up in the bar kitchens of the old country Italians. They called them *cunile*, or something like that, which meant rabbit in Italian. At another local establishment, a favorite story involved how every new cop on the beat was welcomed into the tavern for a meal of rabbit. None but the bar patrons were the wiser as the fresh-faced cop dined on one of Uncle Ansgar's cats.

Uncle Ansgar's house was next door to Grandpa's. Both properties had a house and a couple of acres of land, bought during an era when property went for a relative song. Ansgar's place had no doubt been a fine looking property at one time, with a vineyard of concord grapes in front by the road and a gravel lane leading back to his house. He had augmented his income by growing strawberries and vegetables for sale, and by caponizing roosters for sale to the public. I remember going to his house as a young boy, but I hadn't been back in years. After I was married and had a family, I decided to pay him a visit and picked a few bushels of grapes, for eating and making jelly. I'd heard Pa talking about how Ansgar had, at a rather advanced age, moved in one of the Murphy women, from a clan that lived nearby and whose members were reported to be "not quite right" in the noodle. As I drove up the lane, it was evident that the house had seen better days. He had long since stopped selling chickens, vegetables from his garden, and berries from his berry patch. Uncle Julian had moved into Grandpa's house by this time, and through his biweekly visits to our farm to fetch drinking water, kept us informed about the details of Uncle Ansgar's life, infinitely more exciting than his own. He said that Ansgar had put a bathtub outside by his back door, not being one to care about convention, and whenever he decided to take a bath, would heat the water inside of the house and then carry it out by the bucketful to his tub. He'd peel off his clothes and proceed to soak, as oblivious as a bather on the bank of the Ganges. Although I hoped to be invited inside, it was not to be. Uncle Ansgar met me in front of his house, clad in an almost-white tee shirt and jockey shorts that hung down nearly to his knees, having long since lost their elasticity. We settled on a price for the grapes, he went back inside of the house, and I took the bushel baskets out of the truck. I picked the grapes, snipping off bunches with a scissors, and filled up a couple of baskets. I didn't see him again that day, which was maybe for the best. My secret wish is that we could all meet some day, suffused with love, and saying pleasant things to each other. I was about eight years old when Uncle Ansgar noticed my brother and me, in the course of one his filial visits. He studied us both for a minute or two, then said, pointing to my brother, "This one here is all right." Turning his attention to me, his prediction was "This one here'll wind up in jail." By luck and by golly I'm still a free man.

About this time Aunt Virginia bought his house and land, and he moved into a hotel on the main street of Rustbelt City. Populated almost exclusively by men who were down on their luck it was referred to as the "Heartbreak Hotel" and was located next to the Morpheus theater, now the site of a drive-through bank. In a gesture to urban renewal, the "Heartbreak Hotel" burned to the ground. My parents heard about the fire on the noon news from Rustbelt radio, and rushed to town to see if our uncle was alive or dead. He was still alive, after jumping through a window and landing on his feet. The Germans didn't get him, the barroom fights, the long arm of the law, the fire at the hotel, but in the last round, he was finally taken out by ordinary old age.

Until my brother was born and cramped our style, I had the joy of Ma's undivided attention and the privilege of traveling with her to town. The car had gone to the foundry with my father, so we took the City Line's bus to downtown Rustbelt. As we stood on the main street through town, the wind blew scraps of paper and debris around our feet. Ma said that of all the places she lived, and they'd been many, Rustbelt City was, hands down, the dirtiest. Her life had begun in a rustic village in the Maryland hills, where she had cousins with names like Luttie and Hattie. From there, her parents moved to Illinois looking . . . always looking . . . for work. Ma said that she, her sisters, and her mother stopped at a relative's while her father had gone to another town looking for work. When they told their relatives they were hungry, Ma and her family were directed to a bushel of rotten apples in the basement. She told that story to me many times, and the cruelty of those relatives continues to amaze. Just as famine had influenced Little Grandma, so had hunger and want affected my mother's view of life, and for her love and food became synonymous. When they finally settled in Rockford, the family lived in a house with rent they could afford, since no one wanted to live in a house that was haunted. At night, Ma said that she used to lie awake and hear a thumping sound, supposedly caused by a woman who had died by falling down the stairs. I asked Ma if she was scared, but she would only tell me there was no such thing as ghosts. The dead were just dead, that was that, and they didn't return. Still, I was not quite convinced, now that she had told me the story about the ghost. And hadn't I heard strange sounds in our own house during the night? Big Grandpa died when he was still comparatively young. Ma attributed it to the fact that, in the days when employment was scarce, he worked delivering ice, lugging fifty-pound blocks up the steps in apartment houses that lacked elevators. Pa said that his death was due to biscuits and gravy, and the Southern-style cooking he favored. We never ate biscuits and gravy in our house and I still don't to this day.

Rustbelt City, spread along a river valley, had a steel mill, an oil refinery, chemical plants, and a plant that produced roofing shingles, all emitting fumes that mingled in an acrid bouquet. Despite the stench, a trip to downtown was worth it all. Entering the doors of the nickel and dime, and closing off the outside world of Rustbelt, I could smell the hamburgers frying, the french fries sizzling in their baskets and doughnuts bubbling in hot grease. In the glass cases were chocolate-covered doughnuts just begging to be eaten. I don't remember getting one though, because Ma made doughnuts at home. Like so many other families who lived through the Depression, Ma and Pa never bought anything if it could be made cheaper at home. Ma would take me by the hand and head straight for the fabric counter, admire the brightly colored and patterned bolts of cloth, and make her selection. Then a clerk would pull down the bolt, take out a scissors and cut off the yardage Ma had requested. My interest ran more to the toy section, and I would pull Ma along, imagining Christmas morning with all of this under our tree. One of my favorites was an orange colored iron motorcycle with rubber wheels and a real rider; it lasted thirty years or so, until the iron man lost his head in an accident.

The nickel and dime had a pet section with singing finches, golden warbling canaries, tropical fish, and turtles for sale. The turtles had children's names written on their backs, and their shells were about the size of a quarter. Having been especially quiet and polite during this particular trip, I got my very own turtle with my name on its back, along with a little cardboard box of turtle food. We brought him home, and kept him in a goldfish bowl with water and rocks on the bottom. He didn't do much, except crawl around on his little splayed turtle feet, while I stood on a chair to watch my new pet, and to sprinkle his food in the bowl. I did this many times every day, until the bottom of the bowl was a slurry of turtle food and turtle shit. The turtle grew and the house began to smell, or at least my mother thought so, and one day Ma decided that the turtle had to go. We took a trip to Slickery Creek, to the city park, and dumped my little Isaac out of his snug little bowl into the creek. Slickery Creek emptied into the DesPlaines River, the DesPlaines into the Illinois, the Illinois into the Mississippi, and from there into the Gulf of Mexico. Ma comforted me with the news that this was actually a lucky break for the little turtle; he was growing too big for the little glass bowl and now he could grow, and see the world. Some day he could be sunning himself on a piece of driftwood off Vera Cruz, Mexico. Having already experienced my first failure, now I was forced to live the first of many farewells. Goodbye Isaac turtle. Although I travel yearly to the Gulf of Mexico, I've yet to see a turtle with the name of Isaac printed on its back.

Little Grandma didn't fare much better with her pet, a caged canary that trilled all day long until we covered its cage at night, when the happy little fellow finally shut up and went to sleep. Ma never took a liking to the canary. It sang and sang, even when Ma had a headache and wanted silence. It was a messy eater, too, and required daily applications of fresh newspaper on the cage floor. Little Grandma went to visit her daughter in Kansas City, traveling on the Santa Fe railroad, and, sadly, returned home to an empty canary cage. In her absence, the little critter had died. We were told the story often, as a lesson in how even a dumb animal could have emotions. Ma said that the canary had missed Little Grandma so much that it refused to eat, and died of a broken heart. The story has such a tragically maudlin ring. Besides, who could believe his mother to be a canary killer?

Being of Swedish descent, on Sunday mornings our particular Hallenberg branch could be found in the Lutheran church, marked with one of Rustbelt's tallest steeples. Contrary to common belief it was struck more than once by lightning. The church was a stately, dark brick edifice with beautiful stained glass windows that portrayed events from the Bible. The services, by that time usually held in English, tended to be somber, serious and slow-paced. We knew that people had emotions, but they were not for display inside the church. Sometimes my mother took me to the Tabernacle where her parents attended services. It didn't look like a church to me, but rather, was just a big, open room with metal chairs set into rows. Where were the heavy wooden benches that looked like cattle stalls and the box set way up in the air where the preacher stood? Our Lutheran minister would mount the pulpit, look down at his notes, set his gold-plated pocket watch on the edge of the pulpit, and then commence to preach for the requisite forty-five minutes, so that everyone got their money's worth. The church of my childhood still exists as a Lutheran church, although the neighborhood demographic has long since changed. It fared better than the Tabernacle building which, some years later, was sold to the Masons, who eventually, in turn, sold it to Moe Morales. Moe turned the place into a "tittie bar" showcasing a famous stripper who went by the name of "Bambi". In the very same room where I had, with Ma and Big Grandma, heard hellfire and damnation preached by Rustbelt's answer to Billy Sunday, stood a long runway that ran the length of the bar. Forgetting the religious training of my youth, I sat in Bambi's Tabernacle with my friend, Motorcycle Mack, watching Bambi strut the runway, bumping, grinding and twirling her tassels. The Tabernacle had changed its name to the All-American Club, and just as "Billy" had cautioned in his sermons, was eventually consumed by fire. Back when Big Grandma, Ma and I would attend, the congregants in the tabernacle were encouraged to shout out their "Amens" and "Hallelujahs", to testify and reach out to the spirit, behavior that would have raised eyebrows, not to mention the attention of ushers, in the Lutheran church. At that particular service, a slight, nervous looking woman was sitting behind Big Grandma. Caught up in the elevating frenzy, excitement and sheer joy of salvation, she was up on her chair waving her arms, crying out, and in a state of ecstasy propelled herself into the air. Her spirit willing, but her frail flesh weak, she landed smack on Big Grandma's head, and was further anchored there by the hatpin on grandma's hat. No woman appeared in church or tabernacle hatless, and now Big Grandma sat there, no welterweight herself, with her head unbowed, and her hat adorned by one of God's own. After fellow worshipers removed the woman from atop Big Grandma's head, the service continued as if nothing had happened.

We were still living in Bedford Park, when my father came home from work one night to take us for a ride in his shiny, black Pontiac. He told us how he had bought the car brand new when he was a single fellow. Although I don't believe he meant it, he liked to sing the song with a chorus that went "When I was single, my pockets would jingle. I wish I were single again." It was the last new car he ever owned. Over the course of his life, Pa went through a bizarre collection of autos and farm trucks. Some of the old Pontiacs were hard on gas and didn't always run well, but they were well made and sturdy, with metal fenders so thick, that, if melted down and reconfigured, they could have made a transcontinental jet plane. We had a Ford Model A that was classified as a one ton truck. It smoked so badly, with oily fumes rising up into the cab and stinging our eyes, that the only way to drive it was with both windows open. We had a 1942 Studebaker truck that was often reluctant to start. My brother, a neighbor, and I took it to a fishing hole when we were teenagers and after catching our limit, we decided to head home in the truck. The old Studebaker thought otherwise, and refused to start. We were about fifteen miles from home, fifteen miles of cornfields and pastures between us and the home place, and not a phone to be had, and probably no one to come for us even if we had been able to make a call. We were on our own. We had parked the truck at the foot of the only hill in the county, and, like Sisyphus with his boulder, struggled to push the truck

up the hill. After considerable effort, we managed to get to the top, hop in and let
'er rip down the hill, popping the clutch. Not successful the first time, we persevered
up the opposite side, but again met with failure. We sweated and swore and finally,
after half a dozen tries, the old Studebaker coughed and took off. Not being one to
deny progress, Pa had even owned one of those cars with a push button transmission,
like the one that took out one of Sammy Davis Junior's eyes.

But we still had the shiny, black Pontiac, the snazzy car of Pa's bachelorhood,
when we drove out into the country that early evening. We turned off what was
Newell Ave. onto a gravel road, and pulled into a lane. We got out, and Pa knocked at
the porch door of a large white frame house. We were admitted through a glassed-in
front porch by an older couple who led us through the front door, a large heavy one
with a beveled glass inset. I didn't understand a thing that was said and forgot all
about the visit until our parents said, "Today is moving day."

Ma told us "Stay out of the men's way." My brother and I were hustled upstairs
along with Little Grandma to a small empty room that was lit by a naked light bulb
hanging from the ceiling by a cord. The little room was to be our bedroom, and the
place was to be our "farm" for the rest of Pa and Ma's life together, and the anchor
of our lives. To keep us entertained, Little Grandma read to us from a book about
a character she called "Smiling' Yack". When she flipped the pages of the book, a
little man swung back and forth under his parachute until he reached the ground.
Smiling' Yack had a friend, or as Grandma called him, a "pall" named Downwind.
He was portly with a protruding stomach that was always popping off the buttons
from his shirt. A chicken followed him around, caught the buttons in its beak in
midair, and swallowed them. When Little Grandma tired of reading, we looked out
the window at a roof that sloped downward over the front porch toward an apple
orchard and a vineyard. From the other window we could see a small barn, the
chicken houses, and a triangular shaped hog house. Even farther back, at the property
line where our field abutted the neighbor's pasture, was a fence line of trees, stately
elms and the smaller wild plum trees, from which Ma would go on to make jelly.
There were Osage orange trees as well, with their strange green fruit. Crows would
nest there, since the Osage trees were nearly impossible to climb, and the little ones
would be safe in their nests. Pa told me that when Uncle Ansgar was young he had
managed to climb a tree and capture some young crows before they could fly. He
put them in a cage that he'd built and then split their tongues with a razor blade,
having heard that crows could be taught to talk by doing this. Whether or not he
turned them into prairie parrots was never known, at least to me. I wish now that
I might have had the curiosity to ask him. During that first evening on the farm, I
crawled into bed, tired and happy, squinting my eyes and looking at the silhouettes
of trees growing on the fence line, seeing animal shapes and strange profiles, as my
eyelids grew heavy.

When we first moved to the farm, my brother and I had tea parties in a wooden
feed shed. Atop wooden nail kegs we made make-believe meals of chicken feed and

served them on tin plates from a children's tea set, topped off with a dessert of oats. Luckily we only pretended to dine as, in reality, eating enough raw oats and grains could be lethal; the grains could swell up and burst the innards of heartier eaters. Even in smaller amounts, a major stomach ache could ensue, as recounted by my brother's wife who as a young bride was snacking on barley while making soup, and developed distention and intense stomach pains that almost put her in the hospital. The chicken feed still came in patterned cloth sacks that farm wives used as fabric for clothing, and we recognized the florals and checks in the dresses and blouses worn by the girls at our country school. Our own favorite sacks featured a picture of fighting roosters, the Full-O-Pep brand. There was a wood shed on the farm where Pa stored used lumber; it was open on one side and with a slanting roof on top. I had taken a picture of it with my 127 camera, not so much as to capture the woodshed, but rather the large Norway rat that I saw running along one of the boards. The picture was a favorite possession for years. We had a rat population on the farm, and conveniently blamed it on the proximity of Sampson Sims, his menagerie and their spoiled produce diet. That may or may not have been the whole of it, since we kept feed for our animals and had enough rotten eggs now and then in the chicken houses to attract our own rats. We kept oats and corn in bins in a feed shed, but supplements and the oyster shell and grit were stored in fifty five gallon metal drums. Ma reached into one of the drums without looking first, and was bitten on a finger by a rat. It was the only rat bite that I can remember from our days on the farm, though one of our parents' sayings was to "look before you leap".

When we were old enough, one of our chores was to clean out the chicken houses. As much as we hated doing it, the job had its consolation. In the process of shoveling out the manure, we were able to shoot the fleeing rats. It became, in fact, so much fun that even Uncle Julian, notoriously allergic to farm chores of any kind, liked to help. The chickens roosted at night on wooden perches called drop boards. Beneath the roosts was a feast of chicken manure and an errant egg or two and, as we scooped out the manure with our shovels and pitched it out the window into a wagon, the large fat rats would leap up and head for the holes in the chicken house walls. Our challenge was to drop the shovels, run for our 22 rifles and nail the rats before they escaped. Bullets ricocheted off the cement floor of the chicken house. To finish the job we kept a hay cutter handy for decapitating our kill. By the grace of God, none of us was ever injured, and the rats most often escaped unharmed, to return for more sport another day.

On warm summer Sunday afternoons, my father and Uncle Julian parked their cars outside the garage on the cinder driveway. Pa loved the White Sox and even risked running down the battery to hear the broadcast of their games. He'd turn on the radio, open the car doors and we'd sit outside, listening to the baseball games from Chicago. The old tube-type radios ran down car batteries in a hurry, so just about the time the bases were loaded and the count was 3-2, we had the choice of either turning off the game or starting up the car to charge the battery. The afternoon summer heat, the sounds of the crowd in the background, the announcer's drone and the clack-clack of sportswriters tapping on their Underwoods, all combined to have Uncle Julian and Pa nodding off long before the game was over.

The cinders covering our lane were free for the hauling. We had only to shovel them into our truck from a cinder pile next to the Peerless wallpaper mill and head for home. Our biggest truck, the oil-smoker, was the one we used. A Model A Ford, it was brush-painted black with machinery enamel. Pa worked with Uncle Julian at the mill when the foundry shut down. After having risen to the rank of foreman at the foundry, he found himself working the "bull gang" when he hired on at the paper mill. He had to load trucks all day long with heavy boxes of wallpaper, working with men who were a lot younger and in better shape. There were strikes at the mill and Uncle Julian liked to tell the story of Floyd Pincus, head of the Teamsters local. Julian was walking along the picket line when he looked up at the big glass windows and saw the management "white shirts" looking out and shouting at the picketers. Floyd picked up a brick, yelled "Come out here and say that you *#*%!", reared back and threw the brick through the window. Uncle Julian told me the story, but I didn't meet Floyd myself until many years later. I was on the picket line during a big strike at Heidecke Chemical. We had been out for three months, and things were getting ugly. There were two roads into the plant and we had set up picket lines on both. While I was walking from one line down to the other, a pickup truck pulled along side of me, and the driver said "Jump in. I'm going over there anyway." I got into the truck, and found myself sitting next to Floyd Pincus. He patted the seat of the truck, saying "I've got somethin' under here for 'em." Later on an electric transformer was shot out, and a few truck tires were blown out on the way to the plant. Heidecke had their own trucks, blue in color with a yellow hexagonal design on the doors. One of the company drivers showed me the sawed-off shotgun he was carrying in his truck, most likely so that I'd pass the word on to leave the drivers alone. After the strike was over, the company sold their trucks and went to an outside hauling service. They thanked their drivers for going through the picket lines by laying them off, saying, "The Heidecke hexagon has left the roads."

Uncle Julian had a Plymouth from the 1930's. It had a canvas roof that he periodically repaired with roofing tar. The sparrows using his car for target practice were an on-going source of irritation until he came up with a scheme. "Tell you what, boys," he said. "I'll give you a penny for every one of these sparrows you can kill." Seeing the truck full of pennies in place of cinders, we grabbed our weapons and a couple of gunny sacks, and went to work. We killed as many sparrows as we could with our Red Ryder BB guns and soon exhausted our supply. When we looked into one gunny sack only partially filled with dead birds we knew we'd not even fill my piggy bank, let alone the truck. Being enterprising, we expanded the operation to our neighbor's dairy farm. His barn had plenty of sparrows, and we spread feed and lured them to the bottom part of the barn where the cow stanchions stood, with doors that conveniently slid shut. When we thought we'd lured in enough sparrows, we either managed to shoot them on the wing, or chased them back and forth around the barn until they were exhausted and made easier targets. Some of them just gave up, flying into the glass windows of the barn. When we had what we thought was a hefty supply of dead sparrows, we counted them out, and took them to Uncle Julian. We wanted him to make his count so he wouldn't think he was being cheated. A look of wonder on his face, he turned aside when presented the gunny sacks full of dead birds. He gave us the money, a substantial amount for Uncle Julian, without even counting. I happened to look over toward Pa, who was now standing with his back to Julian, his arms clasped to his front and his shoulders shaking. Julian had never specified that the sparrows could only be from the Hallenberg garage.

One of our playmates, Billy Walker, called Mister Stuyvesant on the phone because a couple of stray dogs were hanging around in back of Bill's house. Mr. Stuyvesant had become the county dog catcher. "Don't do anything, or scare them away until I get there," he said. If no one claimed the dogs within a certain length of time, Mr. Stuyvesant could dispose of them as he saw fit and with the impending scarcity of plow horses, he saw a new source of mink food. Since they, along with humankind, are known to bite the hand that feeds them, the mink had to be fed using special thick bite-proof gloves. The Stuyvesants also had hogs, and when they cleaned out their barn, the smell was acrid and strong at our place, a mile away. Mr. Stuyvesant must have had some clout, as not only was he the county dog catcher, but also held clandestine cock fights in his barn. Although now I wish I had, we were never allowed to see one. One of our friends from Michigan days said that her grandpa in Mexico had a fighting cock with yellow eyes, a fierce bird that greatly frightened her as a little girl on her visits there.

Behind the Stuyvesant farm there were hundreds of acres of woods that belonged to Old Man Gates, who owned a manufacturing plant called Gnarly Gates. Long before the woods became the site of an upscale subdivision we roamed there unhindered, with 22 rifles in our hands. By going through the woods, we were able to sneak up on Doctor Demur's place. He was an eye doctor and owned a large brick house with an outsized brick garage. Above the garage was an apartment, probably a former servant's quarters, but now empty of occupants. There was a formal garden in the back of the house, black walnut trees and a small pond with lily pads. He probably saw me riding onto his property on my bike, filling up a gunny sack with walnuts, and carrying home the sackful on my handlebars. Pa loved those black walnuts, and the cookies Ma made with them. The black walnuts were a lot of work; they had to be husked, the nuts taken out and spread out to dry. Plastic gloves had to be worn as the husks were hard and stained hands a yellow-brown color. When the nuts were dry, Pa broke them open with a hammer and a section of railroad rail, separating the nutmeats from the shells. A tedious job, and pieces of shell were often missed, only to be discovered when biting into one of Ma's black walnut cookies.

We had an army surplus pup tent and, after staying out overnight in the woods, we liked to breakfast on frog legs. The frogs from the doctor's pond were leopard frogs, tiny-legged creatures and hardly a mouthful, but we cooked them over the campfire and ate them, all the time wondering why they were such a highly touted entree. We didn't realize that the fancy French waiters were serving the meatier larger legs of bullfrogs to their discerning customers. One way of catching the frogs was by shining a flashlight in their eyes at night, and dangling a fish line and hook with a piece of red cloth for bait. Bullfrogs, usually caught by spearing, were scarce where we lived; besides, the delicious tang of purloined leopard frog was hard to beat.

We visited back and forth with our city cousins who lived not just anywhere in the city but in its very center, and only a stone's throw from a drugstore and the Eight by Nine Nut Shop. I always attributed any poor health later in life to their daily access to pop, potato chips, and candy bars. With a dime we could walk a few hundred feet to the shop and get not only a candy bar but a bottle of pop to go with it. At home we drank root beer that we bottled ourselves and the results tended to be variable. To make the root beer we mixed water, yeast, root beer extract and sugar in a wash tub, bottled it in glass bottles using caps and a capping apparatus, and then hoped for the best. Sometimes no fizz, but, at other times in the middle of the night we heard the bottles exploding in the basement.

There were six kids in the Von Luden family, and together with their folks (my dad's youngest sister, Ella, and her husband Ned) they lived on the first floor of their house. Ella and Ned rented out the second floor to a young couple, the husband was named Leslie and his wife, as I remember, had bright red hair. Since there was no bathroom on the second floor they had to share the downstairs facility with my relatives. Aunt Ella said that when Leslie and "Red" moved out, they left behind a jug of urine, being just too lazy to visit the toilet in the middle of the night.

The Von Luden bathroom always smelled of Lifebuoy, Cashmere Bouquet and Lava soaps, exotic fragrances all. At home we used Ivory soap, cheap and plain, not believing in conspicuous consumption, even if my folks had had it to spend. The Von Ludens lived life to the fullest, money or no, and their Lionel train set at Christmas was a sight to behold. The layout took up the entire living room and stepping carefully around the whistling billboards, crossing gates, and dump cars to make way through their house was a challenge. Situated on the main north-south thoroughfare and truck route going through Rustbelt City, the house had only a sidewalk and tiny yard separating it from the street. There was always plenty of traffic and noise when we visited, a real treat for country mice like us, and we loved going there. Ma's rule at home was not to come back in the house just to pee, once we had left, as we might be bringing in mud, cow manure, or who knows what. Needless to say, the cousins were scandalized when my brother stood on their curb, pulled down his drawers and let fly into the oncoming southbound traffic. He was more than surprised when his oldest cousin screamed and smacked him upside the head, and the others stood there pointing and laughing. It was his first lesson learned in urban custom, and taught by folks who knew their manners. The garage in back of the house opened up into a dirt alley. Since Uncle Ned didn't have a car at that time we played basketball in the garage. An old bushel basket with the bottom gone served as a hoop, and my cousins were kind enough to let me get a basket now and then. Having height and fine coordination, some of them and their children as well went on to play some pretty good basketball.

Uncle Ned was always a stickler for decorum at the table. At our house, Pa insisted that no one come to the table without a shirt, and no caps were to be worn at table (unless you're Jewish, our father added.) Uncle Ned always wore a white shirt, and every one had not only to mind their manners, but to have a thorough knowledge of them besides. That's why it was so shocking when he drove a newly acquired car through the plate glass widow of the laundromat. He didn't have a car very often, and this particular one he had driven to our house to show it off, proud of its Red Ram engine. Not knowing a good from a bad engine, I dutifully feigned interest and stared at it, a brand new engine that still had the red paint on it instead of the oil that usually coated ours. The first laundromat in Rustbelt city was built a few blocks from their house, and the local paper carried a picture of the new car with the Red Ram engine, now resting atop a wash machine. With the Von Ludens in between cars, we picked up our cousins for Sunday school, everybody vying for a seat by the window. After our sister was born, there were nine of us to compete for three windows. My folks said that people at church commented on the family with such a large number of kids, all crammed into a 1940 Pontiac. The sight was worthy of the circus act where countless clowns tumbled out of a Volkswagen Beetle.

Uncle Ned worked at the Eagle chemical plant in the office, a clean job, prestigious, but not very lucrative on payday. Pa and Uncle Julian, less concerned with prestige and more practical than Uncle Ned, thought he should get a better paying job out in the plant. To further enhance his image of impracticality, Uncle Ned took up the game of golf. When a true sportsman was golfing, he had to dress the part, and far be it from Uncle Ned to deny himself the clean shirt and knickers, topped off with a tam, set at a jaunty angle, that signaled a golfer. Uncle Ansgar told us that he and a friend were driving past a street corner when his friend pointed and said, "Look at that queer." The "queer" in question was Uncle Ned attired in his best golf clothes. "You'd better not say that," Uncle Ansgar told him. "That queer happens to be my brother-in-law." In contrast, my father and Uncle Julian came home in blue work shirts soaked with sweat and dried salt, smelling of sulfur and wallpaper ink. They didn't go upstairs to the bathroom to wash for supper, but instead took their shirts off in the kitchen, where there was a ribbed porcelain sink with a drainer on one end. They leaned over the sink in their undershirts and washed their faces, scrubbing and snorting into the water, while the water ran from their elbows onto the kitchen floor. When they were finished, my mother wiped up the puddles with a rag. It was probably about this time that my mother was having "nerve problems", long before there was much medical interest concerning "the change". She went to see Doctor Stein, our family doctor, and he told her just to go out to the barn and kick the cow when things got too hard.

A vacant lot lay to the south of our cousins' house, with a billboard in front by the sidewalk, and a tavern in back of the lot. On hot summer days we sat on the platform of the billboard and watched the cars go by. The locals, in what was then predominantly an Italian neighborhood, would come out of the tavern, their whistles comfortably whetted, and play a game of "*bocci*" ball. Many years later, on a visit to Paris, I watched locals play a similar game called *boules*, in the sand of a former Roman arena. Behind our cousins' place, on the other side of the alley, lived Arnie Marcus and his family. My cousin Bobby talked about them a lot, especially after Arnie's younger brother died. He was cleaning something with gasoline when it caught fire. Bobby told me all about going to the wake, and seeing his little neighbor in the casket, wearing a Hopalong Cassidy suit. I didn't meet Arnie until many years later, when he and I both rode Harleys. I can't remember what his looked like, but mine was painted a beautiful Mediterranean green-blue, the color of the 1949 Nash Rambler. Back then bikers used to hang out at the Busy Bee restaurant and drink coffee while the night was still young, and hit on the waitress, Angie Nogonis, before going out to become public nuisances. Just as Helen of Troy's was the face that launched a thousand ships, Angie's was the body that launched a thousand Harleys. Before I was discharged from the army, I sent home some money and Pa bought a 1949 Chevrolet for me, the one that had the shape of an upside down bathtub. Late one night I pulled in to an all-night truck stop for a cup of coffee. The waitress was none other than Angie, with the shape that launched a thousand Harleys out into the night, now broad of beam, and her beautiful black hair was stringy and hanging down into her face. I added the impermanence of beauty to my list of experiences.

Almost as much as we loved coming to the "city", our cousins enjoyed being "country mice", and often came out to the farm to spend the night. Evenings were especially fun. After supper we bathed, I can't remember in which particular order, but the bath water must have been pretty rank by the time the last bather had been toweled off. Then we got into our pajamas, had popcorn, and played hangman. The game elements were pencil, paper and dice, and involved drawing appendages on stick men, who eventually went to the gallows. After dark, we turned on the radio and listened to programs like the Lone Ranger, Dick Tracey, the Green Lantern, or The Shadow. Then we went to bed, but our cousins complained that it was difficult to sleep because the crickets were too loud, even though the Von Ludens lived on one of the busiest streets in town. During the day we played baseball in our cow pasture, using roofing shingles for bases. We used to tease each other about sliding into base, never sure where the cow pies might be. Fishing in the creek was always a treat, but first we had to dig for worms. There was a manure pile in back of the barn where we were almost always able to find worms, even in the driest times of the year. During August, though, when the grasshoppers were plentiful we would catch them in the fields or turn over boards to look for crickets. After there was a pouring-down rain, we got to stay up late at night and use our flashlights to hunt for night crawlers. If you spied one sticking out of a hole in the ground you had to be mighty quick but careful, since in the struggle to pull the worm out from its hole it would sometimes break off. We stored our excess night crawlers in an old washtub between sheets of wet newspaper in the fruit cellar where it was damp and cool. We went fishing with metal poles that people in later years would call "pool cues"; they had absolutely no give to them. Bamboo poles were our only other option, and we made them ourselves. There was a store on the East Side that sold plain bamboo poles. We put eyes on the bamboo sticks, using bent wire that we wrapped with thread on both ends, and then painted the thread with lacquer. The cane poles were stored in the rafters of the garage.

Going fishing was an enterprise that required considerable planning. Ma made us our Kool-Aid, preferably red, and poured it into a Mason jar, and then made us sandwiches. When we left, burdened with our poles, a can of worms, a minnow bucket for storing our catch of fish, the mason jar of Kool-Aid and our sandwiches, we were ready for an African safari. To get to the creek, we had to walk down our gravel road to the railroad tracks, and follow the tracks south. The dangerous part of the trip was crossing the wooden railroad trestle. The distance between the ties was vast when your legs are short and, if you looked, it seemed like a long way down to the clay gorge where the cows crossed, going from the lane to the pasture and the creek. The next hazard was crossing the fence without tearing your shirt on the barbed wire. And, once through the fence, we had to stay alert for the Holstein bull that Ma always warned us about when we left to go fishing. The bull was always there, just like the devil that we were also warned to avoid, but the bull never bothered us, being more interested in the cows and the grass than in any little fishermen. Once through the fence and into the pasture, the next step was to find a good fishing spot. If you caught one of the little four inch creek denizens you were immediately mobbed by your buddies, who wanted to get up by your "lucky spot". While we carried home our shiners and chubs from the creek in our minnow bucket, we would raise the lid from time to time to check on them. They never left the bucket, of course, and by the time we got home they were usually floating belly up in the lukewarm water. On a good day, we might be able to catch dozens and Ma always made a big production out of admiring our catch. It's a great feeling to have done something of consequence. We were responsible for scaling and cleaning them, but then Ma would take over, rolling them in flour and frying them in oil in a skillet. No trout could have tasted better than those nearly rotten little chubs and shiners. We took great pride in "bringing home the bacon".

Our mother's dad was the engineer on the tracks that ran near our house. He had spent many years in apprenticeship as a fireman before he could get his hands on the throttle. A man by the name of Massey was the engineer, and Big Grandpa said that Massey was so fat that Grandpa had to push his ass up into the engine. When I was a little kid, we drove to a crossing to watch him go by in the engine. We got up as close as we could, and the ground shook from the weight of the engine going past on the crossing. The steam, the noises, the ground-shaking all combined to scare the daylights out of me, but the whistle didn't blow. Massey was an old grump who wouldn't let Big Grandpa blow the whistle because he'd be wasting steam. After Massey's great rear got boosted to that roundhouse in the sky, Grandpa became the engineer, somebody else had to shovel the coal, and Big Grandpa could toot the whistle as long and as hard as he pleased. Back when he'd been a fireman, Grandpa was always covered with coal dust, and the job was hot and tiring. When he became the engineer, he was a lot cleaner. He always wore bib overalls, had on a striped railroad cap, and carried a big gold watch in his pocket. Even when he wasn't on the train he liked to pull out the big gold watch and look at the time. The railroad line could be seen from our house, and the train puffed by with a coal car behind the engine, a caboose on the end, and in the middle was a string of cars that seemed, to me, to stretch for miles. The railroad men wore red bandannas just like the cowboys did, and as he rode by, Big Grandpa would lean from the engine window, his iron jaw clamped onto a pipe with a curved stem. Ma said that, when she was a little girl, the only time that big Grandpa got irritable was when he ran out of his pipe tobacco. He wasn't a bad looking man, except for the nose that was flattened all over his face. Ma said that was the result of his poker playing. When Grandpa headed south from our place on the train, he had something called a lay-over at the other end of the line. When playing poker, the sore losers had a habit of taking out their losses on the winner's nose, so Grandpa must have been a pretty fair player. For any number of reasons, playing cards was forbidden in our house. We only had Old Maid and a game called Pit, that involved grain bidding and bell ringing. Being a dutiful son I very seldom played poker. To this day I like the horses at the race track instead.

Grandpa hated the "railroad dicks" who, at their best, chased the hobos off of the cars, and at their worst often brutalized them. It was much to his credit that he never forgot the times when he was just as poor as the men who were riding the rails. Ma remembered some poor times as a child, and Pa said that was why she used to go to the basement and check on the fruits and vegetables she had canned. Just as others before her and since, she said food was something that you never take for granted once you've gone without. I read in the paper about a woman who had lived through the war in Europe, and was disgusted when she witnessed a food fight. Having seen plenty of food fights courtesy of Three Stooges shorts, with pie throwers in fancy duds, was as close to food-fighting as I could imagine. Pies, or for that matter desserts of any kind, were scarce in Ma's family when she was growing up. During the times when Big Grandpa struggled to find work and Big Grandma came down with tuberculosis, a lot of the work fell to my mother to take care of the family. She subsequently developed TB herself. A large sepia-toned photograph of Ma hangs in our living room, taken at the time that she developed the disease, which was so often a death sentence. The family thought they should have a picture of her in case she died. She was shipped out to live with my great-grandmother in Auburn, and told me how her grandma used to hang out the long underwear on a clothes line, even in the middle of the winter. When the "long johns" were frozen solid, she used to grab them by the arms and act as if she was waltzing with them into the house. My mother fooled everybody and lived to be eighty-nine years old, the picture of her having been put aside, then passed down to us after she died.

Uncle Ansgar told stories about how he had come back from the trenches of the first World War, and then gone on the bum. One of the local bankers, when Ansgar shipped out, had told him that "Nothing is too good for you boys when you get back home." A lot of them didn't get back home, and the ones that did were greeted by a brief but severe recession in 1919. There being no law in effect that a returning service man should have his old job back, and economic pressures being stronger than promises, Uncle Ansgar jumped a freight train and went to Minnesota. There he was arrested for starting a fire in a forest preserve and for vagrancy. At the time, any cop in a little town could stop you and ask to see if you had any money. Without the required minimum, you could be arraigned before a judge, the sentence being thirty days or thirty dollars. This succeeded in keeping indigent men from some towns, forcing them to others where the laws weren't so strictly enforced. Uncle Ansgar said that he was thrown into the bull pen at the jail, a communal cell where persons were kept temporarily for minor offences like drunkenness. He said the jail in that little hick town in Minnesota was the dirtiest one in which he'd ever enjoyed residence.

When Big Grandpa visited, he was always giving Pa advice on how to run a farm. Usually Pa stayed in the house and just let Grandpa snoop around and inspect everything. Our first cow was named Gertrude, the same name as one of our shirt-tail relatives who taught English in the junior high that we later attended, and my brother and I remembered her for her thousand spelling demons. My brother, a somewhat phonetic speller himself, said that if only we'd paid attention to Gertrude we'd both be able to spell today. Our cow was purchased from the McDuff Riding Stables, and we suspected that she was forever ruined as a family milk cow by having been ridden for sport, as a wild bull substitute. When we first got her, Pa used to stake Gertrude out to eat the grass in the ditch by the road. She would pull him through the yard when they went toward the barn, with him holding on for dear life to the collar around her neck. Every once in a while Pa's heels dug into the ground to try to stop her, but to no avail; the cow never stopped unless it was her idea. She was the first and only Guernsey that we ever had. Once when Big Grandpa was on one of his inspection tours, we looked out from the kitchen window to see him in the pasture with Gertrude. He was bent over looking at clover or checking out a mouse hole, with his rear sticking up like a red flag. Gertrude charged, and Grandpa turned a summersault into the field of timothy and clover. It was a howling good time for us, but when Big Grandpa came back in from the pasture he didn't say a word. And, neither did we. It was our own private joke. Grandpa used to tell us that when he was a young man he was a hired hand, and got up every morning to milk thirty head. "That was by hand," he said, "Not using one of these modern milking machines. Anybody could do that". He thought he knew all that there was to know about cattle, but forever neglected to mention his encounter with Gertrude. Little did he know that we had all witnessed the whole thing.

My brother had a Red Ryder BB gun, and carried it with him wherever he went. He was so young when he got the gun as a present that he couldn't cock it himself, and would say, "Crock it for me." A few years went by, and he was old enough to go out into the pasture and shut the gate behind him. His quest into the pasture was to search for a target, a bird or a mouse, to shoot. Gertrude spied him, however, and the chase was on. My brother had time only for one shot over his back as he was running away. As clever as the cow was, every time my brother circled the field and approached the gate, she would give him a nudge and he'd have to circle the field again. Gertrude was disappointed when Ma saw what was happening and ran out of the house to open the gate. My brother had only one shot in his BB gun before he had to cock it again, and he didn't have time for that. Good thing, for if he'd succeeded in hitting her, Gertrude would have taken the game more seriously.

Big Grandma and Grandpa lived in a Gothic looking, shingle covered, two-story house on a steep hill that overlooked Rustbelt's major railroad yard, although not the one for which Grandpa worked. Anyone living above a valley of tracks and steam engines was certain to have their home and yard blanketed with soot. When visiting we had to walk up a steep sidewalk to the back door. Big Grandpa was usually hiding out in the garage with his dog "Chiggers", trying in vain to avoid Big Grandma, who tended to scream at him continually "Delmer!", in a voice reminiscent of the steam whistles down in the railroad yard. Sometimes when we got home, Pa would imitate my grandmother's clarion call. Unlike Little Grandma, Big Grandma was a tea drinker, and never hesitated to heat up the kettle. We'd all sit down in the kitchen to a cup of green tea, called Irish tea after the memory of some of long forgotten Irish forebear. I never remember having a full meal there until Grandpa died. While the grownups were sitting at the kitchen table and having their tea, I was able to roam around the house. One or the other of my mother's sisters and their husbands and children lived there from time to time. When I went into the parlor, Uncle Angus was sitting in an easy chair reading the paper, and pretending not to notice me. Uncle Angus and Aunt Hepsibah were my godparents, having signed on the dotted line in a King James Bible that I have kept all these years. The walls of the house were covered with wallpaper featuring the large gaudy flowers popular at the time, but sun-faded from exposure to the bay window and gray-tinged from the constant infusion of soot. Instead of the usual landscapes or floral scenes, the walls were hung with framed black and white photos of famous steam engines. The grass in the yard, the house and even the family all tended to be gray as the soot generated by the rail yard. When I was in the army, Ma used to send me letters describing the animals, birds and the flowers around the farm, down to the tiniest colorful detail. In retrospect, I think she was the only member of her family who showed any real awareness of beauty. When Uncle Angus put down his paper and tried to talk to me the words stuck in his throat, with his Adam's apple bobbing up and down. He stuttered something fierce. The family hinted that something happened—an accident, it was always blamed on an accident—at work had affected his nerves, and this was why he couldn't work anymore. The words just wouldn't come, and after a few false starts, he managed, "Huh . . . huh . . . hi. How are you?", then went back to hiding behind his paper. As I grew to adulthood I used to see him downtown in Rustbelt City, holding up the wall at Blitz and Kraut's department store, so that he could ogle the girls walking by on Illinois Street. Pa attributed this to the fact that he was of Scottish extraction, and that meant he was romantic. Pa loved reading the Scottish poet, Robert Burns, and quoted him often. He felt that Uncle Angus just couldn't help himself.

Occasionally, Grandpa's other son-in-law, my Uncle Tom, lived there with my Aunt Ina until my cousins were born. I used to see him when I walked up Jackson street to the high school, sitting out in front of the fire station swapping stories with the firemen. At that time he and my aunt lived in an apartment next door to the fire house. I thought he was funny, and his eyes twinkled when he told a joke or recited baseball statistics. To me he was fat, round and jolly, and so unlike Uncle Angus, but Ma had seen him in his younger days as a mean drunk. He and Aunt Ina were living with my grandparents while my mother was still unmarried and living at home. When Uncle Tom came home drunk one morning, after having spent all night somewhere around Rustbelt City, Aunt Ina locked him out of the house and wouldn't let him in. Since Aunt Ina tipped the scales at about three hundred pounds, Uncle Tom took her seriously, wandered around the neighborhood and finally landed in a drunken heap in the hot August sun. The payment for his night out was sun stroke, and a bath in cold water with ice cubes to bring his temperature down. Uncle Tom never learned to drive a car. If he wanted to go somewhere he walked, took a bus, or called up a taxi cab. Aunt Ina and Uncle Tom used to stop at the farm and say hello to Ma on Saturday evening on their way to Slick Scott's Swing Inn. The place was legendary for its hillbilly music and holes in the ceiling from random gunfire discharged by the celebrants. It was closed down years ago when the owners were accused of watering down the bar whiskey.

Ma told me that when Uncle Tom was young, he wasn't a much of a worker. Having finally inured himself to the necessity of steady work, though, he got a job up near Chicago, and rode the Bluebird bus north every day to the aluminum plant from which he finally retired. Before his Bluebird commuting days, Aunt Ina would pack his lunch each day, and he would leave their place with his lunch bucket in hand, supposedly off to yet another job. Rustbelt City was the county seat, and the old courthouse was a limestone edifice, with a short limestone wall surrounding the grounds. Along with the pigeons, bums and winos tended to congregate there. Anyone who walked by was plagued by requests for a dime for a cup of coffee. Ten of these "cups of coffee" and they could buy a bottle of Monk's Breath wine. Responsible for the death of many a derelict, it contained so much sugar that hunger was satisfied, and, without any food, they died of malnutrition. Someone who knew my aunt and uncle happened to be driving by and saw Uncle Tom perched on the courthouse wall, sharing his lunch with the bums. Poor Aunt Ina thought that he'd been going to work, since he'd neglected to tell her that he had lost the job the week before. After his day "at the job" he was met at the front door by an irate wife, her anger greatly augmented by her size. But I thought his spirit of sharing was to be admired.

For a long time I didn't see him, and he finally ended up in a nursing home after Aunt Ina's death. One of his old acquaintances from the neighborhood was in there with him, and told me the story about how, during the Depression, he had seen Uncle Tom sneaking up on a neighbor's back porch and drinking a bottle of the milk left by the milkman. Sadly, his milk-sucking days were over. Since he had been a walker all his life his body was in good shape, but his mind wandered. He was made to wear a bracelet in the nursing home that set off an alarm should he try to go for an outside stroll. Each new resident was interviewed for the little newspaper published there, and when asked his favorite song Uncle Tom said, appropriately enough, it was Roy Rogers singing "Don't Fence Me In." When I visited him there he assured me that he was going to leave and get an apartment on Rollins Street, remembering the street as it had been forty years before. Now it was gang-ridden and one of the most dangerous streets in town. On his few attempts to go there, his bracelet alarm stopped him at the front door. Never having seen him without a cigar in his mouth, or somewhere in hand, I thought to bring him some. When asked what kind he preferred, he told me, and said that he only smoked the ones that cost a nickel. The nickel cigar had gone the way of Rollins Street, but I continued to bring him his stogies until he was caught throwing lit cigar butts into the waste paper basket. About the last time that I saw him I was accompanied by my wife. When he saw us he wrinkled his brow trying to remember me, and then said, with that great twinkle once again in his now rheumy eyes, "Oh, now I remember. You're the little guy who's married to the big woman."

My mother had an Uncle Bill from Muskegon who used to come to visit. One of his legs was missing and he walked around on a peg leg, smoking vile-smelling cigars. My great-great-grandfather was killed in the Civil War (The War Between The States to some of my relatives) and all six of his children were placed with farmers who lived in the vicinity. Before my great grandfather died, he searched for and found each of his five siblings. Whether any of the families legally adopted their charges isn't known, but all six children ended up with different family names. My mother's Uncle Bill gave me his guitar, probably out of gratitude for having a place to stay when visiting around Rustbelt. He said he'd paid five bucks for it, no doubt a tidy sum during the first World War, and the other soldier got the best of the deal by far. I found that out when I learned to play the guitar and I have kept at it for many years, my wife and I always referring to that particular instrument as the cigar box with strings. There were a lot of radio advertisements as well as ads in the magazines and comic books that promised to help the novice master guitar technique in a few easy steps, leading to pickin' and grinnin' that would in turn lead to personal satisfaction not to mention great popularity. The accompanying pictures always showed a smiling man playing the guitar while he yodeled to a bevy of admiring females. But I learned to play from my friend's dad. Bill Walker was a neighbor whose dad played the guitar, and in exchange for painting his living room, Bill's dad taught me how to play, and even threw in a repair job. The neck of the guitar was pulling away from the body, so he drilled a hole through the neck into the body of the guitar, and held the guitar together with a quarter inch bolt. True to his word, after I did the painting he showed me a few chords and taught me a song to warble along with the chords. He told me to go home and practice the song, "Riding Down the Canyon", a song in the key of F and popularized by Gene Autry, long before he owned a baseball team. Gene was a hero to us kids when we were growing up but the inevitable clay feet were discovered years later, when I worked with John Wizowitz at the chemical plant. He told me that he went to see a parade in his home town of Chicago, and one of the Parade Marshals was to be Gene Autry, riding his horse. He was shocked to see his hero (and mine) literally fall from grace, after having too much to drink, and land on the pavement. After my lesson with Bill's father, I couldn't wait to get home and try out my new skill. I could picture the delighted looks on Ma and Pa's faces, and could only imagine the gaggle of buxom beauties soon to surround me. But my fingers were clumsy, and it didn't sound at all like when Mister Walker was playing. "I tell ya folks it's heaven to go ridin' down the trail, to see the desert sun go down."

Bill's dad also played the banjo and the mandolin as well as an old Martin flat top guitar, which is still prized as an instrument by folk and country singers. He had a brief career on the radio and at amateur shows until he got married, had four boys, and became a plasterer. "If any of my kids become plasterers, I'll break both of their arms on their way to the time clock ", he told us. He didn't have to worry, as wallboard was replacing plaster, except in the homes of the rich and on some commercial projects. My brother and I spent a lot of time hanging around the Walker's place since the oldest, Bill, was one of our buddies. The boys all slept in one large bedroom they called the "dormitory". With his occupation in decline, Ted had time to read and during warmer weather when the window to his bedroom was open, I would see him lying on the bed, reading after he finished his supper. His sons bragged that on more than one occasion, in more erudite conversations, he had been mistaken for a college professor. Mister Walker was the neighborhood renaissance man, and, with the exception of consistently finishing his projects, there was almost nothing he couldn't do. He loved geology and archeology, and had a living room full of rocks collected on trips out West, when he'd had the money to travel. He was a talented woodworker and had a workshop in his basement where he built furniture, but not being skilled in marketing he never made any money. While most children had sandboxes, in the Walker's backyard was an airplane with a wing span of fifteen feet, something unique for his sons to play in, but the wooden framework sat rotting over the years with pieces of canvas covering flapping in the wind. The fireplace almost had a similar fate. A work of art when he finished the stonework, with assorted brightly colored rocks, he proceeded to cut a hole in the living room wall. Meaning to finish the job, but with his attention diverted elsewhere, he had to cover the hole with plastic. With the coming of winter and at the urging of his patient wife this was one job he had to finish before there was measurable snow on the sofa.

When he built the dormitory for the boys, his fellow plasterers showed up to help. They were French Canadians known both for their impressive physical strength and immense capacity for beer. Short on entertainment, we boys all showed up to watch them work, and noted beer stacked by the case out behind the house. The dormitory addition started out smoothly but as beer bottles started to layer the yard, the construction job headed south. Boards were nailed in the wrong place, voices were raised and even though we couldn't understand Quebecois curses, it was evident that things were not going well. We lost interest and wandered off. The next time that I saw Mr. Walker he was complaining bitterly about those damn plastered plasterers. But the job was finished, and on time; he'd had to do it himself.

When the third son was born, Mister Walker enclosed the front yard with some fence posts and chicken wire. It was a new concept in child raising. Since he thought it a waste of time to be changing diapers, he put out child number three in a pen with plenty of shade trees. A safe way for a him to get fresh air, and son number three couldn't run out into the road or get into trouble.

Trouble had followed one of Ted's fellow plasterers, though, and Ted enjoyed telling the cautionary tale. The man tended to stray and had a fondness for chasing women, a trait that did not endear him to his wife. Strangely, he started missing a lot of work and thought perhaps the stress of his busy lifestyle was making him ill. At one point he got so sick that he thought that he was going to die, and went to the hospital, fully expecting the worst. Miraculously he got better and went home. This occurred a number of times. Each time that he improved in the hospital he would go home, only to get sick again On his last visit a clever doctor determined that the plasterer had been poisoned. Apparently his wife had been dosing him all along. He either had an exceptionally strong constitution or his wife wanted to stop short of actually killing him off. After their divorce his health greatly improved and he lived to retirement.

Down the road and on the east side of our place lived the Dolanders. Both Mister Dolander and our father raised bees, but we had our hives close to the house while the Dolanders had theirs on the fence line at the back of their property. One day Ma called us to the kitchen window with a "Come here and look! Quick!" We watched him from the window. It was at least a hundred yards to the back of their place and Mister Dolander was running for the house with his bees in angry pursuit. He would run a ways, then fall to the ground and roll, jump up and run again, then fall and start the whole sequence again, all the way back to the house. Our neighbor must have skimped on the protective clothing that Pa always wore : white coveralls and a bonnet with a wire screen to keep out the bees when working around them. Just like people, the bees were a lot happier on bright, sunny days. It didn't pay to fool with them during cloudy, rainy weather. Pa always blew smoke into the hive to make them tranquil. No one wanted to irritate the bees, since the sting was painful to the stingee and finished off the bee. On Saturday afternoons we bathed and washed our hair, combing it and slicking it down with Wildroot Cream Oil, fragrant with a faint scent of flowers. When the weather allowed we sat in the back yard before supper. Since the singing commercial for Wildroot promised that "the gals'll all pursue ya. They love to run their fingers through your hair.!" we looked forward to attracting the ladies. Not counting on enamored bees, we were surprised when they came to sip our hair tonic nectar, only to find themselves enmeshed in the greasy kid stuff. The harder they tried to disentangle, the angrier they got, with the inevitable result. The Wildroot was put away until winter.

Looking over the pasture and the cornfield, we could observe Mister Dolander, a Polish immigrant, out in his driveway, polishing his pride and joy, his "Hudskin". He went through the ritual at least once a week. His missus liked to walk up the street to chat with Ma. Usually Mrs. Dolander felt even more companionable after drinking Edelweiss beer, and since she drank a lot of Edelweiss, that meant a lot of visits. Empty wooden Edelweiss cases provided us with toy boxes. Rumor had it that the Missus started drinking because of the pain from an operation where the doctor forgot to remove one of the sponges. But to my father, no excuse was good enough to justify drinking. He didn't believe in excuses. When he was growing up, anyone with a family member who seemed a little slow (people being unencumbered with today's myriad diagnoses) would explain that the relative had been kicked in the head by a horse. Pa said there weren't that many horses in the entire county.

We didn't believe a lot of what Missus Dolander said and thought that she was a medium through which the Edelweiss spoke. One time she told us that she was hanging out washing when a deer ran through her yard. Deer hadn't been seen in our area since the 1800's. It was many years later when I totaled a Pontiac after running into a deer on a nearby interstate highway. Who knew that she might have seen the first deer to come back into our county. The Dolanders had only one child, a son, Eddie, who was in the Pacific during the war. He sent them home a sword, supposedly a Samurai sword, and sharp enough to do some damage. It had traveled all across the Pacific to our kitchen, where a tipsy Missus Dolander stood, swinging the sword to demonstrate her prowess as a Samurai warrior. Another day, she ran up the street to our house and arrived out of breath, telling us about how a bomb had fallen on Japan, a bomb that was as hot as the sun. We thought it was the Edelweiss talking again, but the evening the papers proved her right. The atomic bomb had been dropped on Hiroshima.

Old Mister Gates had a pond dug out on his wooded acreage, fed by a small stream with a spillway where the water overflowed at times into Silver Creek. We swam there in the summer after baling hay and ice skated there in the winter. Baling hay was a hot job, made even hotter by having to wear long sleeved shirts so as not to get scratched by the hay. One evening after haying we went to the pond with a couple of guys and Elmer, the hired man on the neighbor's farm. We brought inner tubes to float around on; in Elmer's case it served as a life jacket, since he couldn't swim. Splashing around and just generally having a good time, we decided to have a race to shore. "Last one to the shore's a rotten egg," someone said, and off we went. When we got there we looked around for Elmer. Looking out at the pond we watched as his head showed up, then disappeared, then showed up again, then went under in the muddy water. This process continued until he made it to shore, gasping for breath. He'd fallen off the inner tube, sunk to the floor of the pond, and pushed himself off the bottom, emerging to get a gulp of air, then sinking again, pushing off every time he hit bottom, and gulping air when he reached the surface, and in this way finally reaching the shore.

Elmer the hired man was a few years older than I, and had been to Korea during the war. Although referred to as a police action rather than a war, this little police action killed off more than 35,000 of our young men. Elmer said that he'd been on guard duty when a Korean civilian carried off a Jeep motor. The biggest surprise to Elmer was that someone so small could carry if off with ease. The Korean used an A-frame, and carried it on his back, aided by his strong leg muscles. Elmer didn't have the heart to shoot him, as the army had plenty of Jeep motors. He fired wide, taking care not to hit the enterprising man, as had he not fired he could have been in some major trouble. Having survived Korea, he took a job as a hired man and eventually returned to work at the family farm. It was customary to gain some experience on another farmer's place before going back to work at home. After he left the neighbor's and returned to his family farm, Elmer lost his arm in a corn picker. Before the advent of modern combines, the corn pickers that were pulled behind a tractor were always getting clogged up. The farmers would try to unclog the equipment without shutting it down, and many were the sorrier for it. Old Grandpa Selkirk, in the big dairy farm behind us, got his fingers caught in a corn picker when he was all alone in the field. He had to cut off a few of his fingers with a pocket knife before he could free himself and walk back to the house. All of us farm kids carried a pocket knife in our pockets at an early age. The knife was either a Barlow or what we called a Boy Scout knife, with extra gadgets like a can opener and a pop bottle opener. In fact, I still have a pocket knife, but I've never had to leave any of my fingers behind.

The pond owned by Mister Gates was full of tiny bluegills and, supposedly, much larger bass. Naturalists promoted the idea that if a pond was stocked with bass and bluegills, they would achieve a balance with the bass using the bluegills for food. Sportsmen were supposed to concentrate on catching the bass. But we were kids, not sportsmen, and the pond was soon overrun with bluegills that were getting smaller all the time. We were fishing there one day when Mister Gates pulled up in his Caddy and stuck his head out of the window. He was a nice old man and seemed not to mind dirty-faced little kids, but his wife, sitting next to him, had a look on her face as if she'd just smelled something bad. "It's all right for you kids to fish here," he said, "but you're not keeping any of the little ones, now are you?" "No sir," we answered back. I hoped that he didn't see the little bluegills that I was standing on and trying to hide with my feet. He was a kindly man and probably knew we were apt to keep everything we caught. I was only kicked out from the pond once and that was by old Bloodless, the county coroner. Mr. Gates had been in the process of selling lots on his wooded acreage, for a few prestigious houses and, eventually, for a subdivision. The subdivision had yet to be built when I encountered old Bloodless. I was using a spinner for the bass in the pond, and so was he, flailing away with his expensive pole and not catching a thing, while I caught a nice bass. He kicked me off the property, and told me not to fish there again. I gave him a lip-fart as I held up my bass and disappeared into Stuyvesant's cornfield on my way home for supper.

It was 1945, I believe, when the Chicago Cubs won the pennant. Pa was a White Sox fan and said that the Cubs belonged in the Three-I League, a minor league organization. He said the only way that the Cubs won was because the players were drafted during the war, and the team picked up the old baseball has-beens. Nevertheless, I was heartbroken when the Cubs lost the World Series. My brother and I played our own version of Cubs baseball on the front porch, with little red building blocks. We printed the names of players on each block and imagined the blocks to be Phil Caveretta, Peanuts Lowery, Andy Pafko, Bill Nickolson and Stan Hack, among others. They were the heroes of my youth, and in our imaginary baseball games it was always the same, "Cubs win!! Cubs win!!" My own baseball mitt carried Andy Pafko's signature on the leather, an outfielder for the Cubs who played on the legendary team that actually won games. The glove was hard and inflexible as a roofing shingle and I couldn't hammer a pocket into it, no matter how hard I tried. When I tried to catch a ball, it usually bounced off the stiff leather and dropped to the ground. I would stare at the ball, wondering, "How did the ball get there when it should have been in my glove?" Before I had a regulation ball, Little Grandma made one for me out of cloth, laboriously sewn together, layer upon layer, until it was the size of a regulation hardball. I hit the ball in the backyard, since there was little danger of breaking a window with a cloth ball. It would make a mushy splat sound when hit, and would sail all of ten or fifteen feet. Probably not entirely satisfactory, but how many kids have a grandma who made them calico coated baseballs? When we were old enough for a regulation ball, Uncle Julian took us out behind the barn and showed us how to throw what he called a slow curve. We held the ball on the side and threw it as hard as we could against the wood boards in the back of the barn. We had to imagine the roar of the crowd as the cows soon lost interest and went back to their grass.

When we first moved to the farm and I was still hitting Little Grandma's cloth baseball, the backyard was my baseball diamond every day but one. On Mondays the yard was off limits. Pa put hooks on the garage, the old hen house, and our own house, and then stretched clothes line between the hooks before he left for work. The back yard became a maze of lines with wooden clothes poles holding up them up, the lines sagging with their burden of wet overalls, blue work shirts, floral and plaid house dresses, underwear, sheets and towels. For my mother and grandmother, as for most of the people of that time, there was an appropriate job for each day of the week, even including Sundays. Not only was the backyard off limits on wash days, but so was the basement. We were told horror stories about kids who were fooling around, got too close, and got their hands caught in the rollers of the wringer washing machine. "Get out . . . and stay out," was what we heard when the women were busy. Sunday was the day for frying up a couple of chickens for Sunday dinner. We went to church while Little Grandma stayed home and baked the chicken. At least this is what she did until she was close to ninety years old. Then Ma took over, and had to stay home from church. I'd have gladly preferred the sounds of chicken sizzling to the droning of a forty-five minute sermon, and would have volunteered for the stay-at-home job had I been asked. During those days beef or pork chops tended to be only occasional treats, but chicken was another matter. It was the mainstay of our diet. Franklin Roosevelt made a campaign promise of "two chickens in every pot" and served an unprecedented four terms. Although my great-grandmother died when I was quite young, I still remember a visit to her house in Western Illinois. "My Gawd," she said. "Lookit whose here. It's Kate and Ed." And while my brother and I played on the pump organ in her parlor, she ran outside to the chickens, grabbed a couple who couldn't outrun her, and chopped off their heads. She must have been overjoyed to see us, considering our visit a special occasion. It wasn't every day she'd pick and clean two chickens, and this not even a Sunday!

During the hottest days of the summer, when Ma would be slicing cucumbers for a salad or to put in vinegar, my brother and I would beg her for the cucumber ends. In our illustrated Child's Garden of Verses was a poem called "The Land of Counterpane", wherein a young lad lay in his bed, playing with his tin toy soldiers. Not having tin soldiers, we liked to made soldiers out of the cucumber ends. The tops with their stems intact were officers, of course. The bottom ends and topless tops were the enlistees. They were like the pawns in a chess game. On rainy days, we played on the glassed-in front porch. On each end of the porch was one window that could be slid back to expose a screen, and that way we could get a little cross ventilation, and hear the comforting sound of rain pattering down off the roof. The porch had a wooden floor that sloped from the inside door toward the outside one, and we liked to roll marbles down the floor, two at a time, in a race to find the fastest one. Kept in an old Sir Walter Raleigh tobacco can, every one of the marbles was eventually rolled, eliminating them as we went until we found the grand champion, the fastest marble of them all.

When we tired of marble races, there was always the old Victrola on the porch, along with the old 78 RPM records that it played. They ran a gamut of taste, from First World War songs to the depression era. There were Sousa marches, a record of nothing but bugle calls, a propaganda song called "Just Like Washington Crossed The Delaware, General Pershing Will Cross The Rhine" and one of our all-time favorites, "Yacky Hula Hicky Dula"—a true classic. You can imagine my surprise, many years later, on hearing it played and sung by Bertie Wooster, in the PBS series "Jeeves and Wooster", along with many of the old chestnuts contained in that cardboard box. After selecting a record, we had to wind the crank until it was fully wound, and then place the heavy tone arm with a metal needle onto the spinning record. Out would come a favorite song, albeit with a strange tinny twisted sound. Needles wore out quickly and had to be replaced, the grooves in the record quickly wore down, and with the scratches from our record handling, the song lyrics became more and more indistinct, although by then our favorites had been committed to memory and we would happily sing along.

In the spring of the year, the little chicks were growing like crazy in the brooder house. We bought Leghorn chickens or a Leghorn hybrid as straight run chicks, which meant we got them just as they were hatched. At the time, the Japanese had a monopoly in sexing chickens. I don't know how, but they could determine chicken gender when the chicks were still tiny little things. A job as a Japanese chicken sexer required some speed in that a certain number of chicks must be sexed every hour, and with a high percentage of accuracy. Not having Japanese chicken sexers in the neighborhood, we had to do it our own way. As the chicks grew, the young roosters were identified by their crackly adolescent crowing, and combs that were larger and redder than the females'.

When I was a kid, I always had to go to bed early, much of the time when it was still light out; at eight o'clock it was always "off you go". It was a treat, then, when we got to move the roosters. In what seemed like the middle of the night our parents woke us up to go out and help in the brooder house. Unlike their human counterparts, chickens just naturally go to sleep when it gets dark outside, making them much easier to move. We entered the brooder house with flashlights and hooked wires, and were able to catch the chickens by their legs. Although sleepy at the outset, we soon woke up with the lively flapping wings and the squawks of the frightened roosters. They were carried, three or four at a time, to their new home, to be matured for Sunday dinner. Fattening up was not a Leghorn trait; the roosters ate all the time but never seemed to put on much weight. Leghorns were bred for egg-laying and not for lunch. One friend of mine had a mother who raised Buff Orpingtons, a dual purpose breed. They laid brown eggs, not as many as the Leghorns, but the chickens were larger and meatier.

Eventually the chickens that hadn't been caught jumped off their roosts, and huddled in a corner. We didn't want the hens, only the roosters. The smaller fellows, having been pushed toward the outside, were the first caught. Huddled in the back, closest to the wall, were the largest roosters. These budding CEO's, generals, and politicians were shielded by their smaller and weaker brothers, a lesson learned and taken to adulthood. Eventually, though, all the roosters were caught. The young pullets went off to their own house, complete with nests, feeders, and waterers. Not being Japanese chicken sexers, we would still hear occasional crowing in the pullet house, and would ferret out the rooster who had fooled us into taking him for a hen. The chickens that had formerly occupied the pullet house were taken to the old hens home, where, when their feathers started getting scarcer and their egg production scanty, they were literally in the soup. We butchered some of them ourselves, and advertised the remainder of them for sale in the local paper. Buying an old hen remains to me a symbol of widowhood. Most of our customers were little white-haired ladies, answering the ad to buy the live chickens. To pick and clean them for sale was too much work for too little money. We sold them either live or freshly decapitated. When we butchered our own, we first boiled water in buckets on a kerosene stove down in the basement. After we chopped off their heads in the backyard, we took them down to the basement and dipped them into boiling hot water. The steam and the smell were stifling, and plucking chickens one of the worst jobs imaginable. We scraped off the feathers with our hands, and since we were children, it seemed that our fingers were going to get scalded right off just like the feathers. Once the feathers were plucked, we took the chickens upstairs to the kitchen where Ma and Little Grandma used candles to singe off the hair-like pin feathers. Then the chickens were cut open, the innards removed, and the feet chopped off. Nothing went to waste. After the green sack of bile was cut out of the livers, the heart and the gizzard were taken out. The gizzards had to be cut in half and the stones scraped out. We saved the gizzards for Big Grandpa, since they were his favorite. My brother and I liked the wings, and when they were baking in the oven we used to open up the oven door and tap them with a fork to see if they were crispy enough. My mother's sister, Eva, worked for a while picking and cleaning chickens at the abattoir over on the west side of town, Adler's meats. Pa used to complain that Ma's sisters were lazy and wouldn't work. He had spoken up for them during the Depression, and got them jobs in the shipping department of his foundry, but apparently they were less than pleased with their jobs. Eva must have undergone an epiphany since foundry days, though, because a career picking and cleaning chickens was no joy even for someone with the stoutest work ethic.

My brother, Edwin, grew up, went to the seminary and become a Lutheran minister; later on he switched brands and became a minister in the United Church of Christ. He holds me responsible for his belief in the Almighty. We were always eager to go to the barber shop on Second Avenue, an old fashioned barber shop that smelled of cigar butts and Lucky Tiger hair tonic. It had a magazine stand that no doubt had escaped from a Salvation Army store. Littered with outdated torn magazines, the stand also held comic books. They may have been crumpled and torn, and missing a few pages here and there, but they were the kind that my brother and I liked. To our delight, weirdly dressed super heroes and outright freaks danced and flew through the pages. Pa frowned on such outlandish material, steering us toward what he called "sensible" comic books, with those sweet anthropomorphic animals. He was afraid the super heroes and freaks would warp our developing minds. Little did he know that he was fighting a losing battle. Reading about a sappy mouse, his saccharine girlfriend, and a choleric duck was "like water off a (choleric) duck's back". Nothing would stop us from flowering into our deviate destinies. I especially liked the comics where the protagonist had the wings and head of a hawk, a woman who had a magic bracelet that caused her to spin around like a whirling dervish, and a man who was able to stretch his neck for yards and see around a corner. The barber always gave us a parting gift of used comic books and my brother and I couldn't wait to get home. We'd take our comics to a concrete slab near the back door and sit down in the sunshine to read. Once time I bullied my brother into giving me the best comic, the exotic one with the most bizarre of heroes. But when I lowered my bottom to the warm concrete slab . . . WHAM!! . . . as they say in the comics, I sat down on a wasp. I ran howling into the house, holding my behind. Brother Edwin, now certain that God was in his heaven and all was right the world, and appreciating God's swift justice, picked up his treasured comic book and sat down to read.

Pa loved his cows, and he got up early in the morning for milking. He made a churn from a big crock with a paddle and a broomstick handle, to be plunged up and down, and the milk and churn, together with muscle and patience, provided us with butter, buttermilk and cottage cheese. Pa rigged up an egg candler from an old box, a tad bigger that a cigar box, with a light bulb inside. There was an egg-shaped hole on top where we would place the egg, and since the eggs were made nearly transparent with the light shining from the other side, we could examine the eggs for blood spots and cracks. Ma had egg customers, and nothing but the finest would do. The rejects went into the frying pan for breakfast. Ma had us convinced that eggs with blood spots in them were particularly lucky, and even more so the double or triple-yolked eggs, so I wanted all of those that I could get.

These days when a family has a holiday get-together, after a big meal they stack the dishwasher, then sit around and snooze in front of the television. When I was growing up, the women cooked the meal, cleaned it up and were left with the work, while the men grabbed their shotguns and went out to hunt for rabbit or pheasants. There was brush growing along the fence line, much like the hedgerows made famous in English novels, and we piled more brush and tree limbs in the gully so that we had a decent supply of rabbits. In the snow we tracked rabbits to their hiding places in the weeds. Uncle Julian usually tagged along carrying a Louisville Slugger instead of a shotgun. I thought that a bat was a silly thing to bring hunting, but one day a rabbit jumped out of its hiding place and ran between his legs. Snapping his legs shut, Uncle Julian, just for a brief moment, had the animal trapped but couldn't bring himself to use the bat. We could hardly shoot the rabbit without splatting Uncle Julian with buckshot, so the lucky rabbit lived to run another day.

We used the apples from our apple orchard, but there were two trees with no use other than their beauty in the spring. They were crab apple trees, with tiny mealy fruit that my brother and I collected, cutting the crabapples into pieces with our Barlow knives. We dried the tiny pieces and stored them in match boxes that we got from Uncle Julian. We pretended to be explorers, and when we got hungry on our long voyages, we could snack on dried crabapples. Peonies were planted along our cinder driveway, and I was always fascinated by the ants crawling on the little billiard ball buds of the peony bushes. Ma didn't like the peonies picked for the house, as there were always ants escaping from the blooms. In the front yard we had Martha Washington cherry trees and every year, around the Fourth of July, we fought the battle for the cherries to be used for Ma's pies. Blackbirds came by the hundreds to clean up in one night the cherries we had longed for. Nothing deterred them. I shot them out of the trees, hung the corpses by a string from a branch, and watched as the birds continued gobbling down the cherries even while sitting next to their dead siblings swinging in the breeze. I heard their awful squawking while they pilfered our cherries again, so I grabbed a shotgun and shot at the tree. Not one blackbird fell from the tree, but sadly a brown thrasher, a beautiful singer, dropped down with a plop. Why he was hanging out with that bunch of thieving blackbirds remains a mystery, but apparently, as my mother lectured, even if you're a bird you can get into a lot of trouble running with the wrong crowd.

Summers were hot. When we were older, we punched holes in the bottom of a five gallon calf supplement bucket and dug it into the bank of the creek where we knew there was a spring. Even in the hottest days of the summer, we could dip into the bucket and get a drink of cold water, and no longer. had to carry our water with us in a gallon jar. There was a spot along the railroad tracks, not too far from where we fished, where blackberries grew. Ripening during the most scorching time of the year, the thorns on the canes could make deep scratches in the skin, so when we went to pick blackberries we had to wear long sleeved flannel shirts. We'd carry the buckets home, only to find that the berries on the bottom had already turned to mush. One summer it was so hot and dry that the creek almost dried up. There was a bridge over the creek on Newell Avenue and that summer, under the bridge, Bill Clark caught a large sucker with his bare hands. The sucker was trapped in an isolated pool, waiting for a rain so that it could swim away. Our favorite fishing holes were nearly dry, so we went farther downstream in search of more water, but when we threw in our lines, we pulled out giant crawdads clinging to the worms.

My brother, our dog Prince, Little Grandma, and I used to sit on a rickety wooden porch by the front door. We would have a picnic, eating sandwiches from our school lunch boxes. Grandma sat on the ledge on the side instead of the steps, and down below were large gold and black garden spiders, big as a quarter. They wove their webs between the flowers growing in the clay soil Not understanding that they weren't poisonous, I worried that Grandma would fall off the ledge and be bitten to death by the spiders. Our dog Prince didn't last too long. He roamed the neighborhood at night, and Pa said that one of the neighbors had fed him ground glass in some meat. I remember him being on the front porch, and our parents said to stay away from him because he was suffering and he might bite. I think that I can remember him foaming at the mouth. He never had any of the shots that dogs get now, so it may have been distemper. Anyway, we had to shoot him. Eventually Prince was replaced by a border collie named Duke, but I think that by that time I had left home. Duke wasn't very bright, and his only tricks were fetching apples and chasing his tail. Any time he was fed, he would first enact a charade where he'd chase his tail and bark, as if an invading dog (Duke's tail) wanted Duke's supper. He never tired of either trick and loved to bring an apple to any prospective pitcher, slobber drooling out onto the ground. We always thought that Duke was a dog misogynist, because, in addition to defending his meal from imaginary dogs, he had no use for the real ones either, and chased them away, regardless of gender. When Duke started to become feeble and old in dog years, Pa grabbed an ax handle and went for the inevitable walk in the field with him. When they got far enough out, Duke sensed that this was to be his last walk. He turned and faced Pa, growling deep in his throat and baring his teeth. Pa said that he didn't know which of them was going to go back to the house, so he put the ax handle on his shoulder and came back to the house with Duke trotting behind. Duke's reprieve lasted quite a few more dog years. When we were kids we had Zebra firecrackers, and I had so many that they filled up an old potato chip can. We used to light them and throw them at the cat, just for meanness. But the dog walked over at the wrong time, and they blew up under Duke instead. When there was thunder, Duke would get so scared that he came to the back door and chewed off all the wood around the screen door, until Pa let him in to hide under the basement stairs. After Duke died, Pa said that during a particularly bad storm, something had chewed the wooden door to make a large hole in the tool shed. He was convinced that Duke's ghost had come back to haunt him.

Pa always called school the "fun factory". We weren't so sure, and we told him so. But he insisted that it was a factory of fun, not like the foundry or the wallpaper mill. When I turned five, I was to find out if what he told us was true.

PART TWO

School Days, School Says, Dear Old Golden Rule Days.
The foundation of every nation is the education of its youth.—Diogenes

My formal education began at Thornhill School, not the usual little red schoolhouse but a white frame one-room building trimmed in green, with a green door. It was about a mile to the school and my mother walked with me that first day. Summarily rejected because of my short stature, we were sent home to bring back my birth certificate. The next day I returned alone, birth certificate in hand, and so began my acculturation process. I was fitted into the smallest desk in the room. All eight grades were taught by Miss Lang, who only had one year to go until retirement. Back then it was understood that if a teacher was going to get married and start a family, she had to retire to housewifery, and for this reason elementary school was dominated by spinsters. My school supplies included a jar of white paste, pencils, crayons, and the Dick and Jane books. I was shocked to see a few of my fellow scholars snitching tastes of the minty smelling paste. My own yellow Eberhard-Faber lead pencils, with their frequent trips to the pencil sharpener, paled in comparison to the brightly colored new Eversharps sported by some of the wealthier farm kids. Made of plastic, the pencils contained lead that was dispensed by a twist of the eraser. The Eversharp users also had the larger boxes of Binney and Smith crayons, with exotic colors like "burnt sienna" and "flesh." I did have a head-up on reading, since even before moving to the farm I used to listen on Sundays to Joe Kelley reading the "funnies" from the Tribune. By following along on the pages, I learned to recognize the words he read, printed in the balloons above the heads of Dick Tracy and his villain, Prune Face, though "Thwack", "Bam" or "Pfft" never appeared on the pages of Dick and Jane books.

Central heating at Thornhill was a centrally located cast iron stove in the center of the room. Sitting too close to the stove brought on a sweat to soak your long winter underwear, but over by the wall you were shivering. There was a two-part shed outside the school, one side for corn cobs and the other for coal. The corn cobs were free from the neighboring farms and burned with a hot flame, although the fire didn't last long, just long enough to get the coal burning. It was up to the boys to trudge out to the shed with a coal scuttle and bring in coal and corn cobs. The classroom had a large old oak teacher's desk in front, a blackboard made of slate rock, and pictures of our treasured national forebears, George Washington and Abe Lincoln, framed above the blackboard. We had an American flag, too, but I don't remember when we started reciting the pledge of allegiance, although it's held fast in my memory, along with the 23rd Psalm and snippets from Luther's catechism.

We started our day with a half hour of singing from the Golden Book of Favorite Songs. The eighth grade girls played the piano and we took turns requesting our favorite songs, "Columbia the Gem Of The Ocean" and "Tenting Tonight on the Old Campground." The song book as well as the educational format hadn't changed much since the Civil War. Of course we all had to stand for our singing of "The Star Spangled Banner" and on one of my first days at school, somewhere around "the dawn's early light" my bladder went into overtime. I was dancing and leaning on my little desk at the back of the room, afraid to raise my hand during the anthem, so I peed on the floor. One of the older girls was tapped to show me the toilet and led me to a privy connected to the school house. On entering the front door of the school there was a hallway with a boy's privy and a girl's privy on either side. The vent for the toilets went up through the roof, and sometimes there was an eerie howl when the wind blew across it. We got our drinking water from a green iron pump in the schoolyard, pumping the water into a bucket that we carried back into the classroom and placed on a table at the back of the room. You could raise your hand when you wanted a drink, then go back to the bucket and ladle out your drink. Small wonder that diseases were as communal as our drinking arrangement; if something was "going around" we could usually look forward to catching it. The worst for me was the measles. My mother pulled down the window shades and I had to lie downstairs in a darkened room for two weeks, on the bed in Little Grandma's room. It wasn't all bad, though, as my meals were brought in on a wooden tray, and I got to sit up in bed like a little prince. One day a nurse from the county came to the school and showed us a movie about corpuscles, red and white, blob-shaped, and wearing army helmets. When they were attacked by germs, the white blobs fought the germs until they were destroyed. Any movie was exciting to me, as living in the country I saw so few of them. My city cousins were always telling us about the movies they'd seen, and cousin Bobby talked all about the seven dwarves; from Doc to Sleepy he knew them all by name. Soon after the nurse took her movie and drove away, the bucket and dipper were replaced by a crock filled with water, and we lined up for our drinks holding out little conical paper cups. We were told about a German named Koch and his germ theory. My distrust of things medical began about the time I suffered frostbite on the way to school. Ma always bundled me up for the cold weather with heavy woolen garb and a scarf wrapped around my face. It must have come loose on the way to school, because I arrived with my face solidly frozen. The teacher instructed the older girls to run outside and bring in a pan of snow. Common wisdom of the time was to rub the affected part with ice. Being young and small I couldn't argue with the "cure", but it seemed like a dumb idea. Years later doctors changed their minds about frostbite therapy, but it was too late—they had already lost my trust.

Except for the ability to read and do fractions, I have taken little with me from those years of formal education, but a few impressions remain. I can see four or five of the older kids standing behind their project, a paper mache' model of the United states, set up on a table in front of the room. They pointed out mountains painted brown and white, with green for the more verdant sections of the country east of the Mississippi. There was a book with pictures of birds, but I was more fond of their bright colors than in learning their names. Geography was a blur of countries whose names and borders don't exist anymore and of exports they no longer send. From the readers we used, I remember the story about the sun and wind; they had a wager on which of them could make a man remove his coat. The wind blew fiercely but the man just held on to the coat even harder. Then the sun had its turn, and the man soon broke into a sweat, taking off his coat.

The only other student in my grade was Danny Riley. He was even smaller than I, and certainly thinner. At Ma's suggestion I invited Danny to spend the night, and at bedtime she whispered to me "Why his little legs are blue!" The family lived up the road from the school in an old farm house, the farmer living elsewhere on another property. The house must have been rented on the cheap, since it slowly disintegrated and any vital repairs were neglected. The rent paid, there wasn't much money left over for heat, and Danny was always cold. He marveled at how warm our house was, heated by a coal furnace with steam radiators that hissed and popped when the system had a full head of steam. Before we could go to bed the fire in the furnace had to be "banked", placing the coal higher around the outside of the fire so that it would burn for most of the night. The coal left black "clinkers" of odd shapes, with iridescent purplish splashes. These cinders were carried out and spread on the paths between the chicken houses. The modern age arrived for us when we got a coal stoker that fed smaller pieces of coal automatically into the furnace from a hopper by means of an auger. We took a five gallon bucket, filled it at the coal bin and loaded up the hopper once a day. Every year Eaton's coal company came before winter started, and Mister Eaton, a large muscular man covered in coal dust, shoveled the Pocahontas coal through a door in the basement. No bill was sent as Ma had him come into the house and paid him on the spot. My brother and I had the job of scraping up any coal that was left on the ground outside of the bin, and shoveled it through the metal door. Once, when I hit the door with my shovel, a huge bumble bee came out of hiding. I ran around the house and up the stairs into the kitchen. While I was explaining to my mother about my narrow escape and how I'd outrun him, the bumble bee stung me and it felt as if an ice pick had stabbed me in the back of the neck; he'd been going along for the ride the whole time.

The last time I saw Danny was at the Roxy Theater, where he was working as an usher. He had to wear a red uniform with a round, red hat, a costume vaguely reminiscent of an organ grinder's monkey. The uniforms were ill fitting, worn remnants of the early 1940's but at least there were still ushers in the Roxy, and they carried flashlights to guide patrons to their seats. "Honest John" Roskill had an ushering job too, though short-lived. Everybody's friend, he would open the side doors from the inside, letting us in to see movies for free. I had lost touch with Danny because, after the barn on their rental place burned to the ground, the Rileys moved away. Rumor had it that the kids started the fire, but nothing was ever proven. Barns burned for a lot of reasons: hay baled when it was too wet or green, electrical problems, lightning and, sometimes, when heavily insured, burned by the owners themselves.

It was called the "police call" in the army, when we got up with reveille and combed the area around the barracks for cigarette butts and paper scraps. At Thornhill, before school started in the morning, we were occasionally given sheets of Kleenex and instructed to pick up "balloons" in the schoolyard. Its tall grass and large sheltering trees made it a site for local lovers, and the schoolyard was littered with condoms. Our teacher cautioned us not to touch them without using the Kleenex. One night Art, a farm boy who had already graduated and Joe, the hired man on the dairy farm behind us, climbed the largest tree in the yard and waited with several packs of firecrackers, finally dropping them down on a vehicle parked below them. The prank nearly backfired when a partially dressed black man jumped out of his car with a pistol in hand. Luckily for the boys, he thought better than to shoot up into the tree, and finally returned to his car, slamming the car door, and drove off swearing. Knowing how close they came to tragedy they never pranked any lovers again. Bill Walker tried something similar, but it was when we were older and had our licenses. There was another place to park for lovers, on a dirt road even farther out into the country. Bill had his dad's brand new Ford when he decided to drive up and shine a light on a car parked in lover's lane, but this time the surprised Lothario didn't hesitate. He jumped out of the car and peppered the fleeing trunk of the new car with a blast from his shotgun. I'd like to have been there to hear the story that Bill told to his father about how the car was shot. There were pellet marks in a round pattern on the trunk. In the same often used spot, one of my friends parked there after it had rained. About two o'clock in the morning I was awakened by a hammering on the back door, and my friend wanted to borrow Pa's Allis Chalmers tractor to pull out his car. My father woke up and loaned it to him, and we just went back to bed. In the morning the tractor was back in the barn.

It's an old saying that it isn't the destination, but the journey itself that's important. The road to school had dangers of its own, but nothing like those facing the Greek boys who were escorted to school by their *pedagogos*, slaves who were to protect them from getting buggered on the way to school. Our dangers were different from those of the Athenians, but no less frightening. We had to pass over to the other side of the street when we went by Selkirk's. They had a chow dog, a little fur ball but known to be mean as the devil, and we were warned by Ma to cross the street at Selkirk's place. Then we crossed back over when we got by Stevens' farm. Their Holstein bull was staked out alongside the road to eat grass. The only thing between the bull and the Hallenberg boys was a metal chain of indeterminate length attached to a metal pin in the ground. Some of our schoolmates didn't have to walk, but rode ponies to school instead, tying them to the railing in front of the school yard.

I had company on the way to school, Sonny Selkirk and Lois Sederholm. Her house was first, at the corner of our gravel road and Newell Ave. Her dad, the sauna builder, never went to a job, unlike Pa and my Uncle Julian. Flypaper hung down from their kitchen ceiling and the yellow tacky curl was peppered with fly carcasses. We had to wait while Lois' mother got the older sister ready for her job in town, frizzing and curling her hair with a curling iron, which she kept re-heating on the stove. With the hiss of the hot iron and the smell of burning hair, Lois' sister was well turned out and ready for her day. I would stand there sweating beneath my woolen winter coat, which was too much trouble to remove, and listen to Don McNeil's breakfast club blaring from the Bakelite radio. He always instructed his listeners to "march around the breakfast table ladies," but the Sederholm's kitchen was far too small for parade dress, and by then the missus would be busy trying to get us out the door.

Lois was a few grades ahead of me, and her brother Johnny a few grades behind, so I didn't get to know him very well. Like his father, I think that he took a liking to strong liquor, and on one occasion later on it caused him to run into a tree. The property owner, a cantankerous old woman living alone, came running out of her house with a shotgun, waving it at him and then shooting. He took off running down the railroad tracks, the same ones where Grandpa operated his steam engine, and after running for his life he collapsed and passed out on the tracks. Johnny's idea of getting in shape corresponded to Two Ton Tony Galento's, a boxer of that time, who claimed to stay in shape by drinking beer. He was scheduled to fight Joe Louis, and the results proved disastrous for Two Ton. Happily for Johnny, the old lady finally gave up the chase, shouldered her shotgun and puffed her way back home. Johnny nearly died of hypothermia.

Although I was disappointed that Pa's "fun factory" never kicked in, my first year of school was over before I knew it. Miss Lang retired on schedule, and a new teacher was hired to give it a try. No one told me that teachers didn't last forever and I had no inkling until my arrival for year number two that we had a new teacher. She took to heart the old teacher's college admonition not to crack a smile until after Christmas, and strictness was her middle name. A sea change from Miss Lang, no one liked her from the first day of school, especially the older girls, who started a campaign against her and frightened me with their stories of what she could do to me. Afraid to find out, I found myself idling on someone's lawn, supposedly on my way to school, but Missus Sederholm spied me. She asked what I was doing when I should be in school. Having no ready answer I tried to outrun her, but my short legs let me down. The old lady ran like Paavo Nurmi, The Flying Finn, and I was caught, but not before I managed to grab hold of a sapling. Though I held on with all my might, she eventually pulled me off and marched me home to Ma, who later rocked me in Little Grandma's big yellow rocking chair and explained that it was a law that everyone had to go to school. After I returned to my desk at Thornhill it wasn't long before the new teacher was replaced with one of a plumper, jollier variety.

Springtime was hard for studying—the windows of the schoolroom were open and in the field next to the school we could look out of the window and see Art plowing the field on his "Johnny Popper", an old John Deere single cylinder tractor. Everyone including the teacher knew that he was supposed to be in school, but planting and harvesting took precedence.

WWII was getting started; Germany invaded Poland and France, and the Japanese bombed Pearl Harbor. Back then we were still commemorating Armistice Day from WWI, supposedly the Great War and the war to end all wars, and a moment of silence was always observed at 11:00 on November 11th. Uncle Juluan was living with us so I asked him what an armistice was, and he explained that it was a sort of time-out so that combatants could rest up. As WWII revved up, we took the war effort seriously. My other cousin Bobby chased home and beat up a Japanese kid, only to find that he was a Filipino and that his family had left the Philippines before the Japanese army got there. I don't know if Uncle Angus and Aunt Hepzibah had explained to him that we were allies with the Philippines. Sonny Selkirk and a buddy started following me home. Sonny had a wooden gun and in their eagerness to play solider, he would poke the gun in my back and they'd order me to hold up my hands and march. Sonny's friend lived in a house trailer on the Stevens' place, with his parents and an older sister, probably gratis as they were Stevens relatives. "Let's see how you make a fist," they said to me and, sure enough, they said I made the fist of a German, tucking my thumb the wrong way. There were more pokes in the back as I was marched along toward home. For a time the walk was a terror that loomed large, and there was no one to help; the buddy's older sister just walked along, amused at the proceedings. At the supper table with Little Grandma, Uncle Julian, and my parents all assembled I poured out my heart about my problem, sure that they could give me good advice. "Tell 'em that you're Swedish," someone said.

"Tell them you're neutral and not in the fight," was another suggestion. The forced marches continued, but one day, when Sonny upped the ante and jumped on me, I had had enough and exploded, pinning Sonny down on the ground and beating the shit right out of him. No doubt the element of surprise had helped, and his erstwhile buddy thought it best to engage in a strategic withdrawal. That night my mother got a call from Mrs. Selkirk, and when Ma told me about it, she just smiled. No pretense of neutrality there.

We had a small red night light burning when it was dark above the stairs, because our bathroom was located on a landing halfway between the upstairs bedrooms and the first floor kitchen. One night Mister Selkirk, the local air raid warden during the war, came and stood under the window and yelled up that the red light was showing, when there was supposed to be a blackout. The military orders were to put sheets over the windows in case enemies should attack our little corner of the Midwest. Of course, at the time there wasn't a bomber made that could reach to the Great Lakes from an Axis country. He wore the official tin hat of an air raid warden and took his duties seriously. My father, ignoring his advice about neutrality, told Mr. Selkirk to leave or he'd cram that silly hat down over his ears.

One of our wartime duties at the school was to collect the down from inside of milkweed pods, supposedly for use in life jackets for downed pilots, but I doubt that they were ever used for anything. We had drives to collect metal and paper. Our city cousins had a junk man nearby where they were able to bring their old newspapers and sell them. Sometimes folks were known to weigh down the papers with rocks or wet papers in the middle of the pile, but this didn't fool the scrap men for long. At lunchtime we played war using corn cobs for ammo, and pelted Danny Riley's sister, who seemed to be enjoying the attention, as she probably didn't get much at home. The teacher came out and told us to cease and desist, but since we were just boys on a mission, we didn't realize the harm we might have caused young Miss Riley's psyche.

Our parents had books of stamps which rationed certain items deemed essential to the war effort. Gasoline was one of them and even though we could get gasoline for the tractor and the car, Pa and Uncle Julian rode to work a few times on their old bicycles. It was about 5 miles each way, so this didn't happen too often. Providing for the future was, in some circles, thought unpatriotic and called "hoarding". But when it came to sugar, Ma's patriotism took a back seat; she had a secret stash in the large closet in the second floor hallway, storing her precious bags of sugar there. I was lucky, not having to sob over the effects of war, like the kids in Europe, or sustaining the losses suffered by so many other families. My only tears were those of frustration, as I tried to build model airplanes—p47s, Messerschmitts, Mitsubishis—using glue, tissue paper and balsa wood. The glue and bits of construction scrap stuck to my fingers, and the end results never resembled their mighty namesakes.

The metal lunch boxes we carried usually contained peanut butter and jelly sandwiches and tiny thermos bottles of milk. If they happened to be dropped, the shards of glass inside the thermos made an awful sound, and replacing those thermos inserts had to put a dent in Pa's paycheck. During inclement weather we stayed inside to eat our lunch, playing card games like Authors or Old Maid, or maybe pumping on the player piano. The rolls must have been picked up at an auction or maybe left in the piano bench long ago, as they were all in Polish. No one in the school could speak Polish or were familiar with the songs. Weather permitting we spent our lunch period outside and saved the waxed paper from our sandwiches, to polish up the slide for a really fast ride. We played baseball in the little school yard during warm weather, and "Red Rover, Red Rover, send (insert name) over," where one line of kids would send the named person over, to try to break through the other hand-locked line. Pa and Uncle Bob showed us how to play pig-in-a-hole where each kid had a hole and one player lobbed a ball toward the holes. If the ball landed in your hole you had to run and the kid who lobbed the ball had to get the ball in time to hit you with it. We liked to play marbles, and Annie-I-Over, where someone threw a ball over a building while yelling Annie-I-Over," and a kid on the other side tried to catch it.

Miss Lampeau was the last teacher at Thornhill School. Though incomprehensible to us, she must have had a life beyond the confines of Thornhill, and this included a gentleman friend, a rotund cigar-smoking fellow, never seen without the derby that covered his bald head. He usually picked her up in his Oldsmobile after school. The thought of Miss Lampeau with a boyfriend was just too much for my friend Bill Walker to contain. Arriving at school one morning, the poor teacher was shocked to find an original American primitive drawn on the front door of Thornhill school. Depicting a rather Rubenesque couple, nude and in obvious throes of passion (the gentleman's cigar being somewhat south of his navel), the artist finished off his masterpiece with the unmistakable derby hat on the male's head. How Miss Lampeau identified the artist remains a mystery, but in no time Bill and his father were at the school, painting the front door. There was little social commerce between our neighbors unless something was amiss, and then would follow the telephone call. Soon enough Missus Walker was on the phone with my mother, telling her how embarrassed she was and, since the surrounding homes were on a party line, the entire neighborhood shared her pain.

Wilamina Field was a small airport on old Route 66, only a few miles away. On lazy summer Sunday afternoons we watched biplanes that looked like left-over British Spad Pursuits climb way up in the sky to do acrobatics. One such stunt was called a falling maple leaf, where the plane climbed way up in the sky and then headed down in a spiral. The plane was supposed to pull up before it hit the ground. We thought that the pilots must have had experience flying similar biplanes in WW1 because they never crashed. When nighttime came, we could hear the radio at the Redelsheimer's farm, even though it was at least a mile away. The radio speakers must have been huge, because we could make out from hearing "The William Tell Overture" that "The Lone Ranger" was on. When the Lone Ranger and Tonto were sneaking up on the outlaws, we could hear Mendelssohn's "New Hebrides" overture. Even now when I hear it played on the radio I can imagine Clayton Moore and Jay Silverheels creeping up on the "owlhoots" with guns in hand.

One summer day my brother and I were playing Annie-I-Over by the garage, when an airplane flew over. We knew something was wrong since the plane was flying too low, and the engine was sputtering. There were two men in the plane who were swearing, their voices loud and they flew over close enough that we could hear them on the ground. We stopped throwing the ball to listen, and then all was silent. A short time later we heard the wail of a siren. We took off running through the corn fields and down to the neighbor's pasture, which had a considerable slope as the pasture headed down toward the creek. The plane had embedded itself in the slope in the wrong direction. It couldn't have glided anyway, because it was a wood and canvas WWII trainer, made to look like a fighter plane and without its motor running the plane dropped like a rock. When I got there, one of the older kids in the neighborhood, Roger "Wub" Naylor was helping to pull the bodies from the wreckage. Although I had seen dead persons before, they were at funeral homes, laid out in coffins and made up to appear as lifelike as possible. Seeing the twisted bodies and exposed brains of the two fliers after hearing their final moments was too much to bear, and I ran all the way back home, in a state of shock and pale as a piece of writing paper. Uncle Julian greeted me with "Didn't you hear me? I told you not to go." One of the pilots killed was a son of Floyd Pincus, the union organizer of rock throwing fame whom I was later to meet on a picket line. For months afterwards, curious folks drove cars up to us on our gravel road, asking for directions to the crash site. They were looking for macabre souvenirs, pieces of canvas and wood. Although I felt a profound disgust for them and their odd requests, I saw then that I had led a pretty sheltered life. These folks looked just like my friends' parents and my relatives, no different, and certainly not evil. Perhaps everyday people could harbor these aberrations and, for some, another's tragedy brought them out.

Every since my trips to the Five and Dime with Ma, I have always loved chocolate doughnuts. At school we conducted a science experiment with two white rats kept in separate cages. One was fed oatmeal, apples and other healthy foods while the other rat lived on doughnuts and coffee. It was no surprise when the doughnut-eating rat developed "ratty" looking fur, while the rat on the so-called healthy diet was plump, preening his silky white coat. The experiment having proved the efficacy of oatmeal, we held a drawing for the rats. One of the few prizes I've won in a lifetime, I proudly carried home the "ratty" doughnut eater. We built a cage for it in the basement and started feeding it a better diet, following the pyramidal chain as our teacher had shown us. Although not thriving, Ratty seemed to be doing well enough and I was surprised when, one day, Pa told me that the rat wasn't going to make it, and that he had to kill it. He assured me he had taken care of it humanely. Later on I mustered up the courage to ask "How'd you do it, Pa?" He told me, true to his word, that Ratty hadn't suffered; he'd put him under a coffee can and sprayed in some poison gas, and the little fellow just went to sleep. My bull-shit detector went off, but who was I to gainsay my father. Poisoning the rat was far too dangerous a thing to do. No doubt a well placed heavy boot heel had done the job.

I managed to get through fourth grade before Thornhill School closed down. Illinois had passed the Community Unit Law, that one-room country schools were to be closed and replaced by consolidated schools encompassing the old rural one-room models. Oddly enough, even though the old one-roomer was closed, there was no large new shiny school being built near our neighborhood so, instead of going a mile and a half in one direction, my brother and I went a mile and a half in the other direction toward Rustbelt City, on Newell Avenue. There were still dangers on the way to school, although no Holstein bull or chow dog. These had been replaced with considerably more auto traffic, the railroad tracks for big Grandpa's train, a state route where cars came around a curve too fast, and another set of railroad tracks with two sets of tracks, part of the Rickety, Rustbelt, and Eastern line. Ma made it a point to tell us that we had to walk on the left side of the street facing traffic, because the angels wouldn't watch over us on the other side. My brother was to walk in the gravel on the shoulder of the road because, he being younger, the errant car would hit me first. Whether it's an advantage to see the car that ran over you, or whether it's better to be hit first or last, is wisdom that continues to escape me, but those were her rules, and we stuck to them.

Mom and Pop grocery stores were still thriving in those days, and there were two on our way to school, on the corner of the curving highway and Newell Avenue, and at the corner of Miller Road and Newell Avenue. The couple who owned the little store by the highway were grouchy, probably because they weren't making any money. Some of their stock was so old that when they finally closed down, Bill Walker bought a bottle of near-beer left over from prohibition days. Near-beer looked and smelled like beer but the alcohol content was a lot less than aftershave. One day when Ma didn't have anything for supper she sent me on my bicycle to get something from the store, before Pa and Uncle Julian got home from work. This was, for me, an all new level of responsibility, so I cranked up the bicycle to top speed, easy to do because there was a hill leading down to grandpa's railroad tracks. When I hit the tracks I was really moving, and the bike went out of control. One minute I was flying and the next I was skidding sideways along on the pavement. On getting up and examining the bike, it still seemed to be rideable, so I went on to the store and asked for five pounds of sausages. Without so much as a comment on my appearance, the dour lady who owned the store sold me the sausages. I left the store, skin scraped off my face and the blood from my scraped knees running down my legs; when I got home my mother was horrified. "She didn't say a word when you came in the store?" my mother asked. She wiped off my face with a rag, and found that I had taken off a lot of skin from my face and my knees. Continuing on for the sausages, despite my accident, brought attention and praise that night at supper, and almost made the accident worthwhile.

Most of the traffic on Newell Ave. was heading in the same direction—north toward the school. We were heading that way one morning when we saw old grandmother Sederholm. She was carrying a bag holding her few possessions, and was shuffling along in the other direction. "Where are you going?" we asked. "To Finland," she answered. I told her that she was going in the wrong direction since Finland was north of us and she was going south. I knew what lay ahead for her as Newell Avenue ran out of pavement at the country school and then turned to gravel. There was only one curve in the road until it got to Jimson Creek and the gravel road kept getting smaller and smaller until it was, for all practical purposes, a one lane road. I knew, because Edwin and I together with our friend Bill rode our bikes out to Jimson Creek to fish. It was a memorable trip because a farmer's German Shepherd dog came running after us and tore off the seat of Bill's pants. We were standing up on the bikes trying to pedal as fast as we could. Anyway, old Grandma Sederholm didn't comprehend a word of what we were telling her, and kept trudging south until her family brought her back home, never to see Finland again except in her memory.

On the first day at my new school, Ma walked with me, but I sincerely wished that she hadn't. I remember standing in front of the teacher with my mother by my side, knowing full well that the kids peering at me through the window never had to suffer such an embarrassment. They were all crowding up to the window to see the new kid, and the faces were about equally divided between black and white. Among the kids, one in particular stood out, a dirty-faced kid with long blond hair and a flattened pug nose. He was crowding the other kids out of the way for a good long look, and in that innate way of kids and dogs, I sensed danger. I knew that he meant trouble, sooner or later.

The building was a one-story school made of limestone, just like all of the other city schools, because, at one time, Rustbelt City boasted a number of limestone quarries. Further north on Newell Ave, about a half-mile from the school, was the Michigan Quarry. Pa and Uncle Julian could remember when it was still in operation. There was a dynamite shack at the bottom, and they said that some one had once broken into the shack and stolen dynamite. One of the older boys of Pa's acquaintance had studied his high school chemistry, and showed Pa and his brothers how to make black powder using charcoal, sulfur, and saltpeter (potassium nitrate). Willing students, the brothers and their friend built a home-made cannon and fired it off. Sadly the student who had showed them how to make black powder stopped short of explaining the first law of thermodynamics. The mighty cannon fired off its projectile, but at the same time flew backwards and went right through Grandpa Hallenberg's wooden porch.

Eventually the company that owned Michigan Quarry pulled out the pumps, the quarry filled with water, and by the time I was in grade school we used to go fishing there when Pa got home from work. Across the street was the city dump, which had also been a quarry, but it was being filled with trash. I saw bass lurking in its murky green water, but I never went there to fish. It was the greatest place for shooting rats, though, because they grew as big as cats; mostly the kids went there for target practice.

On one side of Hampton School was Greentree, where the white kids lived, and on the other side was Cannondale, home to the black kids. Across the street from Cannondale was the Lutheran Home for Children, housing not only orphans but kids from various situations that ranged from poverty to outright abuse. And there were the few of us from Thornhill, kids from the country, and the Legges, who lived in a big mansion on the corner of Newell and Mann Road. A creek ran through their property and there was a wooden cabin in back of the house, through the woods, that displayed the trophies from their grandpa's hunting expeditions: heads, horns, and skins, they even included a jaguar skin from a trip to Mexico. Grandpa Dahlhaver made a lot of money, all courtesy of Jackson Ice Company and other business enterprises. Missus Legge was friendly with my mother, and had egalitarian impulses, hoping that sending her Jan through the Rustbelt School System would make a "regular fellow" of him. The experiment was doomed to failure, due more to his personality than to his social standing. But later on in life, my friend Bill reported seeing Jan at a twenty-year high school reunion. He had a young, leggy blonde on his arm and was driving a flashy sports car with the top down. Even had they been from a rental agency, the girl and the car were still quite a coup at a Rustbelt High School reunion.

The school playground was covered with crushed limestone, and had a basketball backboard, a baseball diamond in the grass, and a field out back covered by a luxuriant growth of giant ragweed. The kids would trample down paths in it for play. Don Harlan was the pug-nosed kid who'd shown such interest in me, the newcomer whose mother brought him to school. Don came from a large family in Greentree, all boys save for one girl, and even she had wider shoulders than I did. Dirt was ground into his hands, likely from helping his older brothers work on cars after school. When a new kid came to the school he was given the Harlan treatment, where Don would start a fight to show that he was still "cock of the walk". Not wanting to dispute his status, I hoped to avoid a fight, but knew that a beating was likely hanging over my head; it was just a matter of time. One recess we chose up sides for a football game, and they decided in the huddle that they'd hand off the ball to me. Full of pride and not wanting to let the team down, I started running with the ball, with what looked like the entire male population of the school gaining on me. I put my head down, running as fast as my short legs would allow, and ran smack into the post for the basketball backboard. I must have passed out for a few seconds, but came to, looked up at the stars spinning around my head, and heard someone say, "I've never seen anybody do that before." I'd made it, and was one of the guys, without even getting beat up.

We still liked to play marbles, and even had a tournament once a year. There were official rules and an official size for the circle, and the tournament was held by the city in all the grade schools. The tournament marbles were made of clay instead of the usual glass marbles, and the winner of the tournament got to keep the marbles. Although I couldn't make my own glass marbles, I saw the possibilities for making them out of clay. I went home, dug a hole out by the garden down to the clay layer which started about a foot down from the loam, and made my own marbles, heating them in the oven. Then my brother and I could have our own tournaments, and I had a good chance to win.

When we played marbles, you got to keep the ones that you shot out of the ring, the marbles belonging to the other player. My marble stash usually dwindled, but Don Harlan's was the largest collection, and he kept them in a three pound coffee can. When recess was over, somebody would yell "grabzies", and we scrambled for any marbles left in the ring. Don may not have been the best marble shooter, but he was far and away the best grabber.

The darkest days for the white kids and the brightest for the black kids were after every Joe Louis fight. All the colored kids would be bobbing and weaving by the back door of the school, and I'd wait until the last minute to go in, when the enthusiasm had died down, and shuffle in with the rest of the white kids, much subdued. To tell the truth, though, I never listened to the fights on the radio and didn't care who won. Don Harlan said, "Wait 'til he fights Gus Lesnivitch." Joe Louis beat everything but the Internal Revenue Service: Tony Galento, Billy Conn, and Tammy Maurielo. The sports writers said Maurielo couldn't back up because his heel had been run over by a car and, as everyone knew, the ability to back up was a necessary skill when facing Joe Louis in his prime.

We had an occasional visitor to the school, and they'd always receive a warm welcome if we were getting out of class for an assembly. Any reason to get out of class was a good one, and the "movie man" was no exception. He arrived in a black van, and as soon as he pulled into the school yard he'd be surrounded by kids pounding on the van and screaming for movies. He brought out his projector and the silvery, circular discs that held the precious movies and headed into the school. The movies were well screened for object lessons in behavior, celluloid Aesop's Fables, but the only movie that I remember used Steven Foster's "Beautiful Dreamer" as a theme woven throughout the show. The star played a man who went to court and said that he didn't like the United States, saying "Damn the USA" or something in that vein. Taking him seriously, the judge banished the man from our shores, sentencing him to be shuffled from one boat to another for the rest of his life. "Beautiful Dreamer" rendered by a thousand screeching violins (the sound system being less than mediocre) played in the background while his lady love, whom he would never see again, gazed out to sea. The sad expatriate finally died and was thrown overboard. For some reason the movie left me with a long abiding feeling of anxiety, similar to what I felt for a long time after Ma had read us Black Beauty.

Another assembly featured a clown who came in and entertained, then showed us how to put on clown makeup and walk in floppy shoes. When the show was over, a few of us, more star-struck than the others, hung back and then followed the clown down to the basement, where we found him sitting with the maintenance man. They were taking pulls off a bottle of Four Roses, the cheapest rotgut available at the time, and were engaged in animated conversation. When they looked up and saw us standing there they were quite cordial, but discouraged us from joining the circus just yet. We returned to our classrooms but someone had ratted out our "Bozo" to a teacher. The clown had given his last performance at Hampton school.

I don't remember whether it was the day of the drunken clown or a different day, but someone got the bright idea to swing from the overhead wood beam in the boys toilet. The fun escalated and we soon were swinging, and yodeling like Tarzan of the Apes (played in the movies by ex-Olympic swimmer, Johnny Weismuller). As punishment the teacher had to slap the hand of every errant lad with a ruler, each of us putting our hand flat out on our desk. It worked on everyone but Ronny Hallwood, who pulled his hand back just as the ruler came down, causing the teacher to hit the desk. Without a doubt one of the smartest kids in the room, his became an increasingly sad story. I heard that he had started stealing the spinners off steering wheels. A thing of the past, there are no longer any spinners for sale. They're illegal, perhaps because they were dangerous, since your shirt cuff could get caught, and cause you to have an accident; perhaps, too, some censor decided that the naked chicks in the flashy plastic spinners were too distracting. At any rate, Donny moved up to hub caps, a much hotter commodity, since they could be bought and sold in the parking lot of the local drive-in root beer stand. Thinking logically, Donny thought if hubcaps, why not tires, and finally graduated to just taking the whole car. I never saw him again after sixth grade, and never learned of his eventual fate.

Santo Santorini was another visitor who came to the school. He'd ride up on his bicycle, red white and blue pin wheels spinning on his bike, which was tricked out with all sorts of gadgets. The kids would run after him, screaming, "Santo . . . . Santo's here". He'd give us a lopsided grin while sitting on his bike, and thoroughly enjoyed his celebrity status. Santo lived with his legendary mother in Greentree, and his family was the source of many stories. The kids said that old Mrs. Santorini liked to sit on her front porch, but had blown out the bottom of her chair with a huge fart. She was reported to use the front porch, too, when she'd stand there and trim Santo's pubic hair with a scissors. Old grandpa Santorini was a drinking buddy of Grandpa Hallenberg, and was nicknamed Black Joe. Another Rust Belt City immigrant, he had come over from Sicily. They shared a love of alcohol, and got together to drink "grappa" and tell stories about the old country. Grandpa brewed his own, both beer and hard liquor. He walked along the railroad tracks where he knew that there were some hop plants growing wild, and would gather them for his beer. He made the hard liquor by fermenting potatoes and then distilling off the alcohol, his own version of vodka or aquavit. It was on one of his hops excursions that Grandpa reported having seen and talked with his "*tompte*".

There was an outbreak of the flu during the winter when I was in fifth grade. Kids got dizzy and weak and then passed out on the floor. Stanley (Stosh) Lefarge fell over in class one day and four or five kids picked him up and carried him out of the room. He went out stiff and straight, looking up at the ceiling, in a move that I was sure had been orchestrated by some of the boys to get him out of class. Nobody let me in on the joke, but Stanley was out of school for the rest of the day. He was a good actor, and when we put on our version of "A Christmas Carol", he was given the role of Scrooge's nephew. Ronny Hallwood was Scrooge, and I was envious because that's the role I wanted to play. It was probably type casting when I was given the role of Bob Cratchit, who had more children than he could support and a meaningless job, in his case copying bits of information from one piece of paper to another. Shirley something or other was my wife and our Tiny Tim came from the "crippled kids room." One of the rooms in our school was designated the "crippled kids room," where many of the kids were placed who were left handicapped from the polio epidemics of the 1940's. One of them was picked to play Tiny Tim, and he had to be small enough that I could carry him on my shoulders. Stanley was a big hit with the audience that night, an audience made up of teachers and our parents. He hammed up his part and had a Southern accent that didn't sound at all like his uncle Scrooge. And the play ended with Tiny Tim on my shoulder waving the actual cane that he used, saying, "God bless us, every one." You don't get any more realistic than that.

Once a year there was a benefit for the PTA, where the mothers showed off their cookies, cupcakes, and the like on card tables set up around the outside of the main hall, near the principal's office. For a nickel or a dime you could get all sorts of goodies, and a few things were even priced at a penny. Ma took a great deal of pride in the fact that her popcorn balls sold out every year. As a family, we had healthy eating habits, seldom having any candy around the house. Once or twice a year, though, Ma made popcorn balls or cream puffs. They didn't last for long at school, and they didn't last for long at home either.

The only other time during the year when we could live for an entire day on nothing but Popsicles, ice cream bars, and soda pop, was the day of the Sunday School Picnic. It was held in a wooded park with a large open area, just across the street from the Lutheran orphan home, and went on into the night. There would be a bonfire, with everyone standing around the fire and singing "The stars at night, are big and bright . . . deep in the heart of Texas" (clap, clap, clap). There was no refrigeration in the little park, so the ice cream bars were kept in canvas containers with dry ice; every time they were opened they'd give off a cloud of cold steam. Next to the park was the Rust Belt City Country Club and its golf course. One year, during the picnic, Red Henderson ran out onto the golf course and tried to steal one of the balls. He was caught and punished, not being as fleet of foot as the colored kids from Cannondale who made stealing golf balls into a profitable sideline. They'd run onto the green when they could get away with it and run back into the Cannondale subdivision, and later they'd sell the balls at a discount price to a new group of golfers. Having made it back into Cannondale they were usually safe, since even a rich white guy wouldn't be crazy enough to chase a colored kid into the unpaved street near the Black Crescent Tavern.

Being more than ready for spring, the teachers announced that we were going to have a kite flying contest. It was the first, and last, time that we had anything like this at the school, and on the appointed day—which was very windy—the teachers all stood outside of the school, wearing long-sleeved sweaters with the ever-present handkerchief tucked into the wrist band, and enjoying their break immensely. Since Uncle Julian worked at the wallpaper mill he brought home a roll of paper for my brother and me to use for our kites. We split up a bamboo pole into thin slivers to use for the sticks, and Uncle Julian, somewhat of an artist, helped my brother by drawing a green and gold dragon on the face of his kite. My kite was over four feet high, taller than I was at the time, and on its face I drew a fox. Not having the benefit of Uncle Julian's artistic skill, I drew two eyes on the same side of Mr. Fox's face. Ma and Pa helped out by cutting up old rags into strips which were then tied together, and the tail was carried in a shopping bag. Mason's cord was used for the kite string, strong enough to hold up an elephant without breaking, unlike the fragile string that was actually sold for kites. I don't think a kite with a forty foot tail had ever been seen before in our neighborhood. Two of my proudest achievements in life have been quitting cigarettes and building that kite. Years after I'd left home, the kite (by now referred to as the four eyed fox) hung in the brooder house, long since abandoned by the little chicks Ma used to raise. Mice chewed up the paper and the four-eyed fox to use in their homes. I went in and looked at it wistfully from time to time, remembering a triumph as momentous to me as Lindbergh's flying across the Atlantic.

On the appointed day, I headed for school with both kites because my brother had come down with the measles. Jackie "Polecat" Streets saw me at the school carrying the tail in its shopping bag, and he said, "If that kite flies, I'll be its tail". He was a little fellow at the time, and we called him Polecat because kids chased him home on Newell Avenue heading toward Greentree. There was a ditch alongside of the road with sewerage in it, and if the kids caught Jackie they threw him in the ditch. That's how he got his nickname, and he soon became the fastest runner at Hampson School. Years later, just after he'd been discharged from the Marine Corps, I saw him at Sofie's Club House when he came in to pick up a pizza. Considering his size and his military bearing, calling him Polecat seemed unwise.

The kids from Greentree used old newspapers for their kites, and they were about one-third the size of mine. As my kite rose into the sky, it went up over the school and seemed to be all the way to Cannondale. Stanley Lefarge helped me, and we wrapped the string around a fencepost on the fence between the school property and DeCitto's land. At one point, in spite of its large tail, the kite started spinning around, did a nose dive, and crashed into the ground. More kids rallied round and helped me to get it aloft again. When the contest was called over, it took forever to reel in all the string since the wind was still blowing hard. At the assembly held after the contest, prize winners were announced, and I was given the prize for the highest flying kite. There was a special prize for my brother, having the kite with the best design. Apparently no one else had an uncle who could draw such professional looking dragons.

I loved to eat and was getting fat from a excess of peanut butter. Another favorite was berries, and on the way to school my brother would wait patiently alongside the road while I charged into the brush to forage for berries. In one of my forays I was scratched by some unidentified bush, and came to school with a rash of red bumps on my arm. "It's the seven year itch," Don Harlan said. "You'll get it back again every year at this time for seven years." Since I was diligent about my school work, the teacher thought I'd make a dutiful patrol boy, and after a ceremony where I was given my white patrol boy belt, it was official. My responsibility was to herd the little primary kids to a point where they could safely make it back to their homes. One patrol boy went north along the main drag to Greentree subdivision, and another went south toward the Lutheran orphan home and Cannondale. In the fall the wild grapes were ripening as they crawled up the trees alongside the road, and, just as I'd done with my brother, I went over to the vines and ate the grapes as fast as I could, while the little kids stood and fidgeted by the roadside. The grapes were small and it took a long time for me to fill up. No doubt the teachers wondered how I could walk that slowly and, on returning to school, my purple hands and the purple ring around my mouth told the tale. Eddie Tee Watson got my white belt, and I had to stay in the classroom until the closing bell, while Eddie Tee was out in the sunshine walking the little kids toward home.

Low points for the year were often high points for us kids. One stormy night a fire at DeCitto's house lit up the sky along with the flashing lights from the fire trucks.

In the other-worldly glow, firemen stumbled around with heavy hoses, not taking much notice of the kids from Greentree dancing around in excitement, watching as sparks shot from the roof of the house. The next day at school, you could still smell the scorched wood, and the house on the hill had broken windows and a gaping hole in the roof. Don Harlan said that while they were busy, he'd managed to steal a fireman's hat. "What did you do with it?" we asked. "I ran off with it and wore it for a while. Then I was afraid that somebody would catch me with it so I shit in it and buried it out in the woods." As far as I know, the hat is still under the ground in Greentree, waiting for a future archeologist.

Justice was swift in our grade school, and parents were involved only after punishment had been meted out. Although most punishments were minor, the principal kept a razor strop in her office for major offences. When the strop was used, the door to the office was closed, and we could hear the wails of the offender receiving his punishment after confession.

Miss Loosely was a young teacher who taught one of the lower grades. To be a teacher then was a near certain guarantee of a single life, but Miss Loosely escaped a few years later to a job teaching the dependents of servicemen in Germany, after the war. Somebody dumped stones and gravel into the gas tank of her car. She came out at lunch time to find her gas cap missing, and a suspicious ring of mud and gravel around the place intended for gas. The entire school was assembled on the playground, and Miss Ernest, the principal, held up a shiny fifty cent piece. "You see this?" she said. "The first student to find Miss Loosely's gas cap gets this fifty cent piece." Fifty cents would buy ten bottles of pop at the time, so this was no small reward for the missing cap. Sure enough, one kid ran as fast as he could go, in a straight line, right for the gas cap in some weeds growing in the ditch alongside the road. "You did it, didn't you?" the principal said. The kid denied it, and was squirming under the grip of the stocky Miss Ernest, who hauled him off to the office and closed the door. It's said that confession is good for the soul, and, after a few well placed whacks with the belt, confession was obtained. The next day, from the window of my class, I could see a heavy black lady, sadly and slowly making her way to the principal's office.

By the time we got to sixth grade, Don Harlan and Willie Brown sat in the back of the room, Don thoughtfully chewing on his pencil and Willie with his box of crayons. More conventional students sat closer to the blackboard and the teacher's desk. Don hadn't studied the lesson, but he was plenty bright enough, he just had a different agenda. "What were you doing last night instead of your lessons?" the teacher asked. He replied that he was in a dark closet looking at his atomic bomb ring. Fifty cents and a Cheerios box top could get you one. I knew, because I had one too, but all it did was shoot out sparks in the dark. Probably radioactive, and there are most likely scads of adults with damaged eyeballs, scarred from peering at their atomic bomb ring in darkened closets. Don was faster than the teacher with his comments, though, and I could see she was counting the number of times that he wasn't exhibiting the "proper respect".

None of us had the slightest idea of what a cloak might be, but on one side of the classroom was a walk-in closet with an entrance at one end and an exit at the other, called a cloak room. It was where we hung our coats and stowed our overshoes in the winter. Our mother had just bought us brand new galoshes, the kind with the five buckles up the front. Being practical by experience, she placed a piece of tape in each boot with our names written in indelible ink. When we got to the back door of the school, my brother pulled off his boots (tracking up the floor with dirty boots was a major offense), and then turned around to pick up his lunch bucket. When he turned back again to retrieve his boots, they were gone. The principal and Edwin's teacher went through each room of the school in search of the boots and finally worked their way up to sixth grade. They walked into the cloak room, and there standing beneath Willie's tattered coat were my brother's new boots. Willie hadn't even taken out the identifying tape from inside of the boots; most likely he couldn't read anyhow. "Why did you do it?" the teacher and principal asked. "They was so nice and shiny," he answered, with a pleading look in his eyes as they led him off to the office.

Willie marched to school with his brothers and sisters, single file along the road, with the oldest in front. There were about a dozen in the family, with Willie (or Dog, as he would soon be known) in the lead, then Stony and Red after that, followed by the rest of the little guys, too numerous to name. We were waiting for the bell to ring and the school to open one morning, milling and shuffling around, when Willie decided he just couldn't hold it anymore. He opened his fly and took a piss, right there in the schoolyard. Don Harlan, disgusted by this breach of decorum, commented that "Willie's dick looked like a little brown stick." Insulted, Willie amazed us by brandishing a straight razor. Don took the straight razor from him by grabbing Willie's arm and punching him in the face. "Where'd you get this?" Don asked. "I found it Harlan ! I found it layin' alongside the road." Don took the razor, and stuck it into his boot. It's my razor now," he said. I told this story years later to someone at a plant where I was working, and he didn't believe it. He said nobody could take a razor away from Dog Brown.

In the Summer, there were baseball games between the Greentree Cardinals (as we called ourselves) and the Cannondale Brown Bombers. If we were choosing up sides for a game, I was always the last person picked. When I asked Harlan to tell me the secret of success, he said that it's all in the wrist. During the winter we rolled up giant snowballs and made forts, defending them by throwing snowballs at each other. A good throwing arm came in handy. At the corner of Mann Road and Newell Avenue there was another mom-and-pop grocery store owned by an Italian couple. No doubt a disagreement caused Dog Brown to throw a rock at Chuck Henderson, one of the kids from the orphan home. Dog missed his target, and instead broke the plate glass window of the grocery store. The old man came running out, swearing in Italian and shaking his fist, but the perpetrator and the spectators were already blocks away, having taken off at the first sound of tinkling glass. With people like us for customers, how could you make a dime? Don Harlan went into the store wearing a heavy overcoat and came out smiling. He had slits in the pocket of the overcoat and reached in to hand out big belly button oranges to his lieutenants. Another time, a delivery truck crashed and overturned at the intersection in front of the store. The driver didn't seem too badly hurt and, after he was hauled away by the ambulance, the realization dawned. Although such things happened only in dreams, the truck was filled with candy, now spilled out on the road, and kids from all over flocked to the scene to help themselves, until the cops arrived to shag them away.

Sixth grade proved to be one of the most successful periods of my life. I was elected by my classmates to be the representative of our school at a Junior Red Cross meeting for all the grade schools in the city. Even though I'd handled only a few dollars in my life, I found myself running for the post of treasurer. The meeting was designed to show us what democracy was about, and I got to pick the representatives to go along with me. Looking around the room, it seemed a good idea to pick boys who might enjoy a day away from hum-drum classroom life. The choices were obvious, since all of the boys that I picked where tougher than I was, and I feared reprisal if they were disappointed. So off we went to Gomphrey School, and I vaguely remember being introduced as a candidate. I had to go up onto a stage in front of a lot of kids and teachers. There was a lot of cheering for me, loudly encouraged by Don Harland, Stanley Lefarge, Eddie Tee and Clyde Watson. It seemed there was a good chance of winning, judging from the roar of the crowd, but when the ballots were cast I lost handily. It was a relief, since I wasn't sure just what a Treasurer was supposed to do, besides count money.

When we got back to Hampson school, my representatives said that they couldn't understand how I managed to lose. They said they'd taken Don's suggestion and stood outside the door during a break in the proceedings, asking kids as they came out who they were voting for. If they didn't say "a vote for Hallenberg," then they got a punch in the face. Only a few punched back, and made a real horse race out of the election. Like the junior politicians they were, the dirty rats went back to the auditorium and voted for somebody else, going back on their word. We heard that there were some complaints of voting irregularities, lodged by teachers from the other schools.

Three grades behind me in the school, my brother was whiling away his time, along with our old friend from the neighborhood, Bill Walker, and Jan Legge, his mother's candidate for an egalitarian education. Jan's refined speech and his gentle demeanor labeled him a "sissy", but in our milieu, it only meant that he was kind and ingenuous. When his family finally gave up and moved away, I went to the auction sale at their house, and bought a set of elk horns and a jaguar skin rug. My brother

said it was a shame that I was bidding against a boy scout who could have put the
retired wild life to better use, but I didn't see the young scout. Every year the jaguar
rug got thinner and thinner (it really didn't fit into the decor of married life), until
finally our little son kicked its straw filled head off. I don't know what happened to
the elk horns, but most likely, after making the rounds at the neighborhood yard
sales, they're perched on the hood of some car fancier's vintage Cadillac.

There was a circular drive in back of the Legge house, around a goldfish pond
that was surrounded by rocks and flowers. One morning in class, to my brother's
horror, Jan Legge tattled on his classmates, saying, "Miss Tracey, I saw Archie Nash
and August Jefferson fishing in my fish pond". It was an invitation to a beating.
I told Pa about what Edwin said had happened in his class. Pa told me that once,
when he was younger, he had a kid in his class that everyone thought was different,
and they called him a sissy. The "oddball kid" grew up to become a world famous
naturalist with a number of books to his credit. "So who's got the last laugh now?
He's not working in the foundry!" Archie grew up to own a little eatery on Bass St,
and had a disabled child. August was doing fairly well in the local drug business,
but decided to expand his horizons, and was killed in California.

Television hadn't appeared in homes for our entertainment, so we had talent
shows at the school. The Streets Brothers had a barbershop quartet and sang,
"Goodbye my Coney Island baby, so long my own true love." They dressed up in
striped black and white suits and wore straw hats. Everyone was sad the day the
quartet disbanded, when half the group went to jail for one crime or the other. My
personal favorite was Geraldine Scarpia, one of my classmates. She had naturally
curly black hair, and dressed up in a cowgirl outfit to sing "I didn't know the gun
was loaded." The song was about a woman explaining to the judge about how she
managed to shoot her husband, and the "jury all agreed, that Miss Seppi should be
freed." I can't think of why that young a girl would willingly dress so provocatively,
and sing in front of an audience, unless it was on Major Bowe's Amateur Hour,
and later, on television, the Morris B. Sach's Amateur Hour. She must have had
either a stage father or a stage mother pushing her on. Years later I played poker
with her mother in the back room of Sofia's Club House. Perhaps characteristic
of a stage mother, she always bluffed. Good hand or bad, she bid on every one as
if she were holding four aces. Geraldine showed the same lack of judgment as her
mother, since she sat next to me on the ride into the coal mine at the Museum of
Science and Industry. It was one of our rare field trips; we took a yellow school bus
into Chicago, the bus filled with chattering, smelly kids carrying brown paper sacks
with carefully packed lunches inside. The ride down into the mine in the cars was
dark and scary, and Geraldine jumped into my lap. I don't believe anyone had sat
on my lap before, and I didn't know what to do any more than her mother would
had she been really holding those four aces. After that year I don't remember seeing
Geraldine again—goodbye Coney Island baby.

I graduated from the school, although there was no ceremony involved in leaving sixth grade. Wanting to give my teacher a gift, I dug down in the ground at home until I hit clay and fashioned what I thought looked like an elephant, and baked it in the oven. Then I painted it shit-brindle brown and brought it to my teacher as a going-away present. Edwin was delegated to carry the elephant, in a brown bag, and of course the trunk got knocked off. Somehow I doubt that the trunkless elephant sat for very long in the china closet with the rest of her objets d'art. After cleaning out my desk I walked to the street, and there was Don poking in the ditch with a stick. "Old Miss Delano flunked me." Don had to do it all over again—sit in the back of the room and chew on his pencil. But Miss Delano was on the way up, even though it would appear that Don was on the way down. The principal went to a different school, and Miss Delano assumed the job. I can see the ceremony: the two women meeting in the office behind closed doors, and instead of a ceremonial sword, a passing on of the razor strop.

I saw Don a few times after that, and most people, especially his teachers, didn't see much of a future for him. Maybe he flunked a few more grades, because I saw him running up the stairs in high school with another tough-looking kid, but he dropped out before that first year was over. Then he married a fifteen year old girl. Back then you could do this by running off to Missouri. Eventually he started buying up old houses and selling them, and one of his brothers said that he was working so hard that he dislocated his shoulder. Driving down Washington Street, I saw him standing at the door of the wallpaper mill to get a breath of fresh air. Somehow or other, he got a pipe fitter's card, and later on I saw him at the chemical plant. He was carrying a pipe about twenty feet long, and the pipe was bounding up and down on both ends as he walked.

A fellow employed at the plant, a guy who hadn't been there long, went to the office early in the morning before the big shots arrived and told the night foreman he wanted his money right now. Somebody was coming for him and he felt that, for health reasons, he had better get out of town fast. He shoved the foreman around a little until the foreman opened up the safe and gave him the money out of petty cash. When Don heard about it he came running up "Where's the son-of-a-bitch?" But the miscreant was long gone. The last thing that I heard, Don had bought a plumbing supply business and had a house with ten acres in a ritzy subdivision. And I read in the paper that he and his wife were going to have a celebration for their fortieth wedding anniversary. When it comes to a person's future, I was glad to be reminded that predictions are seldom right.

On graduating, I was sent on to a junior high school, an even bigger limestone prison that was two stories high. The choice was to either get a ride from someone or catch the bus at the corner of the state highway and Newell Avenue, across the street from the grouchy couple's grocery store. While waiting for the bus, I saw Naomi Hougue walking to the store with the home-made pies that her mother made for sale. She walked down the street from Cannondale, and crossed the double railroad tracks of the Rickety, Rustbelt and Eastern where there was a wooden shack along side of the tracks. Next to the orphan home was an old folks home, and one of the old men from the home was given employment as a crossing guard. When a train came, he popped out of his shack to make sure that cars or kids didn't try to cross with a train coming. The train went to Gary, Indiana, and the only kid to ride it that I know of lived at the orphan home. His older brothers were already at the home and were athletes of some note, but he decided he didn't want to be there. One day he hopped a freight car when it slowed down, and rode to Gary. At school he bragged about his adventures, after he was caught and brought back, and we were impressed with his stories. The administration at the orphan home was less impressed, though, and sent him off with a one way ticket. I don't know where he went, but kids at the home who didn't "play ball" were sent off never to return.

The foundry shut down about the time that I was going to junior high, and Pa got a job loading trucks at the same wallpaper mill where Uncle Julian worked. My father had worked at the foundry since he was fourteen, so not only was this was a cut in pay, but the work was physically demanding because he was fifty years old at the time. At home we joked about the hamburger ; at supper they might be seventy-thirties, sixty-forties, or maybe eighty-twenties, the lower figure depending on just how much oatmeal, crushed soda crackers or bread crumbs were used. We were fortunate because we lived on a small farm, and though money might be scarce, we still ate well. I suspect other kids whose dads were laid off lived on a lot less. Not unusual for their time, Pa and Ma had both only finished eighth grade, and there was a long time when Pa didn't work at all. The old saying that "when it rains it pours" was certainly true as Pa had a cut that got infected, and he had to sit in the kitchen soaking his thumb in hot water and Epsom salts. My new school was on the way to the paper mill, so he dropped me off in his black pickup truck. He'd painted it himself with a bucket of enamel and a six inch brush. Although the paint job didn't look like much, it kept off the rain. The only truck older than ours belonged to old man Katzky.

Mister Katzky had a model A Ford, painted green and yellow, with his name in bold letters on the door—as if we didn't know who he was—and in the back of the truck were brooms and the other sundries he sold door-to-door. Usually sitting next to him in the passenger seat was his daughter Celine. Every society must have its deviants, and at my seventh and eighth grade alternative to a coed reform school, the prim Miss Celine stood out. Her hair was drawn up tightly in a bun, whirled around and set smack dab in the middle of her head, and as she stepped from the truck she carried a leather briefcase in her hand. No doubt her parents had encouraged the briefcase, a proper scholarly accoutrement in the old country, but in our milieu anything that smacked of the intellectual would be either derided or just ignored. After all, this was the era of early television and we faithfully watched the roller derby. Good looking women whizzed around a banked oval track, and tried to pull down their opponents by yanking on their hair. My friends talked continually about Chief Don Eagle, Gorgeous George, Bonito Gardeni, who wrestled on television. Celine wore dark colored dresses and thick brown cotton stockings, like the ones my "little Grandma" wore. I can remember being in only one class with Celine, where she made everybody look up and pay attention, no mean feat, when the teacher was talking about music. Celine said that the violin was the greatest of all musical instruments. I was not quite sure whether it was the same thing as a fiddle, but she was firmly established as a crazy. And as in most societies, persons labeled as crazy were usually left alone. If you almost fit in with the rest of the kids, or even if you just wanted to, you were likely picked on. But Celine was just ignored: no slumber parties, no gossip, and no giggling about cute boys.

Once again, the majority opinion of an individual's likely future proved to be wrong. I had forgotten about her by the time I was married, living in an apartment, working midnights in a chemical plant, and greeting a new dependent every other year. In the local paper, I spied a strange article in the letters to the editor, where some young lady extolled the pleasures of what she described as "free love.". Even though I'd been told "there's no such thing as a free lunch," she made sure that every one knew her lunch was free, and she went on with an interesting indictment of conventional morality. Of course, the name at the bottom of the letter was Celine Katzky. Her old country, orthodox father must have been spinning rapidly in his grave. I'm sure that I must have overlooked something while we were watching the girls with tight sweaters and bobby socks.

The school was bounded by city streets, the city football field and Slickery Creek, which had a miniscule amount of water about twenty feet below its concrete walls. Large weeds and green, slimy moss grew in the creek bed due to a large amount of nourishing sewerage. The school grounds had a baseball diamond with shady trees and spectator benches running parallel with the first base line, and there was a cinder track running around the outside of the baseball field. On Sundays local teams would match up against teams from the surrounding towns, and sometimes we'd watch the games. The bleachers on the football field were wooden seats on an iron frame with those handy openings where loose change could fall on the ground. With the lure of easy money being too great, our interest in the game didn't last long, and we were soon combing the ground under the bleachers for loose change. Once when the visiting team was Levelworth-Powkipski, grown-ups who'd come to see the game remarked about the awful smell. and questioned where it came from. We didn't answer, but we knew. The smell was Slickery Creek, which ran in back of the football field. It must have been a dry autumn that year, with more than the usual amount of sewerage growing six-foot weeds in the creek bottom. The older and more athletic students played sandlot football during the noon hour; and it really was an hour. The teachers were glad to get rid of us for an extended period of time, and the superintendent, who wore a suit and had an office, went home for his lunch. Not wanting a trip to the local emergency room, I hung out in the bleachers while my fellow students played tackle football without pads. Don Harlan's brother George was one of the major players; he got his nose broken and bled all over his shirt. One of the brothers from the local Catholic high school came to scout potential talent, and he asked George if he was going on to Catholic High. It was a foolish question because kids weren't automatically passed to the next grade before the 1950's. When my father dropped me off by the front door of the school he said that some kids had to duck their heads to get in through the door. I think that a few of them went right to Korea from grade school.

On summer afternoons, my brother and I used to go with Uncle Julian to watch the baseball games. It never occurred to me at the time that our parents wanted us out of the house for a few hours. My favorite team was the Loran Athletic Club. The players had red socks and wore red caps, and featured stars like Scrappy and Yappy Brozovitch. The Moose, the Elks, the local oil refinery, and athletic clubs from the neighborhoods all had teams that played at half a dozen different ball diamonds around the city. There was no admission charged, but someone always passed the hat during the seventh inning stretch; I noticed that Uncle Julian wasn't overly generous. The Loran AC building is still on Loran Avenue, but now it's just another tavern where customers drink beer and swap lies. I sat on the wooden benches and saw Scrappy hit the ball all the way to Fourth Avenue where it bounced into somebody's yard. And what happens to the heroes of our youth? I lost track of Scrappy, but Yappy got ten years for dropping the ball with the pipe fitter's pension fund.

City line buses brought the kids to school, the ones who lived too far away to walk: one bus from Bedford Park where I would have been if we hadn't moved to the country, and one from Addison Road. "Wub" Naylor, one of the neighbor kids, gravitated right away to the Bedford Park bunch. As soon as they got off the bus, they lit up cigarettes that dangled from the corners of their mouths. The Addison Road bus had both black and white kids, and I soon was hanging out with the white kids from Addison Road. You had to belong to a group; it was insurance from being picked on. The colored kids lived out around the infamous Club Sixty Six, where my friends said club patrons were screwing in the cars in the parking lot. My friends thought that this was unusual at the time, although after the sexual revolution of the sixties, no one would pay much attention unless they were inside of the tavern. The group I hung out with included the Miters and the Roswells. Louie Roswell was a little guy with big muscles, red hair, and a twisted grin. His favorite pastime was finding a pickable kid, pulling off his pants, and throwing them into Slickery Creek. After retrieving his soggy pants from the creek, the victim had to sit in disgusting filth for the rest of the day.

Bells rang to call us into the school, and to mark the canonical hours of the school day. Between classes we marched in a line, even to go to the toilet; since the administration and teachers seemed to feel we might go crazy, we were not given the opportunity. At lunchtime, we had to eat in the stands in the basketball court. There was no hot lunch program; you either carried your food in a paper bag, went hungry, or went to a little neighborhood grocery store for junk food. If I ever had extra money, I would go there for a Dreamsicle, an ice cream bar that had orange sherbet on the outside and vanilla ice cream inside. Stanley Lefarge, my old classmate in grade school, sat behind me and said to his companion," See! He doesn't know me now." I felt bad, because I didn't snub him, I was just shy at the time and didn't see him sitting there. But what he said was true. The colored and the white kids who had grown up together were growing further apart: two different worlds, with two different sets of rules, and even two different national anthems.

When we were finally let out for lunch, we couldn't just walk down the stairs to the lunchroom/basketball stands, we had to run. Miss O' Riley stood at the bottom of the stairs with one crooked arm out, letting in only a few at a time to eat. When I told Pa the name of the teachers at my limestone prison, he said," My god! Those are the same teachers I had at Center School in 1914." Miss O' Riley was short, arthritic, and had the face of a bulldog, accustomed to chewing on kids and spitting them out. That couldn't have been her real hair because it was frizzy, rusty red in color, and stuck straight out and was, I think, a wig. Hungry eighth graders stamped back and forth impatiently, letting out a whoop when they were finally let in for lunch. During one of our runs to the "lunch room" I tripped at the top of the stairs. Trying to catch my balance and stop, I could only succeed in going faster and faster down the stairs and, out of control, I nailed Miss O' Riley at the bottom of the stairs, with her one crooked arm sticking out. I think that she had been trying to say "Stop!" Most of the students, at least the ones that I admired, held me in high esteem for a few weeks, until they forgot the incident and moved on to something else. My punishment was light actually, I just had to stay longer at the quasi-penitentiary, and, on release, I got to walk over to my cousins' house on Chicago Street.

My cousin Nadine met me at the door. She was already released from the high school. The Hallenbergs didn't go out much as a family, but we never missed the operettas at the high school., especially when Nadine was one of the stars. She sang along with two other girls, "Three little girls from seminary . . . life is a joke that's just begun. Wee!" And I said, years later, "It's just not fair! Little Yum-Yum can't be seventy years old." She was in another musical where an Indian girl was serenaded by a Royal Canadian Mountie. I saw it later in movie form, with Nelson Eddy and Jeanette McDonald, at the Countess Theater, a cheap, no-frills movie house in town, its only luxury being the large glass outer doors before you got to the ticket window. Another of our neighbors made the paper when their old grandma tried to walk through the glass door without opening it. Nobody I knew ever made the paper by doing something ordinary.

Besides being the keeper of the lunchroom, Miss O' Riley was also my English teacher. On our first day she gave us the assignment of memorizing the poem about Young Lochinvar; "throughout the wide border, his steed was the best." Hardly the type of thing most of the class could relate to. I made the mistake of going home and memorizing it in one night, and of course Miss O' Riley took this as a sign that she had a prize student on her hands. She soon found out that this was not to be the case; I just had the god-given gift, or curse, of being able to memorize: one look at a racing form, and that's it. Only one other student, Nancy Ragnitz, went home and memorized the same poem in one night, but racing forms and the words to doo-wop songs were probably not going to be her specialty. She had pretty blue eyes and curly blond hair and would never have spoken to me, except that Miss Kelley told her to. I felt embarrassed and foolish when Miss Kelley sent us to the auditorium, to stand in front of the rest of the class and present our poems. She most likely thought she had two kids with some promise, and hoped that some day we might mate and produce a super-race of poetry reciters. For the rest of the year I sat in the back of the room with Don Harlan's older brother George, where I was a bottle rocket of a student rather than an intercontinental missile.

George sat in the back of the room, where he was never called on, cleaning his fingernails with his pocket knife. He must have done something wrong as one time Miss Kelley called George up to her desk., using the mean voice that frightened ninety per cent of the eighth graders. I heard . . . CLUMP, CLUMP. as George headed for the front of the room. He was a real heavyweight, and, from the size of him he must have been held back since Coolidge was President. I wasn't the smartest kid in the class, but I've always been quick to pick up on emotional nuances. The look on Miss Kelley's face turned from strict to wonder and finally to genuine fright. In a voice deep as a basso profundo, George asked what she wanted, and she barely mumbled some lame reason for the summons. When he returned to his seat, George slipped in with his knees resting just under the desk. As I always said, "You can fool the foolers, but you can't shit the shitters". Miss O' Riley might still be able to bully me around, but now I knew that she was just another face, as in The Wizard of Oz. Her bluff could be called.

We had to travel between rooms with a different teacher for each subject; Miss Cube was our geography teacher. Since I never could learn to control my mouth, I probably should have looked for a job as a carnival barker or an auctioneer. When Shirley, the girl who sat in front of me, didn't know the answer to a question, I whispered it to her—"Africa". Striding down the aisle came Miss Cube, and I couldn't figure out right away what was up. With an ego as big as my mouth I figured she was coming down to praise me for being so smart; instead, she punched me right off of my seat onto the floor. It was no pimp slap either, she used her fists like Rocky Graziano. From now on, "Mum's the word," unless you're on a quiz show.

Bernie Bean was in this same geography class, and I had a bad feeling when he started hanging around with this older kid, Anderson. Anderson always had a sly look on his face, as if he had plans to swallow a pretty large canary. Bernie sat one day in geography class groaning in pain. I could even hear him from half way across the room, but the teacher just ignored him, not wanting to get involved with a poor black kid in pain. This was the same teacher with the good right cross. It got everybody's attention though, even the teacher's, when a cop came into the room and pulled Bernie to his feet. Poor Bernie hobbled away with one broken leg, the cop pulling on his shirt. Bernie and Anderson, it turned out, had snatched some old lady's purse, but things went wrong when the police happened to be close by. Bernie escaped by jumping over a fence, but Anderson was caught and squealed, which sent Bernie away to the reformatory in Saint Charles, sometimes known as Uncle Sharkey's. Later on I saw him in high school, but now he was a few grades behind me, and looked as if he had had lots of time to exercise. He had also turned very serious, and was no longer the young guy who got pulled out of geography class. In wrestling, he was one of the best in the state.

When the weather was good, they let us out, and I remember the home rooms playing each other in softball. But if it was raining we had a gym class of sorts, which consisted of Mister Reynolds marching us around in circles on the basketball court. He dressed like a gym coach, with a dark blue tee shirt and navy blue sweat pants. While the rain pattered down outside the iron-barred glass windows, he tapped with a stick on the floor to keep time to our marching, or almost marching, since we just shuffled around and watched the clock each time we circled the court. One of the kids told me that Mr. Reynolds had blue balls that had swelled to enormous proportions. "I know," the kid said, "because my mother's a nurse at he hospital." I listened and nodded my head as if I understood exactly what he was talking about.

My buddies and I hung out on the bleachers in the football field, or played softball, or played tap football between the home rooms. Apparently I was singled out as trustworthy and responsible, and was pulled from the ranks to answer the phone in the superintendent's office. He made the trip across town to go home for his lunch hour, and since rumors of my past failure as a crossing guard had not followed me here, I was asked to sit in the office and answer any calls that came in. It was my first or second day, and the phone rang. The guy on the other end of the line said something, so I said . . . "yah, yah" . . . and hung up the phone and forgot about it. Nobody told me that I was supposed to write down what the caller said. The superintendent was mightily upset when he returned from his lunch, and I lost my job; he told me not to bother coming back. It was all for the best, because now I could spend lunch time with my buddies, and, to my surprise, I felt no guilt over the affair. My parents always said that "Self done is well done", and besides, it wasn't my fault that I had a deceptively responsible appearance.

During the winter we had basketball games between the homerooms, which I remember as interminably long, with me running back and forth on the court with feet encased in lead. I think that it was due to puberty, as I had managed to begin shaving. Even though I was clumsy and awkward, with the basketballs skidding off the end of my toe, the kids from my grade school sat in the stands and cheered for me. I didn't know what had come over me, a perfectly normal human one minute, and a total madman the next. My homeroom was also the biology classroom, and contained taxidermied animals, the prize being a stuffed armadillo. The teacher was a frail little lady with white hair, and seemed forever on the verge of a nervous breakdown. I still feel bad about how I treated her, because even though I detested bullying and discipline, when the shoe was on the other foot, I couldn't help but plague the poor woman. I must have wanted attention any way I could get it, so I pulled off the armadillo's tail and threw it out the second story window. "What happened to its tail?" the teacher wailed. "Someone has ruined the armadillo." And later, when she explained the laws of thermodynamics, I told her that we're all going to go up in a puff of smoke, and that would destroy some energy. Her eyes turned moist thinking about her mortality, and now I know why, but back then I was an immortal eighth grader, with none of the empathy that comes with age.

For my birthday, Pa bought me a telescope to look at the heavens, but what I really wanted was a football and a football helmet. Pa retired the telescope to his dresser upstairs, but he never could get it to work. With adolescence, I had turned into a shit, but it wasn't my fault. The testosterone made me do it.

Miss Motter taught mathematics and even though I had learned how to add, subtract, multiply and divide in the country school, she assigned us math problems to do at home: the same old multiplication and division problems. Instead of something more complicated, she just assigned us more and more. Usually I did a few, and then the problems just sat there unless Ma decided to finish them. She seemed to enjoy doing multiplying and dividing, and she had a primitive adding machine in the basement to add up her egg prices and to make an accounting as to whether she was making money on the chickens. After supper, when it was dark outside, Uncle Julian and I sat at the kitchen table and read "pulp" magazines. The stories were about steely-eyed Texas Rangers who rounded up outlaws and then rode away out onto the lonely prairie while some young, innocent girl pined away for them. We didn't store away the old magazines for long, because the pages started to turn yellow almost before we had finished reading them. They were a lot more enjoyable than long division, and I didn't see the point in doing fifty problems when I already knew how to do one.

The blackboards were made of slate, and I did see a slate quarry in the Upper Peninsula of Michigan where the stone was cut, although now it's just a big abandoned hole in the ground. Slate rock isn't cut anymore for roofing shingles, blackboards, but is still sometimes used for pool tables, and anyone who has ever had to move an old pool table can tell you just how heavy the slate could be. Miss Motter was standing in the front of the room, carrying on a mathematical dissertation that nobody was paying attention to, when the blackboard came loose at the top and settled down onto her head; this, of course, got everybody's attention. I was amazed that no one did anything. We sat there, stunned, as she sank lower and lower under the blackboard's weight, until she seemed to be about three feet off the ground. Finally Gary Gianni jumped up and lifted the slate blackboard off the shrinking teacher's head. Years later I met him in a bar, and he was still a gentleman. He had been in the army airborne, married for a month, got a divorce, and now owned a go-cart track. If the glass mirror over the bar had fallen over onto the head of any of the ladies perched on their bar stools, he would have been the first to lift it from their heads.

There was a talent show at the junior high, and one of the colored girls played boogie-woogie on the piano. I was surprised because usually she was so quiet and reserved. I never knew that she had so much talent. My father had picked up an old upright and I was given piano lessons, but felt that playing the piano was not a very manly thing to do, at least until Don Harlan was talking to my parents and said that he wished that he owned a piano and could take lessons. I had no need to worry about a career in piano, though, as I banged away on the "March of the Elf Men." Being terribly stubborn, I refused to play for company, but my father insisted that I play for my Uncle Ned and the cousins. After being threatened I started to play, and could see the pitying looks on their faces as they listened to this poor musical cripple, with two ball peen hammers for hands, squashing the keys like black and white bugs. Shortly after, the piano lessons came to a halt. Chuck Loomis and his brass quartet was another big hit at our junior high talent show. Chuck played, "When Yuba Played the Tuba Down in Cuba," and, if that wasn't enough, he followed it up with "The Sheik of Araby." Chuck forgot to tell the teachers that his band members would insert "with no pants on" between each line of the song. Tame stuff today, but in the pre-1950's Midwest, such risque' material caused an outrage from the teachers at our junior high.

In shop class I made a bread board, and soldered up a handle on a tin can to make a drinking cup. Hung by the back door on a spigot, the drinking cup banged on the pipe when the wind blew, a sort of primitive wind chime. It hung there for years, and may be hanging there still, even though the farm was sold. Mister Jones, the shop teacher, wore a wrinkled white shirt that smelled of tobacco and body odor, and talked about a lot of weird mechanical things. He even said that cars could have diesel engines. While I was planing down my bread board to a sliver of its former self, the eighth grade girls had a different course, something called home economics, where they were sewing up their white graduation dresses.

We had one dance at the school, a square dance. I slicked down my hair with Wildroot hair tonic, and put on a clean flannel shirt and a nearly new pair of denims, but when I got there, I couldn't work up enough courage to go into the building. One of the real tough kids came up and said, "What're you waitin' for, Casper Milktoast? Are ya goin' in or not?" Casper Milktoast was a weak-kneed cartoon character of that time, who had a big mustache covering up his face. I thought, "I'll show him," and in to the dance I went. "Dosey doe and a little more doe, chicken in the bread pan pickin' out dough," the caller said. And I thought that, well, it wasn't so bad after all, since all the Italian kids were there; I thought a lot of them, and they were all at the dance, so it must be alright. There was some squealing from the Italian girls when they saw Don Gioninni looking in through the gym window. He was the epitome of an eighth grade ladies man, which, at that time, meant that you had your hair trained into a pompadour on top of your head. Meanwhile, I was dancing in a square with a chubby blonde girl, who didn't seem to mind at all that I was dancing on her toes

Miss Hanson taught the business course, where we learned some rudiments of personal finance, like how to write a check. She neglected to explain, though, what happened when there was no money in the account. I was married for five years before I had a checking account, anyway. It used to be that you could pay cash at the bank for your house note, and at the respective businesses for utility bills, and, in rare cases, you could get a money order. Miss Hanson told us that while driving down Newell Avenue she saw members of our class swimming without clothes on in the Michigan Quarry. She claimed to be shocked. Somehow I couldn't believe that a teacher who was reputed to smoke cigars could be shocked over a couple of nude students; I think that she was mostly amused. There was a public beach on one end of the property, in use during the 1920's, but the city said that it was polluted and closed the beach down. The kids that Miss Hanson saw were jumping off the high cliffs on the opposite side from the beach, near the railroad tracks. I think that they finally quit when a young man drowned. The quarry became "clean" again when a local politico bought the property and turned it into a private beach club.

Another of my teachers was a shirttail relative. She taught English, was never married, and ended up raising two nephews who were orphaned. She kept a supply of peanut butter and crackers in her desk for the kids who didn't get breakfast and would otherwise go hungry.

The entire eighth grade had their group picture taken in front of the school, by the big wooden doors that we never entered. Wearing a long-sleeved tee shirt that was too small for me I grinned at the circular flower bed that I'd never noticed before, and left with my picture and my bread board in hand. Now I could go on to the high school, which everyone told me was very large, and would take some getting used to. We should go there ahead of time so that we could find the class rooms. I did, and, no surprise, it was made of limestone, and looked like my previous two schools, only bigger.

For their first year, freshman boys were required to take a one year "shop" course, with six weeks in each shop. In agriculture class, we had to judge cows and other animals as if they were going to a beauty pageant. Your grade was based on how well you judged compared to an expert opinion. Unless the cows were lacking an udder or the sheep had bald patches, the animals all looked the same to me. From my background, a lamb looked good only as a chop, and a cow meant milk and butter. The high point of the class was a field trip to the Chicago stockyards, and we got to look through a glass window at the pigs getting their throats cut. One of the boys threw up. The teacher seemed used to it, though, and every year he probably expected at least one or two regurgitations on the walkway in front of the pig window. The cattle were forced into a pen and smacked on the head with a sledgehammer, not exactly the kind sold at the hardware store but one with a longer handle and a smaller head. By this time, fewer boys were throwing up. When Grandpa Hallenberg came to the area, one of his first jobs was at the stockyards, whacking cattle with a sledgehammer. Everyone was on the assembly line, both the men and the animals; but the Swedes and the Lithuanians were gone. Now black men had the dirty job of" bringing home the bacon".

There was a class called mechanical drawing where the only thing mechanical in the room was the pencil sharpener. We pinned a big piece of paper to an even bigger board and drew pictures of three-dimensional objects. Besides resembling the objects, neatness was a primary concern. My drawings always came with smudges and plenty of eraser marks. Another old standard was the course called print shop, the object being to take lead letters out of a box and write something with them. The skill involved was trying to use your imagination in seeing how the letters would look backwards, the technique first used in printing the Guttenberg Bible.

Most feared of all was the one called "machine shop." The teacher looked like Hitler, with black hair and a mustache, and ran the class like the Gestapo. He was the keeper of large machines in back of his desk, machines that ran back and forth with no other apparent purpose except to cut away at a large iron bar until it became a small iron bar. Everything screeched and hissed in his world, including the teacher, who threw things at kids when anything went wrong. Since his instructions were so minimal, a machine would periodically groan and seize up while trying to do some impossible maneuver. The administration never did anything about the teacher, since they were collecting a comfortable salary at the other end of the school, and avoided going down into the bowels of the building where the machines were located. Meanwhile, the freshmen boys were bullied by the Hitler look-alike.

He tried to push around my cousin Bobby, and got a punch in the snoot. Having flunked a few grades along the way, Bobby was sixteen, and left school as fast as he could to go on the Navy's "Kiddie Cruise." At sixteen years old, you could drop out of high school, sign up for four years in the navy, and get a high school GED certificate by passing a test. Pa said that my aunt and uncle, Angus and Hepzibah, were always telling Bobby that he was bad. Pa said that if you told a kid that he was bad, it would become a self-fulfilling prophecy, and he'd soon live up to his reputation. Bobby fought his way through grade school, and he told my brother and me how he had beat up on a Jap on the way home from school. Hollywood came out with movies during WW II to whip up American fervor, where Japanese pilots with buck teeth dove their Zeros at American planes while, yelling "Yale, class of 1938". We later learned that the Jap he so patriotically beat up was a Filipino, from a family that escaped the war in the Pacific.

Just before he left for the navy, I saw Bobby in front of the bowling alley telling a small audience about how "bad" he was. According to him, he was a bad actor with a bad car that would shatter the glass in store windows because his muffler was so loud. Loud mufflers were a major concern to the police, and a great source of revenue, as a really loud muffler could get you pulled over for a ticket. There was one cop whose territory was the downtown streets, where the rich white kids drove aimlessly around the circuit, and he'd hand out a ticket to anyone who fluttered his eardrum.

There was no grass or campus area connected to the high school. It was bounded by city streets, and on one side was a restaurant, little more that a shack, called "The Fiery Furnace." If you thought you were a tough or wanted to be a "bad" guy, it was necessary to spend as much time as possible in The Fiery Furnace instead of being in class. They served hamburgers, fries, cokes, and the cigarette smoke was so thick that it made your eyes water. I spent as much time there as I could, listening to Les Paul and Mary Ford doing "Hold that Tiger"and "How High The Moon", songs with multiple tracks that made an echo effect. And nobody could complain when we stood on the other side of the street from the school, pitching pennies at the cracks in the sidewalk. The person who threw his penny closest to the crack got to keep all of the pennies. It was probably the only thing to do that was even more boring than the classes across the street.

There was no such thing as air conditioning at Rustbelt High, so on warm days the windows were open and you could smell the fumes from the brewery near the school. I loved the smell, so sickeningly sweet, and it reminded me of the smell coming from Swanson's Tavern, which I passed walking down Jefferson Street on the way to school. That smell was mixed with stale cigarette and cigar smoke blown out onto the sidewalk from the exhaust fans on the side of the building. I never tasted the local beer myself, but Mr. Walker said that it tasted like it was brewed in a hollow log. The brewery has been gone for years. I wonder what the biology department does for specimens now, since the biology teacher claimed that he visited the brewery to replenish his supply of cockroaches for class. During the summer, he worked at a thoroughbred track, and he used to pick the Kentucky Derby: win, place, and show. He didn't get it right every time, but he said that he used the horse's heredity to predict the outcome. The prediction was combined with a lecture about genetics and how the monk, Mendel, studied peas. Even kids who didn't care about peas paid attention when they heard that genetics could pick a horse. The same teacher said that he got his first job out of college because he could play the piano. It was during the depression, when jobs were hard to find, and he had to play the piano at a church on Sunday in order to get the teaching position. That was a while ago, though, and when I went to school he was playing the piano at Blimpy's Tavern, not for God's glory or to keep a job, but just for the fun of it.

We took our chemistry class in a small lecture hall where the seats went up in higher levels, with stairs going up in the middle. There was a lab bench with a sink in the front of the room, equipped with water and gas, so the teacher could demonstrate his skill as an alchemist, and he produced hydrogen. He stuck a flaming stick into the test tube . . . and, POP. Even with the passing of years, when you can no longer balance an equation, you can still remember the pops, the explosions, and the smell of experiments gone wrong. When my brother came along in the same class, the teacher talked to my parents and asked them if he was working too much at a job. It seems that he took the cheap seats in the back of the room, way up high, and leaned his head back against the wall, where he usually fell asleep until the bell woke him up. The teacher loved his chemistry, and found it incomprehensible that anyone could fall asleep in the presence of atoms and molecules. He talked often about the difference between the two. Asking the same old question, and still not getting an answer, the teacher would cock his head with one hairy ear pointing to his audience, and trot up the stairs. He always returned with a black cube with 22.4 printed on the sides, and would beam at his students as if to say, "Com'on! You knew the answer all along. You were just sleepy before lunch, and too delirious from low blood sugar to come up with this obvious answer." Every year he spent one class period reading the life story of John Dalton, from his book about life stories of the great chemists. John Dalton kept a diary in which he was anal retentive about his observations on the weather and such; it was like keeping the statistics on baseball teams. When he read about the part where Dalton finally got where he could barely write, and his hand was shaking, tears welled up in the teacher's eyes. I never knew whether he really was that upset or if it was a show to get our attention.

For biology class I didn't have the cockroach collecting, Kentucky Derby predictor. Instead, the teacher that I got was a single, older lady who probably thought that all boys were after only one thing. I squirted the girl sitting next to me with a pistol-shaped squirt gun. She let out a classroom-shattering scream, and I knew that I was in trouble. The teacher asked her, "What did he do to you?" with the emphasis on DO. I still feel bad that I didn't confess to getting her with the squirt gun, and much to the girl's credit, she wouldn't tell the teacher anything. The teacher was certain that I had felt the girl up, but she didn't come right out and say it. Instead, she stuck me in a vacant storeroom across the hall. The period went on forever, and the stuffed owl looked down at me accusingly. Ma had to come to school and talk to the teacher and the principal about my evil intentions, but luckily, this wasn't grade school and the belt was no longer used. An additional offense was also brought out, that when we were going to look at our blood through the microscopes, I stuck my finger with my pocket knife instead of the proscribed straight pin. The teacher confiscated my best pocket knife, and never gave it back. For all I know, she's sitting in front of the class today, with her feet up on the desk, cleaning her fingernails with my pocket knife. My grade in the class was a D which made us both happy. I didn't have to take biology over and she didn't have to see me again.

Two of my friends in high school were Jim Petersen and Edwardo Sanches. Jim lived off of Addison Road, in an almost all black neighborhood, on a lot that was overgrown with trees and bushes. There was a shack in back of the place made up like a bunk house, where Jim could sleep overnight if he felt like it. The three of us went for a weekend to Indian Creek, to camp out in a tent, and Jim's father drove us

there. Mister Petersen had already got a good start on the weekend; I thought that
he was driving way too fast. The car was filled with the smell of beer and well-used
camping equipment. We waded in the creek, which was full of water snakes. They
hung from the tree limbs over the water, and Jim brought along a 22 caliber pistol
to shoot the snakes out of the trees. I fished them out of the water as Jim shot, and
brought them home as grisly souvenirs. In a twenty percent solution of formaldehyde,
the snakes were kept in glass jars in the fruit cellar, until my folks got sick of looking
at them and threw them out. We had a great weekend, and Jim's dad came to get us
for another hair-raising drive back home.

Jim had a real fascination with guns. We were still in high school when I was
driving home from my summer job at the county poor farm, after having spent the
entire day castrating pigs. Driving past Nolen Park, I saw that someone had taken
down the park fence, and their car was now resting against a tree. Coming closer, I
saw Jim Petersen, with a cop on each side, and they were more or less dragging him
along, away from the car. He was hopping along on one leg and told me later on
that it was broken. Before the cops got there, though, he'd managed to hobble over
to a tree where he tried to dig a hole and bury his nickel plated 1911 Colt 45. But
even while he was scratching in the ground as fast as he could, the cops arrived and
confiscated both his nickel plated beauty and another pistol as well. A city park is a
poor place to bury your pistol anyway.

Jim's dad drank at Zeke Magille's Tavern, conveniently located just a few
hundred yards down the road from their house. It was the first, and probably the
only, integrated tavern in the city. Mister Petersen had a propensity for picking up
strays, and if they were down on their luck he brought them home and gave them a
room. Gunter Lindblad left Germany after the war, and he stayed with the Petersens
for a while with his BSA Shooting Star. He told us war stories, and here was a real
live German, like the ones that the kids in the country school wanted to prod with
their wooden Tommy guns. He was full of fun, and chased a girl in a Caddy all the
way to Peoria on his motorcycle. There was also an old Russian who lived with the
Petersens. He told me that the Russians won the Russo-Japanese war. He'd been a
soldier in that war; it seemed as if everybody that I met was involved in a war. I told
him that the history teacher in our high school said the Russians got their clock
cleaned, but I should have kept my mouth shut. He probably read the Russian
history book, while I had to read the American version.

Edwardo lived on Buff Street, which was next to the river that flowed through
the center of town. It was one of the oldest streets in town, but the area has since
been torn down to make a city park. The street was lined with a lot of two flats that
needed paint jobs, but across the street was one of the engineering marvels of the
century. The Chicago River was flowing backwards and was now heading toward
the Mississippi instead of Lake Michigan. The river smelled like rotten cabbage as
it flowed through Rustbelt City. My Uncle Clint and Aunt Eva lived along Bluff St
when they were first married. Fights used to start in the Paradise Bar and then spill

out into the street, or maybe guys were waiting in the street to settle some argument. One time Uncle Clint looked out the window on two guys beating up on one man, and seeing that the poor fellow might be beaten to death before the cops got there, Uncle Clint went down from the apartment to break up the fight, or at least even it up a little. When the police arrived Uncle Clint was booked along with everyone else. He tried to explain how unfair the fight was, and that he was only trying to even up the sides. As they say, no good deed ever goes unpunished.

When I visited Edwardo in the warm weather he'd come to the door with nothing on but his Jockey shorts. This would have been unthinkable in our family, because decorum was such that we we always had to have on a full set of clothes, even in the warmest weather. When we sat down to eat, we boys had to be wearing shirts, and our caps had better be off. An old weather-beaten women glared at me from the other room, and Edwardo told me that was his grandmother, who didn't speak much English. I found out later that she was really his mother. She looked so old and worn in comparison to my own mother. The family had come North from El Paso, Texas; she had a long-lasting distrust of Anglos and would never speak to me. Edwardo was proud of his Indian appearance and claimed that he was part Apache. He had a cross tattooed between his thumb and forefinger. The symbol was used by a gang of toughs living along the border, and I think that they originated near Fort Bliss in El Paso. He led us to believe that he had girls working for him already in high school, but I never met them if he did. I was next to him in the same history class, and he'd just sit there, never causing trouble and never saying a word. When I was starting to go out with my wife, we met Edwardo and a friend at Magille's. He was wearing a rather garish outfit and had his hair slicked down with an oily pomade that smelled of flowers. My soon-to-be wife later said, "He smelled like a pimp." I told her, "You should go on "What's My Line?", where they guess a person's occupation. You got his right on the first try."

Many years later, I was working with Ernie Reed at a petrochemical plant, and Edwardo's name happened to come up in the conversation. Ernie said that he knew who he was, didn't like him, and that Edwardo was sent to jail after badly beating up some girl. Supposedly he died there, but I'd rather think of him as that quiet Indian-looking kid who sat by me in history class.

Taverns were running wide open in the city while I was in high school. The All Nations Tavern was just a few blocks from the school, and was finally shut down when a mother complained that her fourteen year old daughter was drinking in the bar with a twenty four year old man. Terry Anglehoff was a friend of mine, and sang the lead in our senior class operetta, Gilbert and Sullivan's "HMS Pinafore." Just to loosen up a little before the performance, he stopped in at the All Nations for a few too many cool ones. He was doctored with hot, black coffee and went on stage to sing with a voice better even than the juke box at the All Nations. Everybody said that it was one of the best operettas that the school ever had. He was almost as good as Bing Crosby. I had to take a city lines bus home from high school, but it still dropped us off about a mile from home. There was a bus station downtown, about five or six blocks from the school, and you could go inside in the winter time to warm up. I was just in time for the local radio station to be playing an entire program of Bing Crosby songs, and the program began and ended with "Der Bingle" singing "When the blue of the night meets the gold of the day." When our oldest granddaughter was visiting, I was playing a collection of his songs on the stereo, and told her that it was an entire cassette of Bing Crosby. She said, "Who's Bing Crosby?" Could she have been kidding? Hasn't everybody heard of Bing Crosby?

On Armistice Day there was a ceremony in the gymnasium for the entire school. This started out at the end of the "Great War," and just ignored WW II and the bloody stalemate that was Korea, going strong at that time. The choir sang songs like "The Roses of Picardy" and "Beyond the Blue Horizon," the band played, pretty young girls sang in their ethereal voices, and teachers went to the podium and recited poems. They were introduced as Ensign or Lieutenant or Sergeant. They looked grave and serious as they spoke of a rendezvous with death or the poppies growing in Flanders' fields between the rows of crosses. Oddly enough, the only teacher who had seen some real action in the trenches didn't attend. He was still angry with the army about waiting for the eleventh hour (of the eleventh day of the eleventh month), when, in the last few hours before the armistice, one of his buddies was killed. I was thumbing through the local paper one night, and there he was, in his army uniform, which still fit. He was nearly one hundred years old when the picture was taken, and many of his students were already dead. Back in school he used to show off for his students by mixing a dilute solution of hydrochloric acid in a beaker and gulping it down; apparently there was a malady with his stomach where he didn't produce enough acid.

The Korean conflict was going on at the time, and it infuriated a lot of people in the Midwest that the government refused to call it a war. We watched a program on our old black and white TV called "The Big Picture" that supposedly explained why we were in Asia, and showed rumbling tanks and roaring artillery. But there was no blood, no poetry, no bands, and no choirs of singing girls.

As if five days of school weren't enough, we still had something called confirmation classes to take up our Saturday mornings. Since work weeks back then were often five and a half days, it was a little taste of the adult world: no more fishing in the muddy creek or shooting rabbits. The preacher was a Swede who came to this country with his mother, and lived in the brick parsonage next to the church, where he had, at one time, kept chickens in the back yard. He was bald on the top of his head, dressed in black, and liked to smoke cigars. He didn't want his parishioners to see him smoking, so, if he happened to run into anyone, he would hold the cigar behind his back, and give a quick greeting while the smoke curled upward around his natural tonsure. The room where we met was lined with the framed pictures of every former pastor, in their black clerical garb and all with facial hair of some sort, mutton chops, beard, mustache; they glowered down on us adolescents in the strictest poses they could muster. Humor was not to be the order of the day, but we could "be of good cheer" since the process lasted for only a year. Then we were "examined" in a public ceremony, somewhat of a sham because we were each assigned a question, and given the answer to memorize. "I believe that I cannot by my own reason or strength believe in Jesus Christ or come to Him, but the Holy Spirit has . . . . sanctified and preserved me in the true faith." It's the only thing that I can remember from one year of giving up the pleasures of Saturday morning. None of my fellow confirmands went to jail, that I know of, but perhaps there was more than the usual share of homosexuals and marital failures. There's a saying about a little something or other being a positive thing; I think that it may have been fear and guilt. After our religious education, there seemed to be a reluctance on the part of the former students to mate. The process was summed up for me when I read about a zoo that had monkeys who wouldn't mate. So they were shown some X-rated movies of humans in the process of copulating, and then they got the idea. It takes a lot of movies to get that religious monkey of guilt off your back.

High school, which seemed as if it would last forever, was soon over. I was walking home from our mailbox, which was nailed up with half a dozen others on a two by twelve at the corner of our road and Newell Avenue. As I was reading the grades on my final report card, Sederholm's dog snuck up and bit me in the ass. The nasty old thing ruined a perfectly good pair of denim pants, and just as quickly as it bit, the cur turned around and was gone, back into Sederholm's yard. My mother called Missus Sederholm, who said that I had been chucking rocks at her dog, which was a lie. The truth was that in dog years he was about one hundred, and could barely see. Had he been younger and with good sight, the dog probably would have taken an even bigger chunk out of my ass. It was a fitting end to four years of not paying attention, to be bitten by Sederholm's dog while I was reading my grades.

On the evening of graduation, we went to the Petersens' house afterwards. My parents stayed and visited with Jim's parents, while Jim, Edwardo and I took off for a still active quarry near their house. We drank some beer, and then climbed down the quarry face to the pond below. They were still quarrying stone there, but the pumps were removed in this one area for a pond. The other fellows were much more agile, but I needed a lot of help to climb down. The commencement speech was about leaping bravely into the unknown, but as a portent for the rest of my life, I crept down cautiously on the limestone face of the quarry with a lot of help from my friends.

High school was a time when the answers were pretty much known, and we, as predicted, spit the them back faithfully on test booklets. But my brother told me about a student of philosophy who left school, picked up his guitar, and roamed around to coffee houses reciting poetry and playing the guitar. When one of the students asked one of my teachers what you could do with a degree in philosophy, he answered that you could sell vacuum sweepers. No vacuum cleaners for this former student. He sang, "Goodbye Socrates, and Kant, and Hegel. There ain't no absolutes in this man's town."

PART THREE

WORK IS THE CURSE OF THE DRINKING CLASS

My father makes book on the corner
My mother makes boot—legger gin
My sister makes love for a dollar
My God, how the money rolls in!

(traditional song sung to the tune of My Bonnie Lies Over the Ocean)

We were one of the last to pick field corn by hand. The accepted practice was to use a corn picker pulled by the tractor and run from the power take-off. Now the big combines are used with a corn head, but before all this we husked the corn by hand, throwing the ears into a wagon pulled by our Allis Chalmers model C. If you were really behind the times, the wagon could be pulled by a horse. On one side of the wagon was a "bang board", a wall of boards that you could bounce the ears off. We all worked in the field except for Little Grandma, who had to stay in the house and cook the meal. We kids had to pick one row, while the grown-ups picked two rows at a time. Ma was the fastest picker, and Uncle Julian was way behind, puffing on his pipe while he clenched his teeth to keep the pipe from falling on the ground. Unable or unwilling to keep up, he pretended to check everyone else's rows for corn that they missed. Sometimes it started to snow before we finished and it was hard to husk the corn wearing gloves, but if I took them off, my fingers froze. After we picked the corn, we brought it to the corn bin. We'd shell the ears as needed for the chickens. Pa and Uncle Julian had built the corn crib with wood on the corners, fencing in between, a roof, and a door to open to get to the corn. One of the few times I was allowed to stay home from school was when we painted the new corn crib red, using a sprayer and an air compressor. I had my shirt off, and from the airborne paint I turned red, and pretended to be an Indian. On Saturdays my job was to shell the corn in a corn sheller that had to be cranked by hand. It was a big wooden machine with a handle that spun two plates inside with teeth that separated the corn kernels to fall into a tub placed below, while the cobs continued on through and were spit out of a spout. The ears of corn were always getting stuck, and the machine and the sheller ground to a stop. Then you had to crank the machine backwards, reach in your hand, and try to get out the offending ear without catching one of your fingers. If memory serves me correctly, it took about a dozen bushels to feed those chickens for a week. After the ears were shelled I dumped the kernels into a metal barrel. The adults had the job of cracking the corn by running it through a bur mill. The grinder was powered by an electric quarter horse motor with a leather belt that turned the grinder. You could adjust the fineness of the grind by turning a screw, and we even ground wheat with it to be turned into flour. Other drums lined up in the feed shed held oyster shell (calcium for hard shells on the eggs), grit (tiny pieces of stone so that the birds could digest their food), and a barrel for oats. In the corner were bags of Full-O-Pep chicken mash. After I was married, my son and I even had shirts made from old feed sacks, but sadly enough, I grew too stout for mine, and he eventually grew out of his.

When the eggs were collected, Ma took them to the basement where she washed them and then candled them, looking into our home-made candler to see if there blood spots in the eggs or any cracks in the shells. We ate the rejects and sold the rest. It was traditional on a farm that the wife's job was to take care of the chickens. Ma even carried water to them in five gallon buckets, until I came home from school one day to see freshly dug earth trailing between our house to the chicken houses. We had automatic waterers now, with no more carrying water by hand. I was just a kid at the time, but I never remembered hearing any complaints about the chickens. When Ma was almost ninety years old, I was talking on about the chickens, and how fond she had been of our days as farmers. She looked at me without smiling. "I hated those chickens," she said.

We had a large patch of strawberries. Ma was afraid of snakes, and always pried up the leaves with a stick to see if any snakes were hiding in the strawberries. The snakes were either garter snakes or fox snakes, nothing poisonous, but that did nothing to calm her fears. From an auction sale we must have picked up an old cart with iron wheels, which we used for our strawberry wagon. My brother and I would take the berries Ma had picked and sell them door to door. But since the weather was always hot, toward the end of our route the strawberries were starting to turn to mush in their wooden cartons. We'd manage to get all the way up to the state highway, and then would go down the side streets. When we'd sold nearly all of our wares, we were a long way from home and usually didn't know any of the customers. But one day, when we had made nearly our last sale, I realized we had sold some berries to our old neighbor, who had moved from the farm into the city and started a ready-mix cement business. On the day of the move, his son had fallen off a pick-up truck while they were taking some junk to the dump. The hired man was driving the truck, and was so consumed with remorse and fear that he ran away. I would never have gone to that house if I'd known they lived there, and I can still see the old man walking out to the street and watching us pull the cart down the road, watching us until we disappeared from sight.

I was in first grade when it happened, and his sisters ran all the way from their farm to the one room school, sobbing all the way. The entire school went to the funeral, and I remember the song, "Memories" being done at the funeral, ending with "You left me alone, but still you're my own, in my beautiful memories". Later on, after his cement business was thriving, the father appeared in the local paper with a statement that the state cops were shaking him down for so much that he couldn't make a living. Not long after that he was convicted of income tax evasion. His business passed into history, and some new cement company took its place. Pa said, "I heard that he's got a love nest in Aurora." I was young at the time, but I could hear from the tone of his voice that Pa didn't approve of love nests; in my imagination, I pictured a Turkish harem sort of thing. I hope that old man Selkirk's luck took a turn for the better, but I never heard about him again after he got out of jail.

We raised rabbits, and sold them "dressed," which meant that they were pretty much undressed, without head, entrails or skin. Pa got some wood storage bins from where he worked, and we modified them to make cages. The does had a separate section in their cage, for a nest where they were always giving birth to litters of five or six little rabbits. Not very successful as a money-maker, the rabbits required a lot of work and they were always eating; expensive little rabbit pellets and hay in the winter and, in the summer, we had to pick greens for them, clover from the pasture and surplus lettuce from the garden. Rabbits weren't a favored food around our area, so I ended up selling them to grandpa or other relatives, or we ate them ourselves. The taste wasn't nearly as good as wild rabbit, but at least you didn't have to spit out buckshot.

The hutches sat inside a shed with a galvanized metal roof and wood siding covered with tarpaper. There was a door on one side and a window opposite the door. Pa picked up the window for nothing, and although it was clear glass on the bottom, it had a stained glass section at the top. Imagine our surprise when we came home one day to find a big hole where the window had been. Someone had taken the window right out of the rabbit shed. I guess a stained glass window was a little too fancy for a rabbit shed anyway.

Ma had a driver's license, but it dated back to the time when you just mailed in your money along with an application, and weren't required to take a test. When I got my license, I went to a state police station, went out to the car with a policeman and showed him that I knew how to start it up. Then he got in the car with me and told me to drive over to the prison, where I turned around, and then we drove back to the police station. Mission accomplished. I had done all the essentials: started the car, ran it ahead, and then backed it up. Ma had her license for identification and in case of an emergency, but wouldn't you know it, she decided that she wanted to drive. She learned on the 1936 Chevy pick-up, and I remember riding with her once, when she almost jerked my head off using the stick shift. She delivered the eggs in Bedford Park, and had three accidents in rapid succession, hitting a laundry truck, the post at the entrance to a driveway, and I can't recall the third. After that, though, she got the hang of it and had no more accidents, though she lived to be almost ninety. She must have had a near miss in her eighties, as she decided to quit driving. She flipped a coin to see who should get her car; my family or my brother's. I called it correctly in the air and got a blue Chevy Malibu.

When I was a little boy, we visited my great grandmother in western Illinois, and I stood by the Green River holding my father's hand. Looking out on the placid river we were watching men doing something from a boat. "What are they doing?" I asked my father. "Why, they're clamming. They're going to take the shells to the button factory." At the button factory, the clam shells—I think that they're really called mussels—were made into what was called "mother of pearl" buttons. When my wife and I took a nostalgic trip to my great grandparents' town, the river seemed to have shrunk to the size of a small creek. How could my memory play such a trick on me? I remember the river as being so wide and my father's hands so large. We went to the cemetery to look for the site of my great grandparents' graves, but couldn't find them. The woman who kept the records lived out on a farm and wasn't home at the time, but we met an old man working at the graveyard. He said, "I knew your great grandma. She used to sell cookies. I was just a kid, and the cookies were so very large." Like the Green River and like my father's hand, the cookies might not seem so large if he saw them today.

Great grandpa worked for the railroad, and after he died, my great grandma made cookies and sold them to make a living. When we visited she was so delighted that she ran out into the back yard and killed two chickens for supper. The adults picked and cleaned the chickens, while my brother and I played with the pump organ in the parlor. The house where she lived was an old stage coach stop, and my parents told me that there were bullet holes in the wall from some misunderstanding that happened many years before. It was a shame, but the relatives didn't save the old house or its belongings, and had it torn down after Mary Jane died. Pa had a lot of admiration for her, and said that she was really tough. Pa didn't toss terms like that around very often. She'd even be out in the late fall, barefoot, digging up her potatoes. When Ma was a young girl, she contracted tuberculosis from her mother, and was sent to live with my great grandmother, Mary Jane. It was during this time that my mother's picture was taken by a professional photographer. The picture still hangs in our living room. The studio probably forgot to tell her to say "cheese", because she was given a white dress to wear and she had a serious look on her face without a hint of a smile. Ma said that even in the coldest weather, Mary Jane hung her wash out on the clothes line. Great grandpa's long underwear would freeze solid, and when she and my mother brought in the wash, Mary Jane would pretend to be waltzing the "long johns" into the house.

After I got a social security card, I could get a "real" job, but until then, I had to content myself with working for farmers, mowing lawns, and baling hay. My brother and I saw an advertisement, and we went to work baling hay at the county poor farm, which has since turned into a prison for juvenile criminals, complete with cyclone fence and a razor wire on top. The building where the inmates used to live is now a hive for bureaucrats, and all the farm buildings are gone. Inmates at the farm included the poor who had no family to care for them and no retirement money, retarded people, down-and-outers, alcoholics who were drying out. My brother and I baled hay, but he was put to work in the loft where it was so hot that he got sick and had to stay home the next day. I went back and, as punishment, had a full time job for myself, for a while, at least. The manager and his family lived in the building, and the cast of strange characters lived there with them. You could see them when you worked near the house: a man with red hair who sat in his room and listened to radio soap operas all day long, an old black lady who sat in her room and complimented me on my ladder-climbing skill. She had to have been teasing me, because my legs shook every time I went up that ladder. The inmates were alright as long as they stayed in their rooms and didn't cause the manager any trouble. One of the men, though, liked to sit outside under the spirea bushes and masturbate. When the manager would hear about this from a few of the poor-farmers, he'd find the man, slap him and send him back into the house. Not to be deterred, however, the masturbator would be back at it a week later, with other inmates only too happy to report another sighting to the manager.

I felt that I was really growing up when I drove to work with my own lunch bucket in the old Chevy truck. The lunch bucket was inherited from Uncle Julian, and was an old beauty with a lot of dings, a missing handle replaced by shoelaces, and Uncle Julian's name and address scratched into the paint with a nail. Working with one of the farm residents, who I assumed was there while he rid himself of an addiction, we castrated nearly fifty little pigs in one day, turning them into "barrows". Their loss was our gain because by the time winter snow was blowing, their plump chops would be sizzling in a frying pan. The alcoholic inmate and I put in fence posts after using a post hole digger on the back of a Ford 9N tractor. I was never too good with mechanical things, but when the auger spun around and whacked him on the head, causing him to bleed a lot, he just blamed himself for getting his head in the way. He even kept on working until we put in all the fence posts, using a handkerchief to stop the bleeding.

My last job at the poor farm was to take off all the screens from the front porch and paint them. The screens were about four by eight feet, and were bulky to work with as I took them off, one by one, and painted them on saw horses. There were numbers on metal plates hammered into the wood at the bottom of the screens, and each screen had a corresponding number on the porch. All of them were held in place by hooks that fit into eyes. Not thinking ahead, I removed the numbers while I was painting, and then couldn't remember which number went with which screen. After painting I just hammered back in a number, correct number or not, thinking, "Aw, what the heck. There's enough hooks to hold the screens in place." Although I should have moved the hooks to fit in every eye, at least some of them fit, and so I figured the missing hooks would cause no harm. Who would have ever guessed that one hell of a windstorm would come along at just the wrong time? I drove to work a few days later, my antique lunch bucket sitting on the seat alongside me, and pulled up to the poor farm to discover freshly painted screens scattered all over the yard. Some were crumpled and bent, and some were lying with their screens partially torn out. It was a day that would live in infamy, and it wasn't the last time that I lost a job.

I didn't always show a lack of wit. At the A&P grocery store I misrepresented myself in such a way that the manager thought the assistant manager had hired me. The assistant manager thought that the manager hired me, but at any rate I had a real job, under social security, without actually lying, although it was a slight adjustment of the truth. My job was to bag and carry out groceries, and to stock the cereal aisle. When our oldest son was in high school and working in a grocery store, he said, "Jeez dad, they put the screw-ups in the cereal aisle." I liked to carry out groceries for people because they usually gave you a dime as a tip, and six of these tips could get you a seat at the movies, although without popcorn or candy. The only day that I didn't get enough dimes for a movie was one Saturday when I must have stepped in dog shit, although I couldn't figure out right away what was smelling so bad. Every Saturday, an old lady came in to the store; she drove a black Packard from the 1930's that looked like it was driven right out of a showroom. Every week I made an offer for the car, and every week she turned me down. The beautiful black Packard remains in my memory as an unfulfilled desire. A Chinese lady came into the store with an umbrella she carried to keep off the sun. She was so charming that I carried the groceries two or three blocks to the door of her apartment, as she chattered away in what I presumed to be Mandarin and giggling all the while. On the way back to the store, I got a panicky feeling that a good excuse might be necessary to explain why I'd gone missing for so long a time. But aided by a basic dishonesty of character, I thought of a couple.

When we arrived at the store in the morning, our first job was to bring in the four foot square cardboard boxes of bread, which had been sitting outside of the store since about three or four o'clock in the morning. Having a criminal turn of mind, I always wondered why some hungry or greedy person didn't get up early and steal the bread, but it never happened. People in the 1950's were either less hungry, more honest, or more reluctant to get up that early in the morning. There was a kid who lived in the dormitory of our local college, and I noticed that he always stuck a candy bar in his pocket on his way out of the store. When we unloaded watermelons, sometimes one of them might get "accidentally" dropped and we'd have to eat it, or take the busted melon home. I'm sure that the manager was smart enough to figure things out, but for minor incidents he'd just look the other way.

I lived on the east side of town, and didn't get around much. The west side of town was a mystery to me, and my sense of direction wasn't the best. Kids from the east side only went to the west side to steal hubcaps or tires. The West Side of town was the wealthy side of town, and the two sides of town were bisected by a river and many ancient drawbridges. Most kids didn't own cars back then, so somebody was always asking for a ride home. One kid asked me for a ride, and, wanting to be a good guy, I said "Sure, hop in," and, crossing the bridge to the west side, gave him a ride home. After dropping him off at his house, I took a few turns, and nothing looked familiar. I drove for what seemed hours, and the more panicky I became, the worse was my already impaired sense of direction. Finally, I pulled into a gas station and asked the attendant, "Where's Rustbelt City, Illinois?" He looked at me rather puzzled and said, "You're in it." "Well then. How do I get to the east side?" It was a long time before I tried that again.

A friend told me about his boyhood in Ohio where men caught fish in the irrigation ditches using gill nets. The men got into the ditches and started to walk toward the gill net which was stretched across the water, and they splashed and struck the water to scare the fish toward the net. It worked; the fish were frightened enough to rush into the net, and when they stuck their heads into the squares in the net, they found that they couldn't back out or go forward. Only an extraordinary fish could escape; maybe by swimming through a small space where the nets didn't quite reach the bank, or by swimming backwards through the men's legs. And life, he said was like this, where we were all (except the lucky or fortunate fish) trapped into working. In Africa, I was told, the British arrived and saw that all was good. It was just too good, in fact, to see men sitting around gambling while the women ground grain, and nobody needing any coins. So the British charged a hut tax, and the natives, reaching into their pockets for the coins, found that they had neither coins nor pockets. Going to work for the British to earn the coins for their huts, they found that though they paid off the hut tax, new expenses arose and they never had enough coins to stop working.

Pa said that it could be done, just don't start working that first day. Once you start, there's no turning back. But for some, work is just a temporary thing, with a lot of time off between startings and stoppings. One of my friends said that they were putting their Uncle Johnny on the train when he was drafted for the First World War. He told the family watching at the train station not to worry, because he never held down a job for over six months in his life. And, sure enough, it was 1918 and the war was over in six months just like he said.

I worked for a while at a chemical plant, and it was during this period that three of our children were born. At one time we had three cars: a 1958 Buick Roadbastard that was about half a block long, a 1954 Ford Fairlane, and a 1951 Buick that I bought from my cousin for thirty five dollars, with things that looked like portholes in the hood. Driving to work with three other guys in a car pool, everybody got a kick out of the old Buick because, as we drove by a pasture, the car made so much noise that the steers ran away out into the field. I had more cars than plates, so I tried starting the cars before going to work; the one that started got the plates. A family from Chicago owned the chemical company, or at least, their friends and the family owned most of the stock. The coal mines were on the way down in southern Illinois, so a lot of the workers came up here for jobs. The company was growing; they bought out a small company in Chicago, and rumor was that the previous owners extracted a promise that the company would keep their workers. They were all black and never moved from their homes, but drove down from Chicago every day. Oscar Wills was one of the men from the Chicago company, and he had a steady job of moving drums around on pallets on the loading dock. He got the job because he was burned when a hot amide burped out of the reacting tank and left him a black man but with splotches of yellow on his skin. Bill Eastwald was one of the chemical engineers, and was known to be a bully. With his big round face and stentorian voice, he was out on the dock looking for Oscar, and yelled, "Where is that lazy nigger? When I find him his black ass is going to be sorry." Just then Oscar jumped up from behind the 55 gallon drum where he was hiding. Eastwald ran all the way back to the office where he was safe.

Oscar helped me out when I ran out of gas on a country road heading home from the plant. He conveniently had a length of hose in his trunk, stuck the hose into his own gas tank, and sucked on the hose to get a vacuum and siphon out some of his gas so that I could get home. Since he didn't let go of the hose in time, he drank some of the gas, just enough to stand in the gravel road, coughing and sputtering.

There isn't much in the way of entertainment in a chemical plant, but we found some when the bosses weren't there on the night shifts. There was a scale in the plant for weighing trucks, and we had a contest to see who could pick up the most weight in a 55 gallon drum that we filled with different amounts of water. A short black man came in second; he didn't weigh more than 150 pounds, smoked cigarettes at every opportunity and he coughed all the time. The winner was Johnny Oates, an enormous black man with a chest as big around as the drum. He had a cheery disposition, always smiling and never had a bad word to say to anybody. I was in shock when I came to work and found out that Johnny had shot Oscar, and that Johnny was dead. What had happened the day before made sense to me now; the last time that I'd seen Johnny was on a gravel road leading from the plant. I asked him if there was any trouble, but he smiled and just shook his head no. He seemed to be fooling with something under the dashboard, and it must have been a pistol. Later Johnny caught up with his wife and her boyfriend, stopped at a red light on the south side of Chicago. He plugged them both. A cop was nearby, and he came up and said," Drop the gun", firing at just about the same time. At least, that's the way the story was told to me. Johnny and the boyfriend both died, but the wife was in the hospital only for a day or two, and then she was back out on the streets. We heard that Johnny had shot Oscar Wills, but then somebody said no, it was some other fellow in Chicago with the same name, or maybe they just got the name wrong. At any rate, Oscar showed up for work alive and well. Johnny Oates' body—the strongest but not the luckiest in the chemical plant—was shipped back to Mississippi.

There was a peaceful period when I first started working at the plant, but that didn't last long. The men brought around a petition to have a vote for a union. Pipes leaked in a unit that used liquid phenol, and the operators were burned when it leaked on their skin. The plant sulfonated material using sulfur trioxide, and one night when I was working evenings, there was a leak. The escaping gas combined with a dew to eat the paint job off my car. The company gave me thirty five dollars for a new paint job, and although you could get one for that amount, you had to clean the mud off the car first, or they'd just paint right over it. The guys in one building waded through xylene, and had a lot of other complaints about their health and safety, but what brought in the union was a projected change in benefits that the company offered. I worked with a fellow who was always calculating how rich he was going to be on his retirement, but I was too young and hadn't worked there long enough to care. After one particular midnight shift I had to stay over and listen to some "suit" who came down from Chicago to explain the benefit changes. The talk was too confusing for me to grasp the fine points, but he talked about how necessary the changes were, since the company was getting bigger, and couldn't operate in the same way as a smaller one. He was a slick talker, but those southerners knew when they were getting screwed, and the union was voted in.

The strike was bitter and lasted for three months. The trucks continued to roll right in through the picket lines, but at night a few of the trucks had their tires shot-gunned. There were two roads leading into the plant, and I needed a ride over to the other picket line. A guy in a pick-up truck said," hop in", and I did, and there I was sitting with Floyd Pincus, the old union organizer, the one and the same who threw the brick through the window at the wallpaper mill, and whose son crashed out behind our pasture. He was as crazy as ever, and when he leaned over to say "I've got somethin' for 'em under my seat.", I was only too happy to get to the picket line and get out before it went off. One of the enterprising strikers shot the electric transformer going into the plant, and shut the place down for a little while, and a trucker was roughed up in a phone booth, but the plant continued to spew out toxins with the help of salaried workers and scabs from all over the country. Some time later, when I was out in the yard sitting at our picnic table, a fellow that I used to work with came by. He had been promoted and moved to California, and was back in the area for a visit. He explained to me how I had been blackballed; among other offenses I was probably too enthusiastic about the union. My appearance, too, usually left something to be desired; as my father had told me when he quoted Shakespeare, "All the world's a stage . . . ." and apparently I was coming out on the stage looking shabby. He warned me about wearing my old athletic jacket, the one with the drooling wolf on the back, so old that it was in tatters. He told me that I should put on a better appearance, an appearance that would be eminently promotable, instead of wearing that old wolf jacket with strips of cloth hanging down, and driving a 1949 Chevy that looked like an upside down bathtub. I've looked all over for another jacket with a drooling wolf, but I guess that they just don't make 'em anymore. It confirmed what I had thought all along, though, that all those periodic glowing evaluations shown to you are just bunk. The real ones come from a cigar smoke-filled room, where you're stamped with a label, just like each kid gets growing up in a small town.

The company went through chemical engineers without prejudice. They were especially prone to heart attacks. One young engineer added what he thought was peroxide to a batch, but it was hydrochloric acid. The batch he was making was full of iron, since he was using an unlined tank, and the acid had dissolved some of the insides of the tank. He was a sad and wistful figure, with his lunch bucket in one hand, standing in the road outside of the plant, waiting for a ride home. It was evident that the foremen and engineers who had the heart attacks and were eaten alive were the ones who pledged fealty to the organization, an odd reward for loving the company and trying to do a good job.

Tom Braun was a plant foreman, and ran the plant on the midnight shift. During the day it took a whole team of experts instead of just one man, and work slowed down considerably. All the big egos were busy on the day shift, causing trouble in their desire to outshine each other. Tom was a big old hillbilly, and the guys who lived near him said that he was particularly quarrelsome during the strike. He wanted the strike settled, and didn't like being stuck in the plant to work such long hours. For a while we lived in a little town of seven hundred people, near the chemical plant, and not too far from an oil refinery and an ammunition plant. After the strike was a thing of the past, I met Tom down at Maria's Tavern, and we drank some beer while he told me about how the two of us just about ran the whole plant on the midnight shift. I got a little nervous when I saw a patron with a pool cue walking back and forth behind us. Tom said, "Would you excuse me for a minute?" He was really quick, and before I knew what happened he'd taken the pool cue away from the guy, and then beat him with it. The unsuccessful pool shark's beef was that he had lost forty dollars to Tom in a game, and must have thought he could get it back in a fight. Tom sat back down and continued the conversation from where he'd left off. He wasn't even breathing hard, and didn't seem at all excited—the mark of a really dangerous man. The disgruntled pool player might have had a chance if he just attacked without warning, but instead he grumbled and walked around, trying to work up his courage, and once again proving the validity of that old adage that "he who hesitates is lost".

It didn't take long before the part-time cop, Snuffy Steadfast, came in and said, "What did he do Tom?" The next lesson the pool player got was not to come in and start trouble in a small town. First he lost forty dollars in a pool game, and was wondering how he was going to explain the missing money to his wife. Then he got beaten up, and finally got hauled off to the county jail for disturbing the peace. To add to his troubles, he was bleeding all over a police car. Snuffy had all the latest developments in police technology, and really wanted to try out his can of mace, although opportunities were few. Most of his police calls were for domestic disturbances. Snuffy showed up at a village meeting and requested that they pay for a new shirt. He'd gone to investigate a domestic row at Junior Olson's trailer, and Junior threw him out of the trailer, ripping Snuffy's uniform shirt in the process.

Bill Moravia was driving home from a construction job when he passed Maria's tavern, where two men were fighting in front of the tavern. It was a favorite watering hole for workers from the ammunition plant, on their way home when their shifts let out. Bill saw Snuffy pull up, jump out of his police car and try to break up the fight. Thinking this was the ideal time to try out his new weapon, Snuffy grabbed the mace can, but having it turned backwards he sprayed himself, and the two combatants, finding themselves with a helpless policeman, started punching Snuffy instead. Bill said if he hadn't stopped his truck and come to Snuffy's aid, it's hard to tell what the outcome might have been.

As tough as he was, I thought that a guy like Tom would live forever, but he was burned up in a fire at the chemical plant. He got a call from his old friend, Stumpy Pollard, that there was a problem, and when he walked into the unit it burst into flames. Stumpy was burned but lived through the accident.

Even before the chemical plant, I was shipping gas cylinders and loading trucks with George Benson. He could lift up the 140 pound cylinders by grabbing their caps and picking them up using his arms, and when he did this he smiled at me, his two gold teeth flashing in the middle of his mouth. I don't know whether he had teeth knocked out or he had them done as a decoration. In the summer, we sat out on the loading dock and ate watermelon while we listened to Fats Domino sing "I Got My Thrill on Blueberry Hill" on a 78 RPM record. I wish that I still had it, because George gave it to me, but I lost it somewhere in my many moves. I asked George what other jobs he'd had, and he said he used to be a cook in Chicago. He had a beautiful black Ford coupe, and wanted to sell it to me, but my father talked me out of it. His thinking was that you get a shiny black car, then you get a woman, and then you get kids. He thought I was just a kid myself, and I could get around well enough on my motorcycle.

One morning I pulled up to the plant, and George was getting out of his car. A woman was driving and there were a half a dozen kids, some with their heads sticking out of the windows. I asked George what had happened, and he said that her man wasn't treating her right. George did something about it by punching the man that she was living with. "I had him up against the wall," he said. "I can see that I'm gettin' old and outa shape. I was puffin' hard." And George punched at the air to show me just how that he did it. He went out that weekend with his new-found wife to the Crown Propeller on 63rd Street to celebrate. I wish that I'd been old enough to go because Illinois Jaquette was playing his saxophone that weekend.

George had a barbeque pit on Addison Road, an extra job besides working at the plant. Pa had a deal going with him where we would supply him with chickens, and some chickens we got back for ourselves. It was my job to take the chickens to George's place, then go back and pick them up when they were ready. While we were at work, he showed me a dildo that he was carving out of wood; he didn't use pine, either, but somewhere he'd found a piece of walnut so that he could carve a brown dick. George must have been quite a hand with the ladies, because there were two women who hung out at the barbeque pit, neither of them the woman in the Ford with all the kids. George didn't offer to introduce them, and they stared at me with a not very friendly look.

George was fired for making a mistake on a shipment of chemicals. One of the foremen there was a two-faced creep who kept coming up to George, joking and patting him on the back. Behind his back, though, the foreman kept looking for a reason to get rid of George, and finally found one. When he found the mistake . . . which was a shipment of monoethylamine . . . the foreman asked George, "What does this say?" George replied, "It looks like mama mule to me." The company said that they got rid of him because he couldn't read, but even if that were true, he was smart enough to fake it for four or five years. The foreman, before he was promoted, used to go into the boiler room with the truck drivers after they had loaded their trucks and shoot craps. After his promotion, nobody got away with anything. So, if you want a real Simon Legree on the job, just promote the laziest and most ambitious man in the plant.

My friend's uncle Jerry worked with us, but we knew him better as Slash. He got the name by interfering in an argument between a husband and wife, when the three of them were drinking at Biondi's Tavern. The wife got him with a broken glass when he stood in front of her husband, and, although it would have been more satisfying to have slashed her husband, Larry would have to do. He was taken to the hospital for stitches, and the scar left him with a rakish appearance and a lifelong nickname. Biondi's Tavern was in the heart of what was the Italian neighborhood, called the bloody sixth ward. The sixth ward as we knew it was destroyed by an interstate highway that went through the city in the 1960's, wiping out the Calabasa Ice Cream Shop, the tavern, the Southside Liquor Store, and something called Carnegie Hall, which could be rented for wedding receptions and, when business was slow, a place where stag movies were shown along with barrels of beer to drink, all for one low price.

Every new cop on the beat was invited into Biondi's Tavern for a treat of "cunile" or Italian rabbit, actually a cat, and most of the patrons were in on the joke. They may have picked up one of Uncle Ansgar's cats from the C and M tavern which was only a block down the street. Biondi's was famous for having Joe Pepitone drinking there. He used to travel with the carnivals, where he was billed as the strongest man in the world, and showed off by performing feats of strength, but the most useful thing that he ever did was to pick up the back end of an auto and move it out of the mud. My father said that Joe did this for no financial remuneration, in front of a speakeasy on Washington Street. Slash told me there was a guy at the tavern who considered himself to be a boxer, and he used to come up to Joe Pepitone while he was sitting at the bar, and dance around him throwing imaginary punches that came threateningly close. Joe grabbed him and almost squeezed his neck off.

Slash lived with his parents who had emigrated from Calabria in Italy. The old man was retired, and the only thing he did was take a daily walk to Southside Liquors where he hung out all day. You have to admire his persistence, because he had diabetes and had to have his leg taken off, but still managed to hobble the four or five blocks to Southside on his crutches. Slash blamed his own misfortunes on having married a Northern Italian instead of a Calabrian or Sicilian. The way he told it, he married the "*putani*" after he got back from the war, and she left him for the life of a libertine, which was why he drank so much. Slash told me, "Just wait until you're thirty five. There's all kinds of women out there." He never spoke well of women or married life, and had developed a schizophrenic attitude toward "broads." Slash usually got together with a co-worker, a fellow carouser, and they'd cover for each other when they'd had too much to drink the night before.

George Benson told me not to listen to those guys. He pointed out my father to me and said he was a lot better off than Slash and his drinking buddy. "Married life is a good for a person," he said. "I've been married five times myself." Some of those marriages may have just involved jumping over a broom stick, but marriage, besides being made in heaven, was probably a state of mind for George. And he was there to tell me that it was more to be desired than Slash having a woman in every port, or on every barstool in Rustbelt City.

When I hired on at the oil refinery it was the only time in my life that I was salaried instead of being an hourly worker. Not due to any great ability on my part, the reason for this elevated position in life was due more to the fact that the company needed plenty of salaried workers to run the plant when the union was on strike. Sure enough, as soon as I took the job there was a strike, and now I found myself locked inside the plant instead of out on the picket line. Before the strike started, I had to study the operation of the gasoline and jet fuel treating plant, but the foreman who was supposed to be training me told me not to worry or study too hard, because there probably wasn't going to be a strike. He said that this was an exercise "just in case." Within a few months, I was operating the unit for twelve hours at a stretch, with an old friend taking the other twelve hours. The company thought we could take the place of a half dozen men. It was right at shift change when the plant manager showed up, and I snuck around the back of his truck, leaving my friend to do any explaining, since the ditches along side of the road were filling up with a bubbly solution of gasoline, caustic and lead oxide. I headed for the cafeteria; a holdover from the past, it was once used for meals for the hourly workers, during a more humane era. Now it was opened back up just for the strike. There was plenty of free food, and I ate all that I could, remembering to clean up my plate as Ma told me, since little kids were going hungry somewhere in the world, at least those who weren't lucky enough to be working at an oil refinery. I called home and instructed my wife to tell everybody we knew not to fly until our strike was over, since the jet fuel that we were treating was going by pipeline to O'Hare field; and not to buy gas at our company's gas stations for a while. The unit foreman returned from wherever he was working, and my friend and I were demoted back to being assistants. I brought home plenty of candy bars and soda pop when the strike was over, and the youngest kid was so happy to see me that she lay on the floor and spun around in circles; maybe it was the candy bars.

The company brought in Pullman cars on a railroad siding, but since they were heated by steam from the plant they were too hot, and made sleeping impossible. I got a cot and slept in an old wooden building that had plenty of space. Rob Sidwell stayed in there with me, and he brought plenty of supplies, including a fruit cake. Unfortunately, a rat ate it and, after that, I found it difficult to sleep, imagining that I might wake up with a hungry rat perched on my chest. The strike lasted for three months.

When it was time for shift change, the hourly workers had to wait in a shack until the whistle blew. When it did, they'd walk toward the gate to punch out on the time clock, lunch buckets in hand and shuffling along. Watching them from the window of the wooden shack where I worked, they looked so dispirited, and I used to call it "The March of the Zombies." Salaried workers could drive into the refinery in their cars or pickups, the only demand being that you didn't drive in after the whistle had blown, and that you leave your keys in the ignition in case the refinery was burning up and someone had to move your vehicle. With typical corporate logic, we were told that it was better to be late by two hours than two minutes. You were supposed to go drink coffee somewhere for a few hours if you happened to be late; that way, when you finally showed up it was assumed that you were just returning from an errand. It was the appearance that mattered, as coming in two minutes late wouldn't look good to the hourly guys.

Cap Spuhler was one of a big clan from the town where the refinery was located, and his father and one of his brothers worked there too. When he was going through the gate one evening, he forgot to open up his lunch bucket for the guard's inspection. The company wanted to make sure that no one was taking anything home. The local joke was that one of the kids in first grade, when asked to tell something about where his father worked, said that his daddy worked at the refinery, where they made toilet paper and light bulbs. The guard reached out and spun Chip around; that was his first mistake, and the second was when he got up to receive a second punch in the mush. Chip was fired in yet another case of blind justice. If any of the young guys were arrested locally for a drug offense . . . most of which involved marijuana possession . . . they were laid off from work until the case went to court. If found guilty they were fired, but if they got off the hook, their job was waiting for them. One of the guys working in the tank farm had been convicted of a violent crime, but since no drugs were involved and it was a case of black on black crime, he was free to wander among the tanks out in the dark.

Nick Leary used to come by our shack on his way in to work the afternoon shift. He liked to needle my friend and co-worker, Jim, by poking his head in the open window and say, "How are ya' doin', Jimmy me boy?" Jim hated to be called Jimmy, and he said that the Learys were simpletons for generations back in Ireland. Nick had a bald head, a make-over job for what used to be a hare lip, and sparkly eyes that made him look for all the world like Daddy Warbucks without the white shirt and diamond stick pin. He was hired originally because he was an excellent pitcher for the plant baseball team that played against my favorite team, the Loran AC, the one with Scrappy and Yappy on their roster. But Nick's arm gave out with the usual ailing rotator cuff that plagues pitchers, and he had a job at the refinery until he retired. When the big bosses came up from Texas to visit the plant, Nick was hidden away in the storeroom of the laboratory. Nick's boss was afraid that if the Texans asked Nick a question, the next question might be to his boss, "What's Leary doing here?" Just like most of the guys I worked with at the refinery, Nick was drafted into the army for WW II, and somehow managed to rise to the rank of master sergeant. On the other hand, my buddy Jim, one of the brightest men I ever knew, never made more than corporal in five years. He was drafted at the beginning of the festivities, when the draft was to be only for a year. He came home five years later, after going to England with the Eighth Army Air Corps. Jim said that he'd like to have stayed in the Air Force, but thought that since his folks were getting up in age he should get out and help them take care of the farm. They lived for many more years, of course, so it turned out that there was no hurry to get home.

When I first started out at the refinery, I was told by an older man in the painting department that you only had to remember three things to work there: whip the willing horse, the squeaky wheel gets the grease, and I've long since forgotten the third. It was most likely either shit runs downhill or payday is every second Friday. He also told me that working there was like being a monkey on a string. Every once in a while the company jerked on it, just to see if you were still there and to show you who held the best end of the string. The company was very tolerant of infirmities; Frank Kautz was always taking time off to go to the mental floor of the local hospital. He really was skinny and nervous, continuously smoking cigarettes, or rather he seemed to sucking on them. In addition to "bad nerves", Frank was diagnosed as being suicidal, so it was odd that the company had him train to put

THORNS & ROSES 105

out fires. When a fire actually broke out in the alkalation unit, Jim and Frank were supposed to be on the same hose, but when a huge ball of flame belched out, Frank knocked Jim over in his rush to get the hell out of there. "I guess that he didn't want to die all that badly," Jim said, "At least not by fire."

My nerves weren't doing so well either in the corporate milieu, so at noon I started to leave and take my break under a tree next to a canal which ran through the plant. Reading about Buddhism at the time, I imagined that I was meditating on the meaning of life and was actually trying to meditate, but mostly just dozed off. Having told my fellow workers that it was the bodhi tree, and I was waiting for enlightenment, I'd sit under the tree, but soon slumped over into a more supine position and from there into a full, snoring sleep. I woke up to see a rat, about the size of a cat, his alert little eyes looking at me from about two feet away. Instead of being enlightened, I was scared shitless, and the rat ran away. From what I read, the Gautama (Buddha) covered himself with things like dirt and rat shit, but enlightenment can wait a while for me.

Walter Hinton was the boss. He must have screwed up but, with friends in high places, was granted a reprieve. Poor Walter was sent away from his home in Texas. the state that he loved so much . . . to trade a nice warm research center for a cold northern refinery. But alcohol and downers helped him along, and when he came over to visit his peons in their workplace, he could always lean up against the door jamb to hold a steady course. Walter drove a little Volkswagen beetle which he filled up to overflowing with paperwork. He'd drive to the plant with a cup of coffee in his hand, as a last minute attempt at sobriety for the day. I almost nailed him at an intersection near the plant and don't see how he couldn't have noticed it was me, since I was driving an old chartreuse utility truck that was bought surplus from the electric company. When we got to work, Walter had coffee all down the front of his white shirt, but he didn't seem aware of that, or that it was my truck he'd nearly rammed into. I was glad of that, because we didn't like each other very much, and there was no reason to add fuel to the refinery fire, so to speak.

Rob Sidwell probably reminded Walter of his son, the one who ran away to join the circus or maybe became a hippie. Rob was a surrogate for that son. and Walter didn't like it at all. When the big shots came for an inspection, Rob found a snow shovel and put it in the lab along with a tag that read "For analytical purposes only." Every Friday he'd put signs around the lab that read "Benzene kills", after we'd go to the storeroom to bring back a five gallon can of benzene for use in the coming week. There were signs hanging all around the lab, and you always knew they were Rob's work, since he signed everything with what he called a "bleethel", an amorphous amoeba-like blob. As soon as the signs appeared, they were mysteriously torn down.

Rob was on his way to work one day when he saw a human-sized doll stuck into a garbage can with its feet hanging out. Every weekday morning, the supervisors all assembled at the main office to make their reports to the plant manager. Walter left for the office in his Volkswagen, but failed to notice the passenger behind him, the doll that Rob had retrieved from the garbage and dressed up to look like a refinery worker. He'd tied it up in the back seat, so it didn't fall over, and had placed the requisite hard hat on the doll's head. The plant manager, a choleric individual with a red face even when things were going well, stuck his head out of the window and yelled, "What the hell do you think you're doing Hinton?" Walter passed it on by coming back to the lab and yelling at Rob, who just stared at him with his usual bemused expression. Rob Sidwell quit the oil refinery, bought a farm in Michigan, and raised sheep. Walter stayed at the refinery until it was closed down, and then went back to Texas. I was surprised when some of the former employees showed me a birthday card to Walter and asked if I wanted to sign it. Before I knew what I was doing, my signature was added to the others on the card, if for no other reason than relief that Walter was no longer a part of my life.

The refinery was full of pigeons, and management decided to do something about it. They hired a company that was paid to get rid of the pigeons by trapping them. It seems that they were paid by the pigeon, but when they came to inspect their traps they were usually empty; either the oil refinery pigeons were pretty smart, or the traps were no good. It turned out to be neither, as a guy on the midnight shift was opening the traps and taking the pigeons for himself. He brought the pigeons back to the lab where he picked and cleaned them and, except for a few telltale feathers down the drain, no one was the wiser. Those old pigeons were tough, so he probably had to soften them up in a pressure cooker. When I was growing up, the Italian kids on the south side of town raised pigeons and sold the young ones, called squabs, to the local adults who fixed them for supper. Since spending money was hard to come by for a kid back then, it probably beat having a paper route.

In 1958, the year I went into the army, there was a major flood in Rustbelt City, and Slickery Creek overflowed its banks. The entire sixth ward where the Italians lived was under water. I pulled up to my friend's house in a motor boat that belonged to his uncle, and helped in the clean up. When the water receded the old-country Italian men were hanging out money to dry on their clothes lines. After 1929 that generation didn't trust banks, so their money must have been hidden away in their basements.

Romeo and Johnny were the best of buddies, and worked together at the refinery, but even though they were each other's best friend, they were opposites in life. Johnny was married, while Romeo was single; and Johnny stayed home at night with his loving wife and ate a spaghetti supper, while Romeo had a sandwich and drank a beer. His food came from the snack counter at the racetrack, where he spent his money and his time. In the winter he'd walk around in a shabby coat that would barely keep him warm. Johnny told him to get a good woman like his, who would manage his money, and take care of his needs. "And you've got to think about your old age, Romeo," Johnny told him. "Who's going to take care of you, for Christ's sake?" It got so bad that, rather than hear the usual lecture, Romeo would try to hide out. But Johnny was persistent, and I saw Romeo ducking behind the corner of a shed while Johnny yelled, "Romeo! Hey, Romeo. I see ya. Come over here! I want to talk to ya." But of the two friends, Johnny was the first to die. Romeo married Johnny's widow, and ended up taking Johnny's advice after all. Since Johnny had been such a good provider, and his wife was so thrifty, Romeo didn't have to worry about his old age. He bought a new car, exchanged his old coat for some fine new threads, and made a few deserving horses happy at the racetrack.

Julius was the janitor in our building, but after he went to court he was placed in a work release program and had to fill up tank trucks all day with furnace oil, then return at night to the county jail. He was a tall muscular fellow who could have mangled most people with his fists, but had chosen to empty his revolver at someone, missing all six times. He said that his intended victim had jumped around like a grasshopper, causing him to miss. All skills require practice, and some people just miss out on that lesson; even though I had to practice for thirty minutes a day on the piano, I still wasn't any good at it. Buffalo Bill was asked by General Sherman to organize a hunt for a Russian dignitary, a member of the royal family. This son of the Tsar got himself two Smith and Wessons, fired at buffalo from twenty feet away, and missed all twelve shots; as the saying goes, he couldn't hit a buffalo bull in the ass with a bass fiddle.

Right down the street from the refinery were several bars to help out the men in case they had money left over at the end of the month, Birdie's and Lindbergh's to name a couple. Old man Lindbergh was a widower who needed some extra help now that he was alone, so he hired Bessie, who needed a job, to stock the back storage room and tend bar, so Lindbergh could go home once in a while and get some rest. Bessie was a looker, so business started to pick up. When Bessie told him that she had lost her apartment, and could she set up a cot in the back room, Lindbergh said sure, just be careful sleeping alone in the bar like that. One night Lindbergh sat up in his bed, and thought to himself that maybe he should go down to the bar and check to see if everything was alright. Things were so alright that wedding bells soon rang, and Bessie moved off the cot and up to Lindbergh's house. When he died, Bessie sold the bar, which had been one of the old shot and a beer-types anyway, and bought a fancier place on the east side, close to where I grew up, and named it Bessie's Supper Club. I had the privilege to be there when she was leaving for Florida, after she sold the bar to Ern, who worked for the limestone pit and played the guitar. She left driving a robin's egg blue Caddy, in a dress that sparkled and swished when she walked, and wearing enough jewelry to keep a Mexican silver mine working for a year. It's a great country where a man or woman, regardless of sex—or maybe because of it—can become successful with a little hard work.

I guess that you might call the army a form of work, or at least employment in the sense that it kept you off the street. Every month there was a herd of sorry looking draftees waiting at the train station, and the local American Legion Band played Sousa marches to see them off. The lady from the draft board had the reputation of being tough; people said that she would draft her own mother, but, in retrospect, I wonder about that. Her toughness was likely an act for the right hand, while the left was busy keeping out some mother's darling boy. Probably confused as usual when the lady from the draft board tried to push my poor brother on to the train, I was off in a corner eating my doughnut and drinking coffee supplied by the Salvation Army. I was listening to the American Legion Band play patriotic marches, and wasn't even aware that everyone else had already been loaded up. She said to my brother, "C'mon now, don't be afraid. Lots of men have done this without getting cold feet at the last minute." I finally woke up, took Edwin's place and headed for Fort Leonard Wood (nicknamed Little Korea), and then on to Fort Hood. On the train into Chicago I overheard a quartet of the local boys discussing how they were going to outsmart the government. They said they were going to intentionally do poorly on the mental test and, most likely, be disqualified and sent back home. They must have been just what the army was looking for. I heard later that they were all accepted and sent to Korea. Elvis Presley had gone through basic training just before I got there and my sister, thinking that Fort Hood was a lot smaller than it was, wanted Elvis' autograph. No matter what you did during basic training, the drill sergeants said, "Shit. Elvis did better than that." And I'm sure that he did in my case, when I was supposed to throw a grenade over a large tree trunk and then duck down. My pitching arm has never been the best, so I lobbed the grenade over the tree trunk, but was in such a hurry to duck that the grenade didn't go very far. This time it wasn't necessary to tell me that Elvis could have done better. The face of the drill sergeant, drained of blood, said it all. No doubt he was wondering why in the world he had chosen his occupation.

There was always someone trying to get out while others were trying to get in. Usually they would sign up for a six year hitch just to receive the bonus that was offered. Most of the signees were poor, so the money was soon gone, and they were left facing up to six years of a life they didn't want to lead. Not bathing, screwing up everything, acting crazy, they did just about anything in the hope of getting a section eight discharge. One soldier, Harrison, was so scroungy that he had to sleep outside the barracks in a pup tent. You had to walk a fine line, because some things could get you six months in the stockade, and then a dishonorable discharge.

Major McCully was from Pipestem, Texas, and he was close to retiring, but almost didn't make it back to the Lone Star State. When we went to the field, he slept by himself in a CP (command post) tent, where he had carpet on the floor and wore pajamas at night even though he was in the army. Maybe he had a congressman in the family, because I never saw anyone else who lived like that in the field; he even had an army stove in the tent to burn wood. There was a young private who was trying to get out of the army by screwing up, and the major used him as his personal slave. The screw-up was supposed to keep the tent warm all night by feeding the stove with wood while the major slept the deep sleep of the blessed. In the middle of the night, the tent caught fire, and the major came running out in his pajamas. The young man must have gotten his fondest wish, because I never saw him again.

The same major inspected the mess hall when I was still a "slick sleeve"; in other words, I hadn't been in the army long and was on KP duty. The major had all the cooks pull down their pants to see if they were wearing clean shorts. When he left, the cooks just looked at each other and laughed. It didn't seem to be SOP (standard operating procedure) for the army to check shorts. The cooks got a kick out of the fact that I couldn't understand what they were trying to tell me. I hadn't been around much at this stage of my life, and they had a Mississippi delta accent that was beyond my Midwestern ears. I drank a lot of coffee when I was in the army, and stayed away from lemonade, even though it was terribly hot. Johnny Baxter was another one of the cooks when he wasn't on TDY (temporary duty assignment) to the post boxing team as a heavyweight. I was watching him make lemonade, and saw him add the ingredients to a large kettle, roll up his sleeves, and then proceed to stir up the drink with his huge arm. He smiled at me and asked if I wanted some lemonade. I told him that I never touched the stuff, and preferred coffee, even in the hot weather.

The First Sergeant was "Smilin' Jimmy" Jackson, or at least that's what we called him, because he only smiled when he was about to screw somebody or dish out some ingenious punishment. He was a Southern version of Demosthenes, the Greek who spoke with gravel in his mouth, because he spoke in a gravelly growl. On one of his sleeves he had an 82nd Airborne patch, and we were awe-struck by the rumor that he had bit off a civilian's ear in a bar fight near Leonard Wood. When we were in garrison and not out playing soldier in the field, the sergeant lived in the barracks, but in his own cadre room. He had the predictable habit of being the first person to the toilet in the morning, throwing open the window, and yelling, "You guys got shit in your blood", in that loud growl. Private Colt was an odd duck, but he hadn't done anything to distinguish himself from the rest of the green-suited gob of humanity in the barracks, at least not until one particular morning. As bad luck would have it, the first person to the latrine (no longer the civilian toilet) that day was not Smilin' Jimmy, but just another peon who was probably thinking that he'd do the correct thing before the "first shirt" came in. When he threw open the window, there was an explosion that blew some shards of glass into his face. The First Sergeant went right away for Private Colt, who was taken to a shed. There was some thumping heard, coming from the shed, and a confession was obtained. We never saw Colt again, and nobody ever asked where he'd gone.

When working at a conventional job, you don't get boxes of food from home. PZ and I were the only ones lucky enough to have mothers who sent us cookies; mine were snicker doodles, ginger snaps, and rangers, and PZ got little round

Greek cookies. He was creative, and managed to talk the cooks into a gunny sack full of fruit and other treats from the mess hall. We took the fruit to the home of Sergeant Puckett, who had invited four or five of us peons to his house for a New Year's Day meal. When I asked him why he was in the army, he said there was no work in Louisiana at the time, especially for a black man. Even though it was rude to ask the question, none of the young draftees could figure out why anyone would want to stay in the army. Sergeant Puckett was different in my mind, because he worked in personnel and could memorize the serial numbers of most of the guys in the battalion.

Years later, after I had been discharged from the army, I was shopping in the tool section at Sears and ran into my old first sergeant from firing battery. It was a retirement job for him and he told me that, "Milton was in here. I waited on him, but at first I didn't recognize him." It took a while, but then I remembered who he was talking about. Milton got himself a discharge by a spectacular method. We were headed out to the field, all dressed up wearing our steel pots and field jackets, with the canvas taken down from the vehicles. As we drove in a long line past the barracks from the motor pool, there stood Milton, all dressed up with nowhere to go. I guess he decided that he'd had enough of life in the field, and stood in the doorway, helmet on his head and wearing his field jacket, giving us a military type salute with only one finger. Lucky Milton, he had the color of the winning ticket for an early discharge. I found out later on, from a British engineer, that this was an example of what he called "creative incompetence," and he explained how he'd applied the principle after his honeymoon. He told his wife, "You don't have to make breakfast this morning, dear. I'll do it." So he made breakfast alright, burning the toast and just generally messing everything up. His sweet young wife said, "That was nice dear, but from now on, why don't you just let me make the breakfast?" A job well done, I'm afraid, consigns you to more of the same, with no time off for good behavior.

My excursions into drinking were mostly disasters. Among other ignominious escapades I fell asleep or passed out in the womens' can and had to be carried out. The more pleasant times were drinking beer at sundown, at a picnic table in New Mexico, or reading the "funnies" from a Chicago newspaper in the PX on a Sunday morning.

Somebody must have planned it, because a food strike happened while we were there in garrison, where the men didn't show up to eat one day. I usually took the part of the underdog, but in this case I went to the mess hall and ate. The cooks walked back and forth in front of the door to the mess hall, and couldn't figure out what was happening. They looked so sad, and wondered where the troops were to come in and eat. In all fairness, the food was pretty good for institutional fare; it was just that draftees were unhappy and took it out on the food. The lucky, the halt or the lame, the provident, were all back home drinking beer and parking in lover's lanes with their girl friends or perhaps the girl friends of the soldiers. I didn't think that it was a good idea, and that's the way it turned out. The first battalion commander was a forestry major in college, who became an officer through college ROTC. But the next colonel was a West Pointer, from a long line of military men, and was probably sent by the army to bring discipline to the battalion. He accomplished that, but it became a chicken-shit and cheerless world.

We went to New Mexico to fire off the liquid fueled missiles into the desert, and my job was to calculate the settings for the missile. We were graded on our performance, but we got a poor score when I turned the radar antenna in the wrong direction and pointed it at Mexico. It wasn't the first time, because rumor was that in the early firings, a missile landed in a graveyard in Juarez, and the Mexicans were selling pieces of the missile for souvenirs until the army came down to claim what was theirs. On my discharge from the army, I was called into Colonel Chicken-Shit's office and told that the folks back home wouldn't know any better, but I was unworthy to belong to any veteran's organization, such as The American Legion. I couldn't figure out why he was so pissed off, but finally realized he was still sore about the incident of the radar antenna. He went on and on venting his spleen, and I thought that he was more than a little bit nuts, but just stood stiffly at attention until I could make my escape. This was the same colonel who chewed out his jeep driver for saying hello to the colonel's wife.

When I was discharged, some of the guys took me to town and we ate lingonberry pancakes, and they bought me a cigar. I lit it and standing at the window of the train, smoking my cigar, I waved goodbye. The country was a mystery to me at the time, and we went through a part of Kansas that was devoid of trees. It was flat and you could see for twenty miles with only a few farmhouses in sight, and there were fields of wheat that stretched to the horizon. There was no traffic in sight, but still we managed to hit a semi truck, and the train had to stop. The driver was sitting alongside of the tracks smoking a cigarette, and miraculously wasn't hurt, even though his rig was demolished. I've always wondered why he was crossing the tracks with a train coming, when there was no traffic in sight all the way to the horizon. I made good use of my time by hanging out in the club car. My recollection of Kansas was that it was one long wheat field from east to west.

My parents met me at the station. It was all very formal, because I had forgotten how to act in the two year interval. We went home, sat down for coffee and cookies, and my speech was so correct you'd have thought I was having crumpets with the Queen of England. The bathroom was located on a landing between the first and second floors; I was on my way back down after using the toilet when my Wellington boots slipped on the rubber tread of the steps. Down the stairs I came, unceremoniously bouncing on my ass, and let out with a string of varied cuss words. "Thank goodness . . . our son is home," my mother said. "For a while we didn't even recognize you."

Years later, my young nephew called, and said that he was joining the marines. My brother had probably told him to call and get my opinion, because Edwin didn't think too much of the idea. "What do you think of the service, Uncle Isaac?" I told him that it was regimentation and damnation, but he went ahead and signed up anyway. I got a call from him four years later. "You were right, uncle Isaac: it was regimentation and damnation."

The Clarks were our neighbors, and took over the big dairy farm next to us from the Selkirks when they moved to town. I was riding my bicycle up Newell avenue when I saw Mrs. Clark and the boys heading toward town in their Pontiac. They all had worried looks on their faces; they were headed to the hospital to see Mr. Clark. He'd started lying down after lunch at noon with a pain in his stomach. When he finally went to the hospital they opened him up, and said that there was nothing that they could do for him. So Will took over the farming, along with a hired man, and milked thirty five head of Holsteins even though he was only thirteen years old. He was so embittered against work that he hired on at a utility company as soon as he was able, and for many years didn't come back home to visit his mother and brother. I heard he did finally visit one Christmas, bringing presents, and that there was a reconciliation of sorts. I baled hay for his mother, and can't remember if she ever did pay me. She had the reputation of being tight with a dollar. Everyone thought that she was an eccentric, and they'd watch her wandering around in the cornfield, examining the kernels. Not too long ago she died and left three million dollars in her will, so she must have come up with some good idea while perusing her fields, but she didn't tell Will, and didn't leave her money to him either. It went mostly to charity, because his brother had died. When he was little, the hired man and Will's dad used to send him back to the house to fetch a bottle of beer. He was supposed to bring it to the barn, but used to stop and drink it on the way. Even at five or six years of age he was already chewing snuff that the hired man gave him. He swaggered around and spit, brown juice dribbling off of his chin, and the grown men thought that it was cute to see him imitating his elders. One of Walker's younger brothers told me that, when they were out hunting rabbits with their shotguns, Will threw his hat in the air, just for the hell of it, and blasted it to pieces on the way down. When his wife left him for another man, he more or less did the same thing to himself.

Earl Wilder worked with Pa, and lived in the old Wireman place, which lacked indoor plumbing. One of the last places around with just an outhouse, it must have been a busy place, because he had a wife and twelve kids. Mr. Oreganno, who owned a radio and television shop in town, bought their house, and lived in a new house next to them. He didn't tear down the house until Earl's kids were grown; there wasn't much left of the house by that time, anyway. Pa said he'd seen Earl and his wife downtown crossing the street, and they were holding hands. My father figured that, after twelve kids, the hand-holding period should be over, or maybe couples who continued to hold hands might have more children—up to twelve and counting. One of Earl's jobs at work was to test cylinders. He was unscrewing the main valve while he held the cylinder between his legs, but had forgotten to empty out the gas, so that when the valve was unscrewed, the cylinder took off like an air-filled balloon, and tore down a fence about one hundred feet away. Luckily, Earl's body parts remained intact, and his child producing days weren't over yet.

One day when Earl came home from work, he was met by an anxious wife and a paralyzed kid. The boy couldn't stand up, and his feet wouldn't work. They rushed him to the emergency room, but he burped while the doctor was examining him, and instead of some dreaded neurological disease, he diagnosed intoxication. The youngster had seen where his parents kept the wine bottle, under the sink, and since it seemed to have a beneficial affect on adults, he thought that he'd try some himself. He found that, after drinking the wine, he couldn't even tell the parents what was wrong, since he had lost the power of speech. Large families like this seemed to run in our neighborhood, because the Ottingers had five boys. Bert Ottinger was driving toward town with all five boys in the car, and Bill Walker happened to be following behind them in his car. The boys were so noisy that Bert didn't know the rear door had opened and one of them had fallen out. Bill scooped up the little Ottinger, threw him into his car, and stepped on the gas hard to catch up with Bert. He caught up to him at a stop sign, tucked the little guy under his arm, and gave him back to his rightful owner. Since Bert never even missed him, without much fussing he dusted off his son and continued on toward town. He probably figured that any one dumb enough to fall out of a car couldn't have been hurt too badly.

My brother worked for a while at the plant with our father, and Terry Castenada, a young Italian kid who was working there at the time. Our cousin Bobby was home from the navy, and, still reckless as ever, he was seeing Terry's wife while Terry was away at work. My brother saw Terry loading his pistol after work, and working himself into a rage. "I'm going to get the son of a bitch who's running around with my wife," he told my brother. "Who is it?" Edwin asked. "Do I know the guy?" When Terry named Bobby as the potential target, my brother got to a phone as soon as he could. "Get outta town," he told Bobby. "Castenada's looking for you and he means business." Bob left town and was nowhere to be found. By the time he returned, Terry and was wife had already kissed and made up.

My cousin married a girl whose family owned a lumber yard, and they had two kids. Though he could have spent the rest of his days in the office, with a pencil stuck behind his ear, it was not to be. They got divorced, and he headed for California, which, at that time, was the land of opportunity. He had multiple wives, multiple kids, and ended up being the boss of multiple employees, even though he'd never gone to college. I saw him the last time at Aunt Hepzibah's funeral. He was as congenial as ever, no doubt tipping his hat to all the ladies, but he reeked of whiskey that morning. He thanked me for showing up, and I was glad that I got to see him, as he died of a heart attack soon after, on a crowded expressway in Anaheim. If only he could have settled down at a younger age, worn the green eye shades and lived off the family lumber yard.

Some persons never worked at all. The Macks lived at the corner of our street, and must have inherited some money, because they had two houses. Bob lived in the brick house with his mother, and the house next door was occupied by his aunt, who gave piano lessons, and I remember some young girls who walked the wooden stairs to her upstairs apartment for voice lessons. I don't know what Bob did for kicks, but when I was in the field behind his house I saw him burning a heap of old tires. He raised a lot of black smoke and paid no attention to me wandering around in his field with a shotgun. He was fat as a eunuch, and had no associations with the opposite sex, as far as we could see. Our whole family was invited to his house once, and he showed a movie. I must have been very young, because I can't remember much about the visit, except that the movie was about how things would be in the future. All of the Americans were going to have home grown robots doing our work, and we'd all own airplanes to zip rapidly whereever we wanted to go. I don't remember any purpose for the visit, unless it was a subtle advertisement for a certain brand of church. My parents liked to use the phrase "as lazy as sin," so I don't think the idea of robots doing their work for them would have been appealing, but Bob would have gone for it.

Years went by, and, after I was married, somebody charged clothes and linens to us and to my folks, both at Sears and J.C. Penney's. After talking to the manager at Penney's, we straightened everything out. Whoever charged the clothes used a chicken-scratch signature, and didn't even try to duplicate mine. An investigator from Sears came to talk to Pa, and he hinted at a couple of people that he thought might be suspects. Some of the blame could be attributed to the stores, where they'd have given credit to a canary if it could sign its name. We heard that Bob Mack had filed for bankruptcy, lost his houses and left the state. His mother had died, and he'd acquired a girlfriend with children. He was on the wrong side of forty by then, grossly overweight, and had never had a girlfriend in his life. He rapidly got into the spirit of things, and his money and property were soon gone. From the charge cards at Penney's and Sears, it seemed that, if it was the girlfriend, she had a taste for cheap house dresses. Bob probably had to get a job for the first time in his life.

My old grade school classmate, Dog Brown, parked next to me at Huck's gas station, and he was driving a shiny black Buick. I had an old rattle trap, since we had three kids and I was working the afternoon shift at a chemical plant. Dog began his career as Willie Brown, setting pins in a bowling alley. It was one of the first jobs to be outsourced; he was put out of work by automatic pin setters. Dog made the best of a bad situation, and went into sales. Selling girls and drugs was obviously more lucrative than setting pins, or working in a chemical plant. One of the local narcs said that, thanks to Dog, he had steady employment; if there was no one else to shake down or bust, there was always Willie. So even though he chewed on a crayon in the back of the room, he kept a lot of people in jobs, while I could barely support myself. Was I envious? You bet!

PART FOUR

THERE'S NO LIFE LIKE A LOW LIFE
THE MEN THAT DON'T FIT IN

There's a race of men that don't fit in
    A race that can't stand still;
so they break the hearts of kith and kin'
    And they roam the world at will . . . .

If they just went straight they might go far;
    They are strong and brave and true;
But they're always tired of the things that are
    and they want the strange and new . . . .

Ha, ha! He is one of the Legion Lost;
    He was never meant to win;
He's a rolling stone, and it's bred in the bone;
    He's a man who won't fit in.

poem by Robert W. Service (with many omitted lines)

    That's what Ted Walker told me: "What's born in the blood will come out in the bone!" Dog Brown's bones were developing toward entrepreneurship that involved women and drugs, after automation took away his first job. This is exactly what The University of Chicago economists tell us about capitalism, that it's the filling of voids in order to fulfill peoples' wants and desires. Dog may even have been lucky to be born when he was, for in later times he would have been given a job as a janitor by some well-meaning government organization. He might have spent a lifetime standing in some smelly workshop, holding up a broom, instead of filling the needs and wants of other people.

Since I took care of my needs without him, I lost track of Willie except through articles in the local paper, usually relegated to the back pages. He made the paper when he ran off the street and into a tree on Chicago street. "A ho'net made me do it," he said. The story was that a hornet got into his car and he crashed while swatting at the pest. He made the paper again when the cops raided his apartment. After handing his pistol to one of his girls, he jumped out the window. When the cops broke in, the toilet was still gurgling from things being flushed away, and the pistol was so big that the girl was still holding it; she was lucky not to be shot. Dog tried to make his escape, but he broke one of his legs. He still managed to drag himself a few blocks away before getting picked up. Not too long ago he made the paper for the last time. The picture in the obituary column showed him in a natty black beret, and didn't list the cause of death. He was buried with full honors at the Ezekiel Baptist Church. His brother Stony survived him by only a month or two.

I spent about half of my adult life either trying to get a new job or getting out of the old one. Late one night I was returning from a job interview in Wisconsin., and stopped to have just one beer at a local "titty bar" called Mama's. To my surprise, Edwardo was there, tending bar. He'd gained a lot of weight since the old days, his hair had lost its pomade, and it appeared he wasn't doing real well. His dreams of having girls working for him while he smoked Cuban cigars were apparently on hold. Now he was working for Moe Morales, who owned the bar and employed Martha as his number one artistic dancer. Everybody told me to watch my manners around Martha, since she carried a large purse with not only the usual women's accoutrement, but a revolver as well. Moe gave her the job of manager, and she came down off the stage. This was the first bar that Moe owned; I think he had a paving company also, but may have not been the sole owner. Once in a while, a large man came in and requested Joe's presence back in the office. When this happened, Joe complied in a hurry.

Although Mother's was the exception, his bars had the bad habit of burning down, but, thankfully there was never anyone in the place when they burned. He went from Mother's to a bar called the All American Club. The building used to belong to the Masons, with an upstairs used for wedding receptions, but the Masons sold it. Joe had a stripper who came down from Chicago and put on a great show. Her name was Bambi, and I'm sure that his patrons were stunned and disappointed when the place burned. Although it wasn't as elegant as Mother's, it looked even worse in comparison to his next establishment, another bar, and this one he named "Merry Martha's Lounge". It was divided into two parts: one side with a noisy band and the other with go-go dancers. It had all new upholstery, and none of it yet smoke-damaged.

On the side of the bar where the band played, I met Cotton Harrigan, who Pa said had worked briefly with him at the plant. When Cotton was a young kid he had come North to find work, but didn't stay long at the factory. He played the guitar and sang in country and western bands around the county, and since his wife had died at a young age, he was hanging out at the bars when he wasn't playing. He assuaged his loneliness by offering his house as a refuge for other country singers between jobs: both day jobs and music jobs. Cotton Harrigan complained to me that he'd had to take out his phone. The young, single men were making calls to Georgia and other exotic locations. This was when "Ma Bell" still had a stranglehold on long distance calling, and his phone bills were astronomical. He got rid of the phone, but still had unemployed musicians hanging around. I suppose he needed money, because he sold me a watch, but it only ran for a few weeks and then quit. My wife said,"Where did you get that crummy watch?" And when I told her, she called him "Cottonmouth" Harrigan, assuming that he was some old drinking buddy.

Just at the peak of its fame, Merry Martha's burned to the ground, being yet another victim of what used to be known as a "Jewish haircut". It must have been profitable and prudent, because half of Rustbelt City went this way, turned into parking lots. The car dealers had moved to the west side where there was more money, so Moe took over one of the former auto showrooms and turned it into his next bar. I always thought he was one of the more successful men of the world, because he had both a wife and a girlfriend . . . she would have been called a mistress if he'd been of higher social standing . . . and he had them for about two decades. Usually only very wealthy men or European Heads of State could pull off anything like that. Although I never met his wife, I did see his girlfriend and his kids. When he was still running Kitty's the kids came in to the bar and wanted him to come home. Things were starting to go wrong, and they wanted him to patch things up with their mother, or maybe she had sent them. They missed a really good show, because he had just finished "fooling around" with a female patron, and had her tube top pulled up over her head. Joe told the kids to go back home, that they shouldn't be in there. "Whadda you want? You want to get me in trouble?" He was already in trouble, and it was the end of the beginning, not the beginning of the end.

His real name was Jose, but everybody called him Joe, and Morales wasn't his surname either. He was a good looking man, and appeared to be about ten or fifteen years younger than he really was. Nevertheless, his wife was getting more dissatisfied with her marital situation. Although she had no doubt forgiven Moe for a confessional box full of indiscretions, the crowning blow came when Moe either cosigned, or maybe bought, a Cadillac for his paramour Martha. Since his wife was driving a car not nearly as nice as Martha's, and since Americans judge each other chiefly by their house or car, she was angered by this perceived insult. Moe found out just how angry when he came home and found that his wife had held a yard sale while he was at his tavern. She made only a few hundred dollars, but she had sold his cowboy boots and his leather jacket. The cowboy boots had tips made of lizard skin and had cost him hundreds of dollars, but some old bum walked away with his lizard tips for five bucks. Then she changed the locks on the doors and filed for divorce. Well he lost one woman, but he still had Martha, driving to the tavern every night in her baby blue Caddy. Another one of my admired contemporaries,

Moe proved to be mortal and have feet of clay after all. I always said that when I grow up, I'd like to be just like Moe.

It made sense then for Moe and Martha to move in together to an apartment. She was getting a little age on her, but, except for her sardonic sneer, she still looked like the actress who played Wonder Woman on television. They got along fine as lovers, but things didn't work out when they had the same address. Like the story of the dog with the bone in his mouth who looked at his reflection in the water and lost both bones, Moe now had neither wife nor girlfriend. I would have to look elsewhere for role models. Moe got an apartment of his own, and, last I heard, Martha was working as a hostess at a buffet in a motel near the interstate. We all have to move on and change our persona. She no longer works as an exotic dancer, unless privately, and probably has no need to carry around that short-barreled pistol in her purse.

When we were first married, we were busy having children and living in an apartment in a neighborhood that Pa and Uncle Julian characterized as the "silk stocking district". But like silk stockings that start out pristine and end up with a run or two, the neighborhood had seen its best days long before. My uncle told me how he'd delivered groceries as a young man to the back door of the mansion belonging to O. B. Benson . . . coal and ice. Down Jefferson Street were Swanson's tavern and Whimpy's, where my old biology teacher, of Kentucky Derby and cockroach fame, played the piano for free on the weekends. I heard that his wife was a big drinker, so he would accompany her to the bar and play the piano for the customers. I used to stop in there after working the afternoon shift, and buy a six pack of Blatz . . . all for just ninety cents, and it wasn't as bad as its cheap price might indicate. The really cheap beers back then were Bullfrog or Buckeye. Missus Becky, my widowed landlady while I was in college, drank Bullfrog and chain smoked Spud cigarettes. I couldn't drink either beer without getting an attack of farts bad enough to choke anyone within olfactory range.

Swanson's Tavern was directly across the street on the corner, and was more for the shot and a beer crowd. My friend Roland said he was sitting at the bar in Swanson's, having a drink, when a car careened around the corner and slammed into the front door of the bar. All the patrons jumped off their stools in a hurry, but the bartender (who'd probably seen everything by now), turned a phlegmatic eye toward a stout lady, a member of the sisterhood, who had jumped off her stool and fled in a panic to the shelter of the pinball machine. "One of your customers is here," he said. "He must be in a hell of a hurry!"

The most colorful tavern in the neighborhood was Father Tee's tavern, also known as the Cut Off. It was located on a dark side street, and there was a concrete wall on the other side of the street from the bar, with a railroad track running along the top. My friend was single and used to come to our apartment for supper; afterwards, we'd go out for a beer at the local tavern. A critic of sleazy establishments, still he said, "What kind of a neighborhood do you live in, anyhow?" As we were sitting there, the bartender cut off an old gentleman who was wearing a long brown overcoat that was a little on the threadbare side of new. The old man, whose hair was thinning and whose face was long and gaunt, could have been taken for a retired librarian, but surprised everyone by pulling out a World War II German Luger from his overcoat pocket. He pointed it at the ceiling, and emptied the clip, while patrons jumped off their bar stools and chairs to hug the floor. There was an apartment on the second floor, but no one was hurt. After all the racket there was total silence as the old man calmly walked over to a waste basket and threw in his keepsake. He stood impassively waiting for the police to come, and they didn't disappoint him. My friend never went there with me again.

I didn't go there often, but when I did I was never disappointed by a lack of bizarre action. Cuz was the name of the man who ran the place, and I didn't want to know what his game was. There were plenty of junkies hanging around, and when I came in, Cuz was rubbing the back of the neck of one lady with holes all over her arm. She offered to tell my fortune with a deck of cards, and showed me the queen of spades, saying that meant bad luck. I've been waiting for it ever since. Maybe, though, it only meant that I'd have bad luck if I continued to hang out at a place like that, or maybe that the night would turn bad. As it happened, two of the hookers got into a fight. I didn't find out what caused it, but there was a lot of swearing, punching, hair pulling, blouse ripping, and even attempted eye gouging. One of the customers was heading toward the men's room, but was so drunk that he didn't seem aware that a fight was going on. The girls accidentally knocked him up against the payphone so hard that he sat down on the floor. At the end of the fight, the winner had business all to herself, and the loser had one drink, then moped off down the street, her face looking down at the cracks in the sidewalk.

It wasn't the kind of place where you could just have a peaceful drink and listen to the wistful sad tunes on the juke box. The bar was crowded and noisy, and patrons were dancing on the old wooden floor where the varnish, if there had ever been any, was long ago rubbed off by the shuffling shoes of the dancers. The juke box was suddenly drowned out by the roar of persons pushing and shoving to get out the door and watch the combatants in front of them. The crowd ringed around the fight in a semi circle, and watched as the husband of the disputed woman was beaten up. Then the crowd left him leaning up against a parking meter, and surged back through the door to return to the music. People hailed the winner as if it were an Olympic contest, and said some congratulatory words to him. The only customers who didn't leave were myself and a couple of young Mexican Nortenos who had, judging from their clothes and manner, just recently arrived. They asked me what had just happened and I told them, as best as I could figure it out myself. They said that, where they came from, if you walked into a cantina where your father was drinking, you were by custom supposed to walk backward out of the bar in deference to your father. I thoroughly agreed with them that the lack of decorum and respect in the bar was a shock, but not a surprise.

Jim Petersen had been working on construction until he had an accident and injured his foot. He wasn't the same old Jim from high school days; he had added a lot of weight and muscle. During school he had been quiet and shy around the girls, but turned out to be a late bloomer. When he was tending bar in Coaltown, he had an argument with a patron and threw the guy out the window instead of through the door. His cars started rolling over, and he told me,"you should have seen when the car skidded on its side down the street." During one of his accidents, a girl lost her leg, and Jim decided to move to Las Vegas. Before he left, he was playing in a high stakes poker game in the back room of a tavern and was ahead by plenty of money. That night turned out to be yet another reason why a person shouldn't drink. When Jim woke up, he was in the back seat of his car in the parking lot, broke and feeling sick. When the bar opened, he went back in and they told him that he'd had too much to drink, but before he passed out, he had lost all of his money. Jim told the man in the bar that he was broke, and didn't have enough money to get back home. The man said, "You didn't lose all your money," and fished out a five from his wallet. You could still fill up your gas tank for five bucks at the time. The drink Jim had been given was called a "Mickey Finn". I don't know the origin of the name, but the chemical was probably chloral hydrate, which can take a person to dreamland with the correct dosage, but could cause a permanent nap if the dose was too strong. Pa said that in the early days of the West, Jim would have been the sheriff, but opportunities for some one with his abilities were limited during the button-down-mind period of the 1950's.

Before our paths headed in different directions, Jim, Edwardo and I were driving down the street past the tavern off to the left on Bluff street. Edwardo lived in an apartment on Bluff, and as we were passing the tavern . . . with the appealing name of the Paradise Inn . . . a man and woman burst through the door of the tavern, out onto the sidewalk, and she seemed to be fighting him off. She was holding her own, except for the fact that she had lost her blouse. The brakes squealed and Jim jumped out of the car to even up the fight. He punched the daylights out of the man, but the woman was screeching at Jim and jumped on his back. Just trying to be a "good guy", Jim was surprised, but interspersed between a string of expletives, we figured out that a perfectly good Friday night had been ruined for the couple. Apparently it was an example of taxing and abrasive foreplay.

There was an anthropologist who found time between marriages to take trips to exotic lands like New Guinea. In one of her books, she wrote about two tribes with different methods of courtship. One tribe was cuddly, and loving, and kind to children. Their courtship involved holding hands and smooching and listening to irrelevant conversations. The other tribe got right down to business; they started a fight, and the stronger of the two drug the weaker off into the bushes. Scratching and fighting was in vogue as foreplay for their tribe. I got Sex Education 101 without the expense of a trip to the New Guinea bush, just from observing Friday night at the Paradise Bar.

Jim called me and wanted my help just before he left town for a while. There was a dispute involving a girl who lived out in the country, as well as her brothers, and their friends. Jim had Edwardo, his cousins, and his friends packed into two cars, and we parked off the road on both sides of a bridge. The object was that they were going to pull up the cars and block the bridge when the girl's brothers and friends drove by. I felt lucky that they never showed, and, beginning to think that my friends were a little bit over my head, I never saw much of them after that.

Motorcycle Mack and I sat in my car in the parking lot of the oil refinery and smoked cigarettes. I had just quit the place and bought twenty five acres in Michigan with an inadequate house and a magnificent barn, and to condone the move the radio was playing Bob Dylan's song about "Any day now, any way now, I shall be released." Mack lived in a house with four other young refinery engineers, and rode through the Illinois winters with no conveyance other than his motorcycle. I'd sold my twelve string guitar to a man who played and sang in coffee houses, and had a pottery shop, but had neglected to collect my money. He said that he would come up with the money soon, and wanted to try the guitar out first. This was obviously during a period when I was long on heart and lacking on head. The lack of payment went on until, finally, I told Motorcycle Mack and another motorcycle rider about my predicament. They dressed up in their finest biker array, complete with chains wrapped around their necks, and rode to get my money or my guitar back. Although they came back without the guitar, they had the money. I asked them how it went. "He was slippin' on his shit, he was in such a hurry to get the money," they told me. The money was soon spent. I should have asked for the guitar.

Mack left the men's barracks after having met a girl. She had an apartment in Stonydale that was level with the sidewalk. The neighborhood where she lived used to alternate between residences and bars. At one time, the bars stayed open all night, but with new shorter hours, some of them had closed down and been made into apartments. Mack rode his motorcycle through the front door and kept it in the living room. During a boom time when they were looking for Americans and Englishmen, Mack went to Saudi Arabia. The girl took off with a tennis instructor.

On our way back and forth between Illinois and Michigan, we had a tradition of stopping for food at a greasy spoon called Ma's. It was right off the expressway, and featured hot beef sandwiches and other similar cheap eats. It had red naugahyde booths and large glass windows that served as a launching pad for the flies that looked down enviously at your burger and fries. Instead of being in individual packets, the ketchup was kept in red plastic bottles that made a fart sound when turned upside down and squeezed. The toilets were in some kind of a basement, and to get to them you had to go outside of the building and down some steps, where the local health department had apparently never gone. But I'd go back to Ma's any time rather than eat at the sterile corporate food establishments of today. The folks at the restaurant could have straightened everything out by changing the name, though, because the writer Nelson Algren (and some say that he got this from a man in prison) said to never eat in a place called Ma's. I suppose he was right, but I stopped in there for years. They always had the same old waitress, skinny—as if she had never tasted the the food she served, with a sad face and a plastered beehive hairdo. Many years later I stopped in and she was still there; but she hadn't had enough, now she was the owner.

We moved to our new home in Michigan, and one of the first persons that we met was Wolfman. The Statue of Liberty wanted our tired, our weary, our huddled masses yearning to breathe free, but it looked as if someone had hung a sign outside of our house, asking for any misfits the Statue of Liberty had rejected. Wolfman's real name was something prosaic, like Larry Post, but he had taken on this other persona, probably from a comic book or a TV program. His wife was in a mental institution back in Ann Arbor and her parents had their kids, but he had a scheme to get them back. He'd submitted an article to a local paper that made a big deal about how he was going to walk all the way back, about a hundred or so miles, to a court proceeding just to get his kids. It must pay to advertise, because he got his kids back, though I seriously doubt that he walked the whole one hundred miles. When my wife was working at the school, his kids showed up smelling strongly of kerosene, after they'd tried to fill up a space heater by themselves. My wife drove home to get them a clean change of clothes. Wolfman no doubt had had something else to walk for, which meant that he wasn't home.

After what little we had seen we should have known better, but Wolfman came by and asked if he could drop off the kids just for a day as he had to take care of something important. The day came and went and we still had the kids: two days, a week, then several weeks. Their home life hadn't hurt and probably helped the oldest boy, who was clever and resourceful, and I always wondered what happened to him. With his father's example he could be either a captain of industry or a master criminal by now. The youngest boy disappeared for a time, but we finally found him hiding behind the piano. Wolfman eventually returned but he never asked us for another favor.

I worked in a machine shop and as a part-time bartender, and started spending so much time at the bar that I was almost a part-time machinist and full-time bartender. We had to drive about five miles into town, passing over the White River. On one of our trips, our oldest boy looked down as we passed over the river on the bridge, and said, "There's April Ritz in the river with no clothes on." Her coming to town made a big splash, all right; she must have had either a mania for cleanliness or an urge to show off her body. Another time we'd left our son at home while the rest of us ran errands and, when we returned, he told us that April had come to the house and asked to use the bathroom. He told her "Sure," as that in itself wouldn't be considered odd. He said that she went in and took a bath, and came out in her birthday suit, carrying her clothes over her arm. When I was tending bar, she came in wearing bib overalls and no shirt. She wanted everybody to see the puppy she had on her chest with its head poking out the top of her overalls. The owner, Rudd

Ness, was standing next to me. Paying no attention to the fact that her breasts were exposed, he said, "You can't bring that dog in here. The liquor inspector'll close the place down." I was working at a real class establishment. The other tavern, inside of town, was owned by Angelo Stellani; he was reputed to have mob ties, but this was probably just local legend. If you misbehaved in his tavern, you'd receive a registered letter informing you that you were no longer welcome. Naturally any self respecting hoodlum in the county had to receive a letter from Angelo to sustain his image, leaving my place of employment the only one in the area where a miscreant could drink publicly.

It was almost predictable that Wolfman and April would find a way to get together. They had a wedding—the kind where participants jump over a broom handle to seal the pact—out in the country at Wolfman's place. The wedding celebration was great fun until a motorcycle gang heard about the festivities and arrived in full throttle. Then the party really got started, and somebody blew a hole in the ceiling with a shotgun. After all the excitement you'd think that the new couple would settle down to a quiet married life. But April took off with the kids for Chicago, and Wolfman went after them yet again to get his kids back. Actually I think they got as far as Berwyn, home of the Freight Train Bar, the final destination for the local marijuana crop and, incidentally, for my antique railroad lantern. I'd gotten it from the storeroom at the oil refinery because they were going to throw it out. It had been used in a test that the railroad wanted run on the kerosene they used in the lanterns. We hung it as a decoration on a pole by the road in front of our house, but some one stole it. Samuel Carter came to tell me specifically that he wasn't guilty This meant, I supposed, that he knew who did it, and told me that it was now a decoration at the bar in Berwyn. Raising reefer and transporting it to the big city was a cottage industry in the area, and I was told to be careful about fishing along the White River during harvest time. My friend Don told me that Hank slept out in the field with his shotgun to protect his crop. Samuel came by to talk to me, hoping to stay on my good side, because he didn't want me to stop buying the books which he would bring around to our house. I never asked about where they came from, but they were books he considered to be collectors items. One of them was a collection of Aesop's Fables using words of no more than one syllable. I wish that I still had the book today. It's probably worth a lot of money, but it disappeared in one of our changes of residence. Samuel had a long black beard and plenty of hair, and liked to dress in buckskin, trying to look like a Mountain Man from the Old West. Another walking archetype seen on the streets during the period of the 70's was the men who looked like wandering Ostragoths. When I first moved up to the Northwoods I met Samuel during a snow storm, and invited him in to a restaurant for pie and coffee. While the snow swirled around the windows of the restaurant, he told me about the first winter that he spent in the area, when he ran out of wood for his wood stove. He'd had to sleep next to his horse for warmth. Samuel's reputation in the area was that of a thief, but he claimed he never stole anything from me, presumably because I showed him a small amount of kindness. Once when I was helping a neighbor build an addition onto his barn, my neighbor told me that someone had taken his weed whacker, and when Samuel offered to sell him one, the neighbor realized he was about to buy back his own stolen garden tool. Samuel had a black powder reproduction of a 50 caliber Sharps rifle, which he used to shoot deer and then sell them to unsuccessful hunters from the "big city". He cast his own bullets by melting down the lead plates from old auto batteries, and I believe I still have one somewhere as a keepsake. When he was arrested he was given a haircut and shaved off his beard, except for a mustache. I never really realized that he was a good looking man under all that hair. On the other hand, I looked pretty conventional, my haircut still right out of the 1950's. In fact, I looked so good that Samuel and Tom Herndon asked if I'd like to make extra money by transporting some "bridle path brown" to the Chicago area. Due to the fact that I had four children to support, and couldn't bear thinking about being in jail with a three hundred pound cellmate, I politely declined.

Our oldest son was walking around the gravel road by the lake, which was only a half mile away, when he saw that a house trailer alongside the road had caught on fire. Always a man of action, he ran into the house trailer and rousted the inhabitants, Rose and her three children. Later, my wife said that he should have saved the kids and thrown Rose back into the fire. With nowhere to go, they moved in with us temporarily, or so we thought, until they could find a place to live. Now we had a real houseful, and temporary turned to tedious, but she had a new van that we could use until the repo men came and got it. I never took off my belt and used it on a kid until her oldest boy took a rifle and shot a hole in the window of the barn. The only thing that we were strict about was that we didn't want any of her men friends coming to the house. One guy in particular was known for being crazy, and besides, things were always being stolen. The area was poor . . . a rural "poverty pocket" . . . and one of our friends even had his claw foot bathtub stolen when he was remodeling his bathroom. While working on the floor, he'd put the tub in the front yard and when he came out of the house to get it, the tub was gone. The young fellow who snitched the tub got hard time for stealing a bathtub, which probably didn't make him public enemy number one in the joint. Only a mile or two down the sand road where our friend lived was the grocery store of an eccentric. His store was just a shack, and the merchandise was so crowded into the aisles that a person nearly had to walk sideways to get through the store. It was unheated, even in the winter, and there was a cooler with nickel soda pop. Even in the 1970's, this was probably the last place in the USA where you could buy pop for a nickel. Our friend found the heavy tub at the store, and the thief was arrested when the store owner willingly supplied his name. In fact, I bought a chain saw from the store owner. He went out to one of his disintegrating antique autos out in a field, and pulled the Poulan chainsaw out of the trunk. I never did get the opportunity to visit his house, but we heard the rumor that he and his wife heated the house with bushels of rotting apples, and that gave off enough heat to just keep them from freezing to death.

We went to town and when we returned, our four geese were gone. Geese are supposed to be as good as watch dogs because they're mean and make so much noise at intruders, but their honking must have been muffled by the gunnysacks as they were hauled away. I didn't think of it at the time, but I should have driven around the area the next Sunday to see if I could smell geese roasting. Just before Rose moved in with us, we butchered a couple of feeder pigs. In the stock yards, the saying was they used everything but the squeal, so our pigs were gone, all except for the heads, which we were saving to make head cheese. Rose must have been curious as to what was down there, or maybe she was looking for a secret beer stash, so she opened the door and proceeded down the stairs to the basement. She let out a terrible scream and almost passed out after being greeted by the heads of our two dead pigs, smiling up at her from the bottom of the stairs.

She stayed until she wore out her welcome. I was tending bar until one o'clock in the morning, so it was quite late by the time that I got home, but one night I was greeted by both my wife and Rose, who must have found my secret beer cache, because they were both babbling at once, and they remembered things that I had done and forgot to do all the way back to kindergarten. So much for Moslems and their four wives. I couldn't even manage two women, and with four it would be anarchy.

Our friend and neighbor down the road from us came to the rescue, and decided after a few months that something had to be done, since we couldn't manage to evict her on our own. He showed up in his pickup truck, and told Rose that she was moving to Grand Rapids. She asked when she was moving, thinking he might just be making conversation, but he said, "In fifteen minutes." There weren't many possessions to move, so in no time at all the astonished kids and Rose were in the back of the truck heading for a new life. They knew an old lady in Grand Rapids they could live with, but Rose always returned because there was more excitement in our little neighborhood. She returned all right, but I only saw her at the bar, and then without the kids. She was there one night and, on a challenge from some guys, streaked around the bar with no clothes on for a six pack of beer. She was skinny and not much to look at, but I thought that it was a long way to run, and, since I still smoked back then, I don't know whether I could have done it myself.

The Tower was a large tavern with a dance floor that had once been used as a roller skating rink. The floor was a classic, made of tongue and groove hard maple instead of the usual oak, and there was a large picture window that overlooked the lake. Besides a beautiful view, the lake also served a purpose in sobering up George, the drummer in the band that played on weekends. He showed up in no condition to play with the band on a Saturday night, after having spent the day drinking and smoking. His girl friend drove him to the bar, where we took off his clothes and hauled him down to the lake. We dunked him in the cold lake waters and then fed him strong coffee. Before the night was over he was back up on the stage beating away on the drums. In the meantime, a patron from the audience had been filling in for George on drums, and was disappointed when he had to quit.

I watched from the window of the bar the day our adolescent son accidentally burned down his math teacher's ice fishing shack. He was lucky that he only singed some hair, because the kerosene heater used in ice fishing shacks went up in flames and took the wooden shack with it. Then he built his own and hauled it out on the ice with our Massey Harris tractor. It stayed out on the ice a little too late. I was busy, but I should have been taking care of business; apparently there was a state deadline for removing ice fishing shacks from the lakes. Rudd, the owner of the bar, told me, "You'd better get that shack off the ice soon." I think that the fine for sinking your ice fishing shack into the lake was five hundred dollars. But the ice got thinner, the shack started tipping (as a warning to all procrastinators), and finally sank into the lake, to become a well made home for the fish.

When Rose' returned, Rudd thought that I had some control over her—definitely not true—and he relied on me to take action one night, when he said,"Rose's got Benny Rumsfeld cornered in the men's john, and nobody can get in to take a piss." They were in the entry, a narrow hallway, and the line to get in was beginning to back up. I went to talk to her—plead with her was more like it—because Benny wouldn't come out until she went away. I should have received extra pay for my work in pleading for lost causes. Rudd asked me to talk to Samuel about selling reefer; since Rudd was paying the taxes and it was his business, he didn't want someone conducting other business on the premises. If Samuel wanted a business, he should buy a place of his own. I talked to him, just like Rudd said . . . but tactfully. Personally, I didn't care if he was selling Rudd's barstools in the men's john. My job was to keep the tavern owner happy, keep Samuel happy, and everybody else happy all at the same time.

During deer hunting season, hunters came up from the big Midwestern cities and hunting knives were carried on their belts into the bar. We took the knives as they came in and gave them a receipt which they used to pick up their knives when they left the bar. The hunters came back every year, and during deer season we had to keep our goats locked up in the barn. Unless a goat was a pure white Saanen, it looked a lot like a deer from a distance. And we warned the kids not to walk into the woods behind the house. It wasn't unusual to have somebody try to pawn an item on me at the bar. Samuel came up and wanted some money for drinking, so I gave him a ten, and he left his knife as security. It was a beauty of a home made knife, and he pulled it out from a sheath from behind his neck. I hoped he wouldn't come up with the money, so that I could keep the knife, but no such luck. I wonder who got to keep the knife when he went to Jackson?

The band at the bar was called Day-Trix, and they imitated other groups who were popular at the time, mostly the Eagles. Before that Lead Kelly and the Outriders played, but he had to quit when he lost an arm in a corn picker accident. Lead was a black man with an integrated band that played rock and country music. He was going with Tina Van Hayden, whose dad worked on the ferry that traveled back and forth across Lake Michigan. When she got drunk, Tina used to dance on the tables, which was a dangerous stunt, in my opinion, because she could fall off, break a leg and sue the bar. She and Lead used to come up to the bar late in the evening, and ask me to taste their drinks. Lead Kelley said that there wasn't enough liquor in his drink, and could I add another shot. Of course, Rudd was standing at the end of the bar watching. If I'd given them more alcohol in their drinks, Rudd would have been pissed off; and, if I didn't give them another shot, I'd be pissing off Lead and his girlfriend, who hinted that I didn't want to drink from the same glass as a black man. Rudd stood at one end of the bar staring at me (awaiting my decision), and Kelley stood in front of me with his glass in his hand (awaiting my decision). Another case of heads I lose and tails I lose.

At the end of a dance number, I had to go out on the dance floor with a broom and a dust pan, and sweep up the hair that used to belong to Benny Rumsfeld. He was one of those young men who, if there was trouble of any kind, would be right in the middle. When the weather allowed, he rode to the bar on an old Harley pan head that I'd liked to have owned. "Isn't that pathetic," an old man said to me. The old man must have been in his seventies or eighties, and said that was a pitiful example of a fight between men. In one of its past incarnations as a dance hall, the old man said he used to come here, and that he'd been involved in an altercation with an obviously much bigger and stronger man. Long before anybody had heard of Kung Foo, he instinctively jumped up in the air, and kicked the man in the throat. When he went home, his father criticized him for winning in such a cowardly fashion; he should have just stood there and taken his lickin' like a man. The old man told me that the world had come to a sorry state when grown men settled their disputes by hair pulling.

The "bad penny" returned yet again, in the form of Rose, and since she still didn't have a car after the Repo men took back her van, she'd gotten a Korean guy to drive her up from Grand Rapids. She must have promised him something and told him about the fun he could have in "the great north woods", but he didn't seem to be having too much fun, and left quickly, without Rose. "She's grabbing the nuts of all the men in the bar," Rudd told me. "Can't you do something about it?" I went once more into the fray, but alcohol had befuddled her brain, and she didn't appear to hear a word I said. Busy with my job of dispensing drinks, I looked up to see her leaving with a young Mexican guy. After I was done tending bar, I walked outside to my car, and there was Rose' sitting under the large maple tree in the center of the parking lot. She had lost her shirt and her shoes, and was missing a twenty dollar bill. "I don't suppose that I could stay at your place, just for tonight? "I told her that she had supposed correctly, but she was nice about it and said to stop in if I was ever was in Grand Rapids. She promised to wash my hair if I came; I couldn't tell whether that was a euphemism for something else or that she'd picked up on the fact that I didn't shampoo very often. I've never seen Grand Rapids.

Actually, a patron sitting in the parking lot after hours with no shirt on was pretty tame stuff at the tavern. One night, after closing, I came out to see a young man on the hood of a car. With one hand he was holding on to the windshield wiper, and with the other he was beating on the windshield with a beer bottle. The driver of the car was spinning around the parking lot in circles, trying to throw him off. It was an auto rodeo, but the rider didn't stay the ten seconds; instead he flew off with a wiper blade in hand.

Lane Bumstead warned me that I was driving my Pontiac station wagon too slowly, and that I'd better speed it up or it would soon need a valve job. He was right. I took the car to the local automotive shop that belonged to Art Schiffer and Dave Mettille, where they worked on cars and did whatever else they had to do to make a living. The painter working for them was called Wild Bill, and they said he was a little crazy since the time that he was incarcerated in Jackson. When I came with the Pontiac, Wild Bill was painting a car while everyone else stood around, urging him to hurry up and "paint the car green"—the color of money—so that they could get to the bar before the action started. Dave took periodic trips to Detroit, and came back with an assortment of vehicles for sale. Parked in back of the building were fire engines, emergency vehicles, and even some military surplus. I met a couple of young kids who drank at the bar, and they told me that once when they were following Art on the way home after closing time, he was driving his pickup, and there seemed to be a brouhaha going on inside the truck. The passenger door flew open, and Art's girlfriend flew out on her ass. Luckily, they weren't going very fast and since she was a plump thing, she wasn't badly hurt. The kids told me that, feeling sorry for her, they stopped and picked her up. When they drove off, they found that Art had doubled back, and now he was going after them, goosing their car with his pickup. They got out of his way, but went to the county mountie headquarters to tell them about the incident. Never hearing any more about it, they called up the police to find out what they were doing about it. "Oh yeah," the police said, "We went to their shop, and we had to fine them 'cause they didn't have a business license." There was no mention of the girlfriend or the reckless driving.

I dropped off my car at the unlicensed business. On the way home I stopped to say hello to Samuel and his lady, Karen, at their place. It was in the woods, with a small pond on the property. Samuel wasn't there, so I just had a quick cup of coffee with Karen and walked on toward home. Samuel had once surprised Art Schiffer when he was visiting Karen in Samuel's absence. Art took off in a hurry with his motorcycle helmet dangling from the handle bars, and Samuel shot a hole through the helmet with his rifle. Their place could have stood in a state park as a re-creation of how early settlers might have lived. They had an old fashioned bed with rope strung between the sides to hold up the mattress, and there was a wagon wheel that hung down in the center of the cabin with candles for lights. It was a shame, but somebody burned the cabin to the ground when Samuel was arrested. He'd been stopped while driving a car with a busted tail light, and the police were "so surprised" to find a bag of marijuana in the trunk. Somebody new probably took his place as the official reefer salesman of the county whose job was to snitch on any other budding salesmen to the narcs.

After I drank my coffee I walked up their gravel road toward the paved county road we lived on. Although their road did have a name, thanks to government largesse and the cleverness of the folks who lived along it the locals just called it "welfare row." Seth Akre lived on that road. He made his money with ponies. Local kids paid to go to Seth's and ride on his ponies. The kids went on hay rack rides pulled by Seth's ponies, and he had a replica of a Conestoga wagon that could be used for official events. Another resident of "welfare row" approached me on horseback, looking like one of those Ostragoths. He was a member of the notorious Leiter family, and asked, none too friendly, what I was doing there. When I told him I'd been visiting Samuel and Karen, that seemed to satisfy him. It didn't seem wise to remind the man that we were on a public road; and he rode away on his horse.

On a busy Friday night, I was washing up when I heard something. I looked up over the top of the bar to see a pair of glasses go skidding across the floor. Art Schiffer was the belligerent, and one of the Kennetts was crawling along the floor looking for his glasses. Art must have never heard the rule about hitting a man with glasses. I asked somebody what the argument was about, and was told that the Kennett kid owed Walt five bucks. "Holy shit," I said. "I owe him ninety!" My clunker of a Pontiac had just been picked up and was running better, but I still owed him ninety dollars for repairs. It was in my best interest to pay him as soon as I could, but I figured that even if he'd hit a man wearing glasses, he probably wouldn't hit his bartender. And he didn't.

Everything was going fine as long as Day-Trix was the band at the bar, playing songs from the Eagles and Bob Seger. "I'm Going To Katmandu" was a favorite, and just about everybody got up, danced and shook body parts when that song started up. The owners switched to a country and western band for a while, and the fights became more frequent, more serious, and lasted longer. One night there wasn't a table left standing. We heard that two groups had taken the fight into town, and were still fighting on the main street of the little town of seven hundred, which was five miles away. This meant no profits for the owners, because the bar was closed by the time that the cops came. On the map, most of our area was part of a national forest, and the county headquarters was at least twenty miles away. The country and western music was usually sad, and if that wasn't bad enough, the songs involved men and women running around with the wrong partner. The songs really got patrons to thinking, and too often their conclusion, enough liquor having been consumed, was that the song might be personal, and involve a neighbor. Dave Mettille hit Will Homan while he was on the way to the toilet. He sucker punched him without a bit of warning. I wasn't in the same weight class with either of the two combatants, but I learned early on that most men . . . and women, for that matter . . . aren't professionals, and can't put up a good show for more than a minute or two. By that time they're tired and winded, and you can break up the fight without risking much harm to yourself. Will Homan lived near us in a house on the lake where the tavern was located, and he was angry. He wouldn't speak to me after the fight; he felt that I broke up the fight just as he was starting to get the upper hand. Although this may have been true, at first I just thought he was joking. It seems that we all have something we take seriously.

The incident of the five dollars still wasn't over. The entire Kennett clan came in one night, and sat in a long row on the bar stools. They'd come to avenge the punching of the young Kennett with the glasses, and they'd brought their top gun, a large farm boy with blond hair and no glasses. They didn't start the proceedings, but just sat there on the bar stools, looking menacing. Dave and Art were sitting a few tables away, and appeared not to notice the presence of the Kennett clan, lined up along the bar. At a nod from Art, Dave Mettille moved swiftly to the bar and kicked the stool out from under the big guy. It was so quick and unexpected that nobody did a thing while Dave's boots kicked the stuffing out of the farm kid. I ran around the bar and got there just in time to stop the attack before it went any further. Seeing their champion so easily defeated took all of the enthusiasm from the Kennetts, and they were more than eager to cooperate in removing the big fellow from the bar. The next week, I looked up to see the fellow standing in front of me. He held out his hand, and wanted to shake mine, though I thought it might be some sort of trick. After hesitating, I took his hand and he said, "I want to thank you for stopping the fight. If you hadn't stopped him, he mighta killed me. I got two busted ribs."

Rex was the only member of the Kennett clan that I saw on a regular basis. He was nowhere near as bad a person as the judge made him out to be when he told Rex that he was an habitual criminal, and the judge wanted to lock him up for life. Rex's rap sheet showed an arson and a statutory rape. He'd been married to the daughter of Roscoe Bittner, who owned the local sawmill. The mill was a major employer in the area . . . where little work was to be had . . . and we kept extra in the till on Friday nights to cash paychecks for the men who worked at Bittners. Rex was standing at the bar early one Saturday night, sipping his Jim Beam and water. He looked wistfully out over the dance floor, and told me he was here to meet his ex-wife, and hoped for a reconciliation. A nostalgic song was playing on the juke box, putting Rex in a conciliatory mood, and since his wife was late, he ambled over and asked some young thing to dance. About the time that they were cheek and jowl, Rex's ex appeared in the doorway, took in the scene and left in disgust. Rex had once again screwed up. Timing is everything in life, and Rex's was just off. If the ex-wife had arrived only a few minutes earlier, Rex might have been back with his lady.

On weekends, four or five guys from the Freight Train Tavern in Berwyn started hanging out at the bar. They stuck out because it was obvious they weren't "pine cone hillbillies". The only ones I knew by name were Angelo and the roughneck who was his right hand man, nicknamed Hot Dog. I assumed they were coming for business reasons, but rumor had it that Angelo was getting a little too chummy with Karen, Samuel's wife. One night Samuel came into the bar with Karen walking behind him. In spite of the normal cheery atmosphere I soon picked up on some bad vibrations; Angelo was there with his buddies, and he and Samuel had began a staring contest with more and more intimidating looks. That soon escalated when Angelo sent Hot Dog over to do his dirty work. Looking up over the bar while washing glasses, I saw Samuel and Hot Dog facing each other down at the edge of the dance floor. Things had just gotten to the insult stage, and they were puffing out their chests, exchanging curses. I ran around the bar, to all appearances breaking up a potential fight. But as I tried to shove Hot Dog out of harm's way, Samuel got him right over the top of my head; one of the few times being short in stature was in my favor, and, apparently, in Samuel's. It wasn't really much of a fight, just a lot of scuffling and a few punches thrown. The advantage in this case went to the home team, and the spectators went back to the task of becoming seriously inebriated. Before the bar closed, Samuel left with Karen still walking dutifully behind him, but as they got to the door she paused momentarily, turned around, and gave Angelo a wink.

My wife and the kids went to Roscoe Bittner's sawmill to look for wood. We burned oak slabs in our wood stove, and we sided our bedroom with cherry wood that was classified as "offs", rejected for furniture use, having too many loose knots or other blemishes. One time they filled a huge box with some especially nice oak lathes, about four inches wide by a foot and a half long, and Roscoe just charged them a dollar for the whole box. As our truck was pulling out, Roscoe's wife came running out after them, screaming that she wanted those oak lathes, and they weren't for sale. Apparently she had been saving the wood for something, or at least said that she was; some ongoing family argument was always going on at the Bittners. This time Roscoe had gotten the better of her, and it was too late as she watched her oak lathes disappear down the road. We used the oak to shingle an outhouse that we built back in the woods. First we framed the outhouse, and installed a window that faced out onto the woods for an aesthetic view. Then we nailed stringers running around the outhouse, and nailed Mrs. Bittner's oak shingles to the stringers. Oak splits if it's nailed, so we had to drill holes in the shingles before nailing them. It was a lot of work, but it turned out to be the Taj Mahal of privies, and I've always been sorry that we have no picture of it. The privy had to be used every spring. If we had torrential rains, since we lived next to Bobcat Swamp and the water table would come up higher than the septic field, it was a good idea to have an alternate plan.

Even though Rose had left the area, she had a brother who came into the bar, but I'd only seen him a few times and didn't pay much attention to him. I wasn't working at the bar that day, and was home baking bread when I looked out the big glass window in the kitchen to see two men walking up the driveway. And they were wearing suits. I couldn't remember the last time I'd seen anyone wearing a suit, and no one wears one just to walk up a lane to a farm house, unless it's in the joke about a salesman and the farmer's daughter. They knocked on the door, and when I answered they asked if I knew Eddie Bonet (Rose's brother). My mouth was still hanging open in astonishment when I gave them the classic line, "Never heard of the guy!" As soon as they got to their car I grabbed the phone and called the bar. Rudd answered, and I told him that two men in suits were looking for Eddie, and to spread the word. Eddie disappeared along with the shiny Pontiac for which somebody was imprudent enough to loan him money. The repo men or the bank never did get the car until it was found, some time later, abandoned on a remote two-track in the woods. The elusive car had kept changing locations until Eddie vanished from the north woods.

Fishing was good at the lake across from the bar, until it got too warm. We fished off a pier that belonged to Carrie and Lane Bumstead, who lived in a house trailer on a hill above the lake and the pier. Lane was a huge bear of a man, but he had gout and some other physical infirmities, so he was on a disability pension. He had to check in to the hospital periodically, and when he did, his cronies always managed to sneak in a case of beer—probably not the prescribed treatment for gout. At one time he'd owned a tavern in West Bend, but had dumped one of the local college students on the sidewalk in front of the bar . . . head first. He told me he kept calling the hospital every hour to see if the kid was still alive. He also told me how, during a strike, he'd sabotaged a building belonging to the company. These were just a few of the reasons, along with his health, that he was living out in the Michigan woods.

It wasn't that Lane didn't believe in discipline; he just thought it should apply to everyone else. Once when Carrie was visiting one of her girlfriends, a neighbor who also lived on the lake, they spent the afternoon drinking beer instead of knitting or finding some worthwhile way of occupying their time. She was late for supper, and when she came home Lane was waiting with a stick. He went charging after her into the woods, but couldn't catch her because of his bad legs. Carrie didn't come back until the next day, and by then Lane had cooked his own supper. A few days later, everything seemed to be back to normal. It was really unusual when Lane was barred from The Tower for a few weeks, after an incident concerning his stepson and the alleged theft of a car battery. When Rudd made a remark about it that Lane didn't like, he leaned over the bar, where Rudd was bent down washing glasses, and hit him on top of the head. Lane had to drink his beer at home for a while. Incidents like that were the reason I always kept one eye on the glasses I was washing, and the other on potentially unhappy patrons.

Lane's wife told me how she had gone to visit Missus Leiter, the *grand dame* and reigning matriarch of the Leiter clan. I'd only met the men, the first one being the

Ostragoth with the long, blond hair and mustache on horseback out on welfare row. His brother Wally was perched on top of my car engine when I went to see if my valve job was finished. Another Leiter lived in a house that was covered with dirt, except for one side that had windows and a door. Ahead of its time, the house was energy efficient even though it didn't look like much from the street. On receiving her visitor, Mrs. Leiter said, "Boys, I told you to get that dead dog out of here three days ago!" Carrie said there was a dead dog lying behind the wood stove. She stayed for coffee, not wanting to offend, and watched as the younger members of the clan, who were still living at home, dragged the dog feet first out the door.

Rudd and I weren't the only bartenders working at the tavern. Terry Hotchner worked with me on the weekends, and the owners, Rudd and Bea, treated him like family. His mother was an over-the-road trucker, and his dad was long gone without even the excuse of a truck to drive. Terry wasn't lacking for smarts. He could add up the price of four or five different drinks in his head without using a calculator. Rudd and Bea had him over at their house a lot, next to the bar, because they hated to see him living on a diet of junk food and alcohol. Terry liked to fight. When he showed up for work, he usually had a head start after drinking at a bar in some other town, and often came in bruised and battered. "Lost another one," he'd say, and bragged that he had never won a fight in his life. But whenever one broke out, he was first to join in the fray. Before jumping in, though, he'd spit out the bridge he wore since his front teeth were missing. It was remarkable how fast he could spit out his teeth before he went around the bar, and more often than not he'd come skidding back the way he'd just come.

Terry fell in love, and married a Mexican girl from a large family. I know it was love because, when we first moved to the woods we were down by the swimming hole at the lake, and I saw them standing on the shore hugging and kissing. But his marriage had a half-life of about three months, and they were soon separated due to Terry's love of drinking and philandering. Nevertheless, his wife wanted him back, although Terry seemed to prefer a young, blond waitress. Before the waitresses would arrive, we had to bring the orders to the customers sitting at their tables. Terry started out with a tray full of drinks when I saw two young men run in giant leaps for the side door, so quick that I didn't get a good look at them. Terry was holding his face with one hand, and said, "those Mexicans just cut me." By this time, the two "cuchilleros" were in their car and out of the parking lot. It was just a subtle message from his wife. Terry was nothing if not steadfast in his determination to return to the single life. His in-laws were just as determined. In the next round he came to work with some knots on his head. "Someone was knocking on the door at two o'clock in the morning," he said. "I opened the door, and there were two of my wife's relatives." They didn't cut him this time; just left him on the floor after they beat him up and gave him another warning.

His wife played her last card. Gomez showed up at the bar to talk to Terry. Gomez used to be a professional boxer, and he coached the local golden gloves team for their fights in Detroit. I saw him in front of Terry, talking to him, and when Gomez grinned, there was a flash of gold teeth in the front of his mouth. This was supposed to intimidate him, but both knew that Gomez would have been in a lot of trouble if he hit Terry. The intimidation didn't work. Terry's father-in-law came in and sat at a table where he could swear at Terry in Spanish, and glower at him through the smoke-filled air. The father-in-law was angry and drunk enough to make me more than just a little nervous. After a while he cursed and slunk out of the bar, but a few minutes later a girl came in and said that there was an old man in the parking lot with a deer rifle. Terry grabbed the 357 Magnum that we kept under the bar, but when he got to the parking lot the old man was gone. The soon to be ex-wife finally gave up, and moved to Muskegon to live with her relatives.

Terry wasn't the only one getting beaten up. I went to throw out a drunk who didn't want to leave, and he did a nose dive before I got him to the door. With one hand I had him in a half-nelson, and the other hand was on the seat of his pants. Some unknown admirer gave me two or three quick shots to the head while both of my hands were occupied, and then disappeared into the crowd. I got some backup help and we threw the rascal out, but when I went to bed that night it felt as if I had an electric shock in my neck, and it bothered me for years afterwards.

The only close call that I had was with a woman patron. There was a disturbance at one of the tables near the dance floor, and soon a ring of spectators was encircling the combatants. I went around the bar figuring that it was just some minor tiff, but it was a lot more serious than I thought. Two women of very husky proportions were facing each other, one of them was holding her face, where she'd been cut by a broken beer glass. Looking on was the object of the fight, a short, husky guy with curly dark hair. The one lady was bleeding on the floor from a cut on her face. Before she could do any more damage, I grabbed the wrist of the woman holding the busted glass. She was a lot stronger than I expected and was in a fighting mood, so she turned the glass on me. I had to hold her wrist with both hands as we did a *pas de deux,* with me jumping from one leg to the other while she tried to kick me in the balls. I yelled for help, of course, but none came because everybody thought that it funny. After I tripped her and we rolled around on the floor, some help came to break it up. The quarrelsome three left, and I went back to bartending, but only after a couple shots of Southern Comfort nerve tonic.

This happened on a Saturday night and the following Monday I was with our youngest son at the grocery store. There, standing by the check-out counter, was the husky slasher with her curly headed man. She didn't say that she was sorry or anything, but bought a big candy sucker with beautiful swirling colors, and walked over and gave it to the boy, who was two or three years old at the time. To a little kid, an all-day sucker tops an apology any time.

Actually, incidents like these were few and far between, and seldom was anyone seriously injured. There was one exception that I can think of, an argument one night between two young swains. Each thought he was the number one boyfriend of a nice looking girl in a braless tee-shirt. As the night went on, they both became extremely drunk and faced each other off on the dance floor. One suitor pulled a knife, and the other was so drunk that he fell forward onto the knife. "Boo hoo hoo," the pretty girl cried, and she asked, "What's going to happen?" She sat across the bar from me looking distraught as her two boyfriends were hauled off. "Nothing serious," I told her. The boy friend who was cut was taken to the hospital and stitched up. I explained how it used to be a mark of honor to get cut up like that at German universities. The other suitor was taken to the county jail. Since the owner of the bar also served the public as local bail bondsman, I told her that Rudd would get him out as soon as they set his bail, so there was nothing to worry about. She was still sniffling a little when a bearded man in bib overalls came up to the bar and asked her to dance. When I looked over the rail atop the bar, she was dancing with abandon, and appeared to be at least partially consoled. The hippie in overalls was her third suitor in just one evening.

If it wasn't bad enough that we lived next to a swamp, down the road and around the curve was a junkyard belonging to the Stylers. They lived on twenty or thirty acres littered with old cars and car parts. My wife said some friends told her about a wedding reception held in the Styler's basement. It might have been when Ron and Effie were married, but the reception almost turned into a tragedy when our friend's little boy fell into the sump hole and could have drowned. Effie was a thin little slip of a girl, not much to look at, but must have had some kind of appeal to Al Jimenez, who was Ron's best friend, and living in a house that belonged to Jan Staunton. There were two couples who lived with a group of others in what used to be a commune down the road from our house. Jan and Ray Staunton were married to each other, and Gil and Kay Bing were the other couple. Ray Staunton and Kay Bing took off one morning and didn't come back for months. They said that they had visited Wavy Gravy at the Hog Farm, and stopped at other hippie landmarks along the way. Ray couldn't understand why his old friend Gil was so angry when he and Kay returned. Didn't we all love one another, and we were all one big family? But Gil was angry, and the upshot of the thing was that they just switched partners. Then Kay built on her property, a house called "Kay's shack". That arrangement hadn't lasted long when Gil Bing bought a sailboat, on which he and Jan Staunton sailed off on Lake Michigan, to go down the Mississippi River to the gulf of Mexico. And Al Jimenez moved in to Kay's shack.

Al told me that he did drugs that got him into a paranoid state and that he'd spent an entire night hiding up in the roof rafters with a hunting knife. But drugs probably weren't the only reason for hiding. Ron found out that Al was seeing Effie when he was gone. Ron came to the shack, decided to do the civilized thing, and sat down with Al to discuss their situation. They were drinking wine and smoking a little reefer, which cleared their thinking enough that they came to a conclusion. They'd have it out with knives. One of them said there was a suitable field on the other side of town where they could have privacy. They got in a pickup truck, but on their way to fight they ran off the road and into a tree. Neither man was seriously hurt, just a few minor injuries that sent them to the emergency room.

There was no further reason for them to injure each other. Effie decided that she wanted neither Al nor Ron; she opted for Uncle Sam instead, and joined the army. Ron had a congenital bad leg and he played it to the hilt during the divorce proceedings. He limped into the courtroom, and managed to get a decision that Effie should pay him alimony. After moving back to Rustbelt City, we went back to the woods for a visit, and who should I see but Ron Styler on a motorcycle, riding slowly along the edge of the road while looking into the gully. I stopped to say hi, and ask what he was doing. He said that he'd lost a bag, and was searching for it. Someone must have been a little too close to the truth, or to Ron, and he'd had to ditch some reefer. Between his bags and his alimony checks he seemed to be doing fine.

Smokey and his woman lived next door to the bar, in a converted chicken house. Every time that I passed his place, he was always in the front yard working on his car which was up on blocks. He was a regular, and always came in on Saturday nights to get drunk. He'd leave for home before the festivities got started, with the young kids dancing to the latest tunes. Drinking hard liquor it wasn't long before his speech was slurred, and his request was always the same. "I wanna hear Wildwood Flower," he yelled when the band came in, and soon after he either passed out or had staggered back home. His wife never came with him, though it was a long term relationship . . . and it may have been long term suffering from the pinched look on her face. During the day when I passed by he was usually out in the yard working on the old car that was always up on blocks with the wheels off. Lane told me that Smokey had a claim through workman's comp, and after a long wait, the eagle finally shit out thirteen grand. At that time a person could live for a year on thirteen grand if he was prudent. But Smokey never knew that he had so many friends. They came from all over, and soon they were drinking and gambling all over the county. As the saying goes, all good things must come to an end, and the settlement money was soon gone. Smokey still came to see me on Saturday nights, but he only had enough money to get drunk one night a week, and his friends had disappeared. He sat there drinking all alone and calling for the band to play Wildwood Flower. On our last visit, I drove past Smokey's place. The car was in the front yard, its wheels off, and sitting back up on the blocks.

Parents find something to worry about with their kids, and we were worried about our oldest, who seemed to be tired all the time, even though he went upstairs to bed at a reasonable hour. His school work was suffering and he was getting thin in spite of all that rest. Al Jimenez stopped by and told me that, "I don't like to snitch on anybody, but I saw your boy at a party up in Holtzville at two o'clock in the morning." Holtzville must have been about twenty miles away, and since he didn't have a driver's license, it was a long way to go. I didn't know whether to believe Al or not.

The chicken house, the pigs, the goats, the outhouse, the barn all were on the east side of the house. The only reason to be on the west side was to dig up the septic tank or unplug the septic field from the tree roots. Something went wrong with the septic system at least once a year, so I looked up while I was digging in the Michigan sand. I wondered where my long ladder had gone, and there it was, leading up to the west bedroom window on the second floor. Just like Jacob's ladder, it could lead up to heavenly delights, but more likely downward to the delights earth had to offer.

There was even more trouble to be found in just staying at home. Moose Malone had a lively daughter, and a wife who thought that Moose should set things right for the young miss whenever they went wrong. He'd catch his daughter in woods and backseats all over the county, and finally took a bat to one of her young men, who ended up in the ICU of the local hospital to convalesce. Since they were from one of the old and respected families in the area, the judge didn't do much to Moose except to take away his Louisville Slugger. One night we were fast asleep when I awoke to a lot of noise coming from upstairs. I yelled, "Hey! What's going on up there?" And before I could get going, there was the thunder of many feet running down the stairs, and then the squeal of tires heading out of the driveway. Since all was quiet after that, I figured, "Aw, what the hell," and went back to sleep. Thinking that was the end of it, I came home the next night to find my wife on the phone with none other than Missus Moose. It seemed that Miss Moose was one of the partygoers on the second floor . . . in fact, she was the only female guest. So right away she squealed, and named our house as the place and our son as chief participant in the debauchery. "What do you think she is? A Vestal Virgin?" screamed my wife. The phone was plunked down and the conversation ended. But as you know it's a small world, and not long afterward, when I had filled up my pickup at the gas station and was heading in to pay, who should I see but Moose Malone at the pumps. As luck would have it the weather was cold, so I pulled the coat up over my head. He probably had fresh problems on his mind by then and he didn't notice me.

Another of our acquaintances was Rudy, who called himself J. Rudolph Selyers. I met him first at the local hippie co-op, where he rang me up, bagged up my purchases, and said, like Roy Rogers, "Happy trails" as, unlike Roy Rogers, he threw a joint into my grocery bag. Rudy was a man of many parts. He retired from the Marine Corps, taught chemistry at an East Coast prep school, and moved to Michigan where he joined a church where the members were devout vegetarians. He lived with Annie and her son (who had a mania about Spiderman . . . that's all he could ever talk about), and they raised goats. He was very bright, used five dollar words, and was one of the guiding lights in the co-op food store.

One night, while Rudy and his woman were visiting another local couple, the FBI charged the house with their guns drawn, acting as if they had just cornered a rustic John Dillinger. The arrest was not concerning anything that he'd done since moving to the country but was from a charge made years ago, back in Detroit. He was accused of conspiracy to produce drugs, and we found out that he'd been using his chemistry skills outside the classroom, and under a different name. Ray Staunton volunteered to represent him, since he was really a lawyer before he had begun his hippie incarnation. Rudy was unhappy with his representation., and thought he should have been acquitted, instead of getting a year in prison. Sent to a minimum security establishment, Rudy said that on Sundays all the cons at his country club prison were supposed to stand up and give uplifting phony talks about their on-going rehabilitation process, more of an exercise in acting than soul-searching. Rudy couldn't help himself, and, when it was his turn, gave a lecture on Lama Govinda and "The Way of the White Clouds." Apparently he said something wrong, because the next day Rudy was in the warden's office. The warden was fondling a piece of paper with the word "Dangerous" stamped in red, and Rudy was sent to finish out his sentence at Leavenworth.

His lady friend, Annie, meanwhile was home alone with just her little son to help with the goats, and needed help with the milking. She went up the road and asked their friend, a former dirt bike rider who went by the name of Sam Bike, to help her out, and it wasn't long before Annie and her goatherd were a couple. Sam was also an ex-marine, like Rudy. When he was released, Rudy went to see the new couple, and I was told he made Sam snap to attention while he chewed his ass out. Once a Marine, always a Marine.

Sam lived in a farm house high up on a hill that was so steep my pickup truck could barely climb to the house. For that reason his garden was planted on flat ground down by the road. It was a sandy back road, not often traveled, but apparently, there being no such thing as a small enemy, someone had ratted Sam out. He was arrested for growing marijuana. Sam told the judge that it was done as a companion planting, and that the mary jane kept the bugs out of his potatoes. But the judge didn't buy it, and Sam languished in the county jail until he could come up with the fine. We had a benefit to get him out of jail. A bandstand was built, tickets were sold to what presumably was a "festival", where you could bring a tent and stay overnight. It was meant to be a mini-Woodstock, still fresh in everybody's memory. I had to tend bar that night, but our son helped park cars in the field, and my wife and the other kids helped cook and hand out food. It was a great success, and Sam got out of jail just in time to see the bugs chewing big holes in his potato plants.

Sam had plenty of friends who visited the house often and Annie, free spirit that she was, took off with one of them. She got a job as a waitress at the Plugged Nickel restaurant, and Sam found religion. A family we knew had belonged to a rather loosely structured Christian commune, and they found a wife for Sam. He'd already had at least another one, from his days as an engineer in the City, so this was three strikes and you're out. Before long, however, the marriage started to go bad, and the lady ran away. Sam and our friend Luke drove after her and, when they found her, they kidnapped the lady and brought her back to the marital bed. But later on she left again; this time for good.

Rudy left, and we heard that he was in the western part of Illinois with a woman who was a fortune teller. Ron Styler died from botulism, from home canned sausages that had gone bad. Everybody said that he might have lived if he'd have quit pulling out the IV and the oxygen canula. Samuel was stopped by the cops when they saw he had a broken tail light. It was probably a set-up, because I drove pickups without any tail lights at all, and nobody stopped me. My take was that only one person could be the county reefer salesman, and as long as he snitched on everyone else, he could have the territory to himself. It was just time for someone else to have the job. Samuel's cabin in the woods was burned down, and his wife Karen took their two kids and moved to a resort area, to work in a hotel. Al Jimenez moved back to Puerto Rico, where he was receiving money for being disabled . . . a bad back. Our farmer neighbor, one of the few originals left in the area from the old hippie days, ran for state representative and won. His opponent probably helped get him to the state house by labeling him "the granola candidate". Although it was supposed to be an insult, the label caught on and got him elected

I was starting a new job and was back in my home town. For old times sake, I stopped in at Father Tee's tavern. The sign outside the front of the tavern now read "Widder Brown's," and when I walked in I was greeted by a sea of black and brown faces. Everybody turned to look at me, friendly enough while I sipped my beer, but probably thinking I was either a city official, a narc, or a nut to be the only white man in the bar. Cuz and all the low lives were gone.

The world had changed. America had gotten rich, or at least acted that way. A self indulgent wind had come and blown all these people away, and I was blown to a new place where they didn't exist any more.

PART FIVE

WE ENTERTAINED OUR ANGELS UNAWARE

Tack fur roserna vid vagen
Tack fur tornet ibland dem
Tack fur resta himlastagen
Tack fur ever trygatt hem.

Thanks for the roses along the way
Thanks for the thorns among them
Thanks for the ladder leading to heaven
Thanks for the ever protecting home.

From a placard hanging on the wall in Swedish homes

When I got out of the army, I went back to college. My friends took me to the train station, after a breakfast of lingonberry pancakes, and sent me off with waves and a big cigar. Looking from the window of the train I waved back until the train platform and my army buddies disappeared from sight. Cigar in hand I headed for the club car, where I bought a deck of playing cards with pictures of passenger trains on their faces. It was a long ride back, and the cigar, so pleasantly aromatic before it was lit, gave off a dense cloud of choking blue smoke in the confines of the club car. Later on that year I boarded a different train, to head out for the college where I would finish my degree. I remember an older man on the train who was busy the entire trip, showing a lot of interest in the young women who boarded along the route. Beautiful and full of life, they were heading to the same small Midwestern college and, for once in my life, I was confident that the train and I were on the right track.

At the station I grabbed my suitcase and headed up toward the school. It was seven or eight blocks away, but I needed the money more than I needed a taxi. The town was a decaying industrial mecca similar to my own, and as I walked along I passed a rail yard that looked just like the scene below my maternal grandparents' house. The boxcars were lined up single file on myriad tracks criss-crossing each other, and led to a rusty old metal building with soot-stained windows. Then came the downtown area; its busiest street, "The Strip", was filled with night clubs and honkytonks.

Making my way towards the college, I found myself joined by a middle-aged man, wearing a suit and walking briskly. "Where are you going?" he asked. As if the suitcase weren't answer enough, I wore that expectant look on my face that always heralded new adventures. Looking up I saw the golden dome of the main building shining through the trees. Sitting high on a hill, the building emphasized the gravity of the enterprise, and I told him that, having recently gotten out of the army, I was headed for college. "You don't need that," he said. The man was a prickly sort, shoulders thrown back and hair sticking straight up in the air. He bristled as he spoke, telling me, "I know Latin. I know Greek. I've studied all the great books. And all without ever having gone to college." He told me not to go. "If it's just a job you want, go get a carpenter's card," he said, and seemed so cock-sure. I just couldn't help myself and went on to college anyway, but I've only had one job in a lifetime that actually required a degree. Thinking about this chance meeting I've often wondered if he was a real person, or maybe just a shade, like Grandpa Hallenberg's *tomte*. Was he actually a representative of me in some future life, in a sort of time bleed-through, or was he a heavenly messenger sent to put me on a right path? Most likely he just another nosy busybody who didn't know enough to mind his own business.

As soon as I registered for classes, I headed for "The Strip" and found myself in a bar called "The Porthole", where a black lady sang and played the piano. Her name was Sedonia, and she sang a genre of songs that used to known as "party songs" in the old days. One of her signature tunes was called "Hot Nuts", about a peanut vendor, and she'd sing "Hot nuts, hot nuts, get'em while you can ! See that man against the wall. He ain't got no nuts at all. Hot nuts !" She'd usually point at one hapless drunk, to the relief of all the other hapless drunks in the bar. Another song was about the talents of a big burly and very talented handyman, with "hair" that reached down to the floor. I laughed and drank my beer and said to myself that this sure as hell beat the army, and I might actually learn something to boot. Like all good things, though, it came to an end. One of the professors at the college, who happened to teach political science, ran for mayor on a platform that "The Strip" had to go. He was a reformer, teaching in a college that venerated reformers, and he envisioned a sparkling new world where honkytonks were a thing of the past, replaced by art galleries and antique "shoppes" selling high priced junk, and any other establishments of an uplifting (and expensive) nature. In the end, he didn't get to finish off the strip after all. There was a fire, and with the old buildings so close together, "The Strip" burned to the ground. Sedonia moved on to another rusty old river town where she may still be singing her "party songs", or maybe just croons lullabies to her great-grandchildren. And now, on this "sad height" as the poem goes, I'd like to walk along with the dapper little man one more time, just to give him some advice right back. Latin was useful only to priests and pharmacists. But you could make good use of your Greek by hanging out with the produce men on Market Street in Chicago.

Bill Summerall's father knew Greek and Latin. Bill was a friend of ours from Michigan days. He and Tim Stott bought a sand covered farm with an old farmhouse, and moved in with their girlfriends. Stott took the old house and started working on it, while Summerall lived in a house trailer on the property. Bill said that although both of them came from Ann Arbor, he had grown up in a series of drafty, old houses and preferred the house trailer. As a child, he remembered such a draft coming in through the front door that when the wind blew, the rug lifted up in the air. Bill's dad was a scholar who ignored the more mundane aspects of life, sitting oblivious at the kitchen table while he read the classics in Latin and Greek. He earned a marginal living writing columns as a music and arts critic for the local paper. Bill and Tim had played football together on their high school team, and showed me pictures of themselves in uniform, back when they were short-haired and beardless, back when they looked so young. The Viet Nam and hippie era had arrived, though, and now the men were sporting beards and long hair, with the same degree of conformity they'd shown in the team pictures of so many years ago. I asked Tim about the Summeralls, and he told me how the entire family used to go for walks, with everyone strung out along the sidewalk, walking in order of their birth. When Bill's father left to take a job working for a paper in another city—I think that it was called an "Irish divorce" . . . his mother bought a pair of work boots and got a job tending the furnace in a boiler room. Bill got a call from this distant city telling him that his father was in a hospital, and the chances were very good that he was dying. He went to see his father, and said later that it was the only time in his father's life that Bill had seen him smile.

Bill Summerall's woman left to work for a publishing company on the West coast and Bill went back to Ann Arbor and repaired television sets; I told him I thought that sounded interesting. Back in the days when television sets had tubes there was plenty of work for repairmen, but Bill said he hated TV sets. And then he met Ella Mae. She was really creative, a lot of fun, and liked to make up songs to go with stories—like Scrooge and The Christmas Carol, that she sang while playing the guitar. She even entertained the inmates at Jackson Prison. Together they moved back up north, and rented a place. We went up to visit them, and sat around a bonfire singing one night, until Ella Mae slipped backwards into the fire and burned her butt. We slept in a greenhouse while we were there; though the view of the night sky was beautiful, all that glass made for mighty cold sleeping conditions. Ella Mae found a job tending bar, but by this time Bill had pretty much talked himself out of working and, whether it was heredity, marijuana or a combination, he kept getting more and more strange. Ella Mae finally left him, moving in with a fellow who worked as a carpenter. Ella Mae was attractive and full of energy, so it was no small wonder that the strange man on the way to college had told me to get a carpenter's card. Bill came and went in the lives of his friends and acquaintances, landing wherever he could, and came to visit us one time when we were putting an addition on the house. He stayed overnight and in the morning, after breakfast, I handed him a shovel. At the time we were digging out the footing for the foundation and it seemed to us, that since he was eating and sleeping at our house, he could help out. From the astonished look on his face, you'd have thought I slapped him. After we moved back to Rustbelt City, we heard from friends that he had gone to Ella Mae and her now husband, the carpenter, and tried to get money from them. If they'd pay him a sort of alimony, he told them, he'd be content to go away and leave the happy couple alone. Since Bill had never seen fit to ask for Ella Mae's hand in marriage, he left their home empty-handed.

We hadn't seen him in years and were somewhat, but not altogether, surprised when he showed up at our house in the country near Rustbelt with just a back pack and the clothes he had on. "Let's celebrate," I said. "I'll run in to town and get some steaks." He said that he couldn't eat anything like that. He hadn't eaten in three days, and only sporadically before that, so he had to start out easy. I couldn't remember ever missing a meal, so this was astonishing to me. Bill slept on our sofa with his shirt off, and the kids were still young enough that they crowded around while he was sleeping, to see the tattooed sailing ship that covered his chest. We told him we could get him a job at a landscape and nursery business where our son worked after school, and since a friend was storing his slide-in camper in our back yard, all we had to do was run an electric cord out to the camper and he could live there free. Nothing could induce him to stay, though, so we had a farewell outing at a local pizzeria. On my way to work the following day I dropped him off at the interstate, and he waved goodbye. That night I told my wife that I'd stuck a twenty in his back-pack and she laughed, saying, "So did I". Our son chimed in with, "I put a twenty in there, too!" We never saw or heard from Bill again.

In my college years I majored in science courses and beer drinking. At closing time at a bar up the hill from the school, I was drinking with a friend when he convinced me we could drive to Milwaukee and stay at his girlfriend's place. We were going to take his Volkswagen Beetle and surprise her; she had a job up there as a school teacher. Since he was too drunk to drive, I took the wheel and was soon careening around the curves like a race car driver. The last thing that I remember him saying was, "You sure do know how to take these curves." I was complimented on knowing just when to accelerate on the curve. The police report stated that the Volkswagen skidded three hundred and fifty feet, flipped over, and came to rest on its top with all four wheels spinning. It looked like the VW Beetle turned into a turtle on its back. With the help of a few fellow drunks who happened along, we rolled the VW upright, back on its wheels, but the top was crushed and the windshield was gone. About this time the cops came, and since we were bleeding all over our jackets, an ambulance was called and we were transported to a nearby hospital. Since I'd gotten a good blow to the head, my thinking was a little fuzzy. As soon as I got out of the ambulance, I thought I should make my escape, but got into a wrestling match with an orderly. I lost, and soon a sympathetic doctor was stitching up our heads. They gave each of us a tetanus shot, and let us go. The doctor must have seen military service, and because we were young and wearing our old army jackets, never sent either of us a bill. Yet another case where someone did me a favor, and I never got a chance to say thanks.

The police gave me a traffic ticket, but they didn't so much as smell my breath or make me walk a straight line. My guardian angels must have hovering around while the police gave us a ride back to the Volkswagen without handing out a DUI. The car surprised us by starting and running (a tribute to German engineering), but the top was so low that I had to duck my head to drive, so as not to bump the squashed roof. The only bad piece of luck was that now the snow had started, and I was shaking due to the cold, the lack of windshield, and the shock of too much beer and a head-blow. We were only thirty miles or so from making it back when we stopped at a cross-roads restaurant. Going in, we sat down and when the waitress came over, said that we'd like two cups of strong coffee. We must have looked worse than we realized, with blood still on the front of our jackets and on our heads, because she went into a case of shock almost as bad as ours. After we had some coffee and warmed up a little, we went out to the parking lot and crawled back into the car, ready to travel those last thirty miles. We got to the intersection by the restaurant when a cop pulled up and said, "Where do you think you're going in THAT?" He told us to park it, and, in the cold light of early morning the car, even to us, looked like it had been in a demolition derby for Volkswagens. We had to think of some other way to get home.

My brother got a wake-up call, and showed up with a tow bar that he'd gotten from some place. He was wearing heavy winter clothing and a scowl fearsome enough that I needed no accompanying lecture on prudence and sobriety. It was a pretty quiet ride back. After our return, the Dean of Men requested my presence in his office for a little chat. I'd seen him around campus, he was the coach of the tennis team, and maybe he'd already heard about me and my forays to "The Strip", since every time he saw me he gave me a look that said I'd probably just robbed a liquor store, and had the evidence on me. The dean had gone to divinity school, but had given up a career of saving souls in general, to concentrate on the college. He wanted to save it from evil doers, and relied on a little help from his friends, a cadre of juvenile finks, who kept him apprised of potential trouble makers. The gist of our little talk was that if he heard about me one more time (or if the newspaper gave the college a black eye by describing my exploits), he would send me packing from the school and I'd have to seek honest employment.

It could have been a lot worse, since I still had to show up for the court appearance on a charge of reckless driving. I convinced a friend (not the owner of the VW) to give me a ride to court. He probably didn't help my case any because he looked like a Chicago gangster and talked out the side of his mouth. The presiding Justice of the Peace had a two or three day growth of beard, and was wearing a shirt that looked as if he'd slept in it; in short, he looked as if he'd just crawled out from under a railroad car. But you can't tell a book by its cover, and the seedy JP only fined me thirty dollars. First a policeman had to testify, though, and he said there were a dozen beer cans on the floor behind the front seats. We hadn't been the ones to toss the beer cans there, but what could I do? If I'd said they weren't mine, the Justice of the Peace would have fined me one hundred and thirty dollars for being a liar. Apparently on the night prior to our expedition, the car had been loaned to another buddy, who'd borrowed the car to take his date to a drive-in movie From that day forward, I've always checked a car over before getting in, to see who or what might be lying in the back.

After a brief stay in the men's dorm, I moved to a rooming house owned by Mrs. Eckstrom. She lived downstairs, and that part of house resembled all I've read about the black hole of Calcutta. Roomers were not allowed to use the stove . . . even if it worked . . . but were allowed to keep cold cuts and beer in the refrigerator. Mrs. E probably hadn't used the stove since her husband died, and most likely couldn't even find it. The neighbors said that the old lady underwent a drastic change after her husband's death. She used to put out decorations at Christmas that her Mr. E had made, with even a plywood Santa in a sleigh pulled by reindeer displayed on the roof. But now she kept to herself, and for income she rented out the rooms upstairs to young students like me. The rooms were clean. There was a sign above the bathtub that read "Clean the tub when you finish with your bath." She had hearing aids, but her batteries were usually dead or dying." Is that you?" she was always asking, because I had a key to let myself in. As I walked up the creaky stairs to the second floor, she cawed like a crow, "That isn't a girl with you, is there?". It wasn't a matter of morals; she didn't want her place being placed off-limits by the college. The college hadn't inspected the house for years, or we probably would have to move back into the men's dormitory. She was usually found sitting in the parlor smoking Spud cigarettes and drinking Bullfrog beer; not the premium brands, but the cheapest way she could fuel her addictions. In the entire time that I lived there, I never saw her eating a meal of solid food. One night, after misplacing my key somewhere, I knocked and pounded on the front door for Mrs. Eckstrom to hear, but no one came. Thinking I'd have better success at the rear entrance, I went around the house to the back door, knocking and pounding again. It was a nearly fatal mistake. Mrs. E must have just put in new batteries, because she heard it now and the back door flew open. She stood there, pointing a revolver at my chest. Never in my wildest dreams did I think she owned one and, throwing up my hands in the air, I stood there shaking, as she said, squinting through the cigarette smoke, "Is that you?" It's a good thing that she was in her usual state; if she were sober, she might have killed me.

Ron Hayley lived with me in the rooming house. He'd been one of my brother's roommates in the dormitory, but after a while moved out to rent a room at Mrs. E's boarding house. In the mornings, he just refused to get up and go to class, so I'd serenade him with my guitar, banging open the door to his room and singing "Old Shep" or maybe "Riding Down the Canyon". He had less ambition and less energy than anyone that I had met before Bill Summerall. My father met Ron a few times, and he rode with my folks when they drove to Minnesota for my brother's wedding. Another of Pa's predictions gone wrong, he said of Hayley that "he'll never amount to anything". The last we heard, Ron had been written up a few times in the Arts sections of various papers, running a unique coffee house that attracted all kinds of people. He played old records of Frank Sinatra and Count Basie, among others, and served his coffee in old bone china cups picked up at auctions and junk shops. Ron must have hung out in college for six or seven years and finally, at the end of his matriculation, wasn't even taking any classes. But I finally graduated. My sheepskin was cut right out of the animal's ass.

Back in Rustbelt City there was an old tavern, the C and M, that stood on what used to be the main street of the town, before Rustbelt City moved out to gobble up the cornfields on the west side. It was a venerable old watering hole and, at one time, had even enclosed Uncle Ansgar in its murky darkness. There was a gentle old man, who also happened to be an uncle, who was in the habit of coming for a drink after he received his social security and pension check. His good-for-nothing nephew used to come in when his uncle was there, and shake him down for money. The nephew was big and mean, and he would threaten his timid little uncle until he handed over cash for the nephew's pursuits. One evening, after having enough of this treatment, when the nephew came in and made his usual demands, his uncle was ready for him. "Say your prayers," the old man told him "Cause this is your last day on earth." The nephew said, "C'mon old man. you're not goin' to do anything, fool ! Just hand over the money." And the old uncle pulled out his pistol, emptying it into the nephew while everybody in the bar watched. He ran out the back door, and threw his pistol into the dumpster. No longer could he come in to the C and M and enjoy his limited social life and his pension money. For two years the man lay low, more and more of a recluse, but his conscience tortured him. Even though he never heard a word from the police, there were plenty of witnesses, and his fingerprints were all over the gun. Finally, when he could stand it no longer, he went to the police station, to unburden himself and get the memory of the crime off his chest. He walked in and approached the desk, pouring out the cares of his heart to the officer. The policeman told him, "Oh yeah, that guy. I remember the murder. That guy had been giving us nothing but trouble for years." The cop said that he hadn't heard a word the old man said, and to get the hell out of the station. All these years he had suffered for nothing, as is the way with most suffering. The uncle was only one of many who were glad to see the bully's demise. Crime isn't always punished, nor is virtue always rewarded.

It seems that the big fish are far out in the middle of the lake. It's too easy to think the best fish might be hanging out by the boat ramp, and anyway, popular opinion has it that anything worth while can only be obtained by hard work. The family has always liked fishing, so I built a boat in Pa's basement. We called it the peapod, because it could carry so many "peas" and, riding high in water, looked just like its namesake. When we went to take the boat out and launch it, we remembered why Noah built his ark outside. Just as in all the boat-building jokes, we could barely get it out of the basement, and the bottom took a pretty good scraping. When I'd painted my motorcycle years before, a rich Mediterranean green-blue, the color of the 1949 Nash Rambler, I'd gone to the same store where I went now, to pick out a bright blue color for the boat. Except for a scraped bottom, it surely was shiny when Pa, Edwin and I left for the backwaters, armed with all our fishing equipment and the usual high hopes. An old black lady sat on the bank watching us put in the shiny new boat. She was holding an old cane pole with only a few feet of line. She couldn't heave the line out as far into the water as we could, with our spin casting reels and flexible fiberglass poles. But she was comfortable sitting underneath a shade tree, and she could go to her car and get something to eat or drink whenever she felt like it.

We spent a long day out in the sun, burnt red as lobsters. There was plenty of exercise as we spent our time rowing around looking for the "deep holes" where the big fish hung out, rather than just fishing. When we finally pulled the peapod up to the bank and beached it, the lady with the cane pole smiled at us. She didn't have to say a thing, looking at our empty stringers. She pulled up another bluegill, dangling from the four feet of line at the end of her pole, removed the hook and plopped the fish into a wire basket she pulled up from the water. It was full of sunfish and bluegills. We struggled to put the wooden boat on the car carriers, and slowly put our gear away. Although I didn't think of it at the time, I wish that I'd walked over and wished that lady *bon apetit*.

This was during a period when the rivers were so polluted that they were devoid of game fish. Carp were the only fish that survived, and sometimes the tiny black bullheads we called "spikes." We made dough balls to fish for carp by mixing flour and corn meal, then boiling it in water. Sometimes my wife would add exotic flavorings to the mix, but plain old vanilla seemed to work best. Dough balls were called "*munka*" bait and one of the guys I worked with said the word meant bread dough in Polish also. The dough had a hard time staying on the hook, so we used treble hooks, sometimes adding cotton balls to help keep the dough on. Carp were wily and hard to catch, often stealing the dough ball from the line, and when you reeled in your line there'd be nothing on the hook. Although I threw the smaller fish back, I kept the big ones. When we were first married and I was working midnights, I used to go to the river on my way home, fishing until I'd unwind and get tired. Too tired to clean my catch one morning, I brought them home, a couple of lively fifteen pounders, ran some water into the bathtub and threw them in. I figured that first I'd sleep, and could clean them when I got up. Gone on some errands when I got home, later that day my wife decided on a bath, and let out a scream when she found two huge scaly fish in our bathtub, their big lips sucking scum off the water in the tub.

We tried everything to make carp edible: Italian recipes with tomato sauce, English recipes, French, and Oriental recipes. Nothing worked. If you soaked them overnight in brine and smoked them, though, they weren't too bad. Usually I ate the smoked carp as a snack, with beer to wash it down, which no doubt enhanced that carpy flavor. I'd built a sort of smoke house at my folks' place using concrete blocks, an old wooden pig feeder, a metal drum for the fire, and tile to carry the smoke and warmth upwards to the smoke house. The carp was placed on racks in the smoke house, over a fire built in the drum; the drum had an opening that could be used as a damper. Since there had to be more smoke than heat, it took a long time to smoke the fish. Once Pa and I decided to go fishing while we had a batch of carp smoking. We left Ma to tend the fire and keep the smoking process going while we were gone, but on our return we found the smoke house burned to the ground. I was heartbroken, but Pa had a funny look on his face, the look that said he should have known better. No doubt we should have taken Ma along with us, and smoked the fish some other time.

The polluted waters provided us not only with carp, but also with snapping turtle. I brought one home; it was a big snapper, and had a shell that was a few feet in diameter. I asked my wife to try making turtle soup. She looked up a recipe and did the best she could, the result being a sort of vegetable turtle. My wife set out the bowls, one for each of us and smaller bowls for kids (I think we had three at the time) and ladled out the soup. Starting to slurp our way through the soup course, we noticed the broth being somewhat gritty, and black sludge began to appear in the bowls. My wife cried out, "Stop"! She hurriedly scooped up the bowls from in front of the kids and whisked them away. I was left sitting at the table, my bowl still before me, trying to decide whether or not I wanted to eat the rest of it; you know, waste not want not. My wife didn't hesitate to spare our kids the polluted soup, but I was on my own.

All work and no play made me a dull boy, so I went with my buddy Rick to the harness races. It could be an expensive hobby, but then most hobbies are. There was a charge to park your car, and then you tipped the attendant in order to get a spot close to a tunnel that led into the track. Then there was money to get in to the track, an extra charge for the club house, and then more money for box seats, the ones high up by the windows so you could look down and see the trotters and pacers as they crossed the finish line. Even then the spending wasn't over since you had to buy a program, and how could you go the race track without one of Lucky Laughton's tip sheets? Finally settled in your place, you discover that you really could use a cup of coffee and a cigarette. It seems pretty cheap to get your coffee and to be having so much fun, when the poor lady behind the coffee counter is making chump change, so you hand her a five for the coffee. But what a thrill, with the lights shining down on the track, the drivers perched high on their sulkies, wearing their colorful outfits and warming up their noble steeds who make that welcome "clip-clop" sound you've been anticipating. And the drivers seem like so many happy bandits, winking and blinking at each other, looking forward to another night of screwing the patrons and raising their blood pressure. Down in the cheap seats, that Rick called "the boiler room", it was especially tense. Disgruntled bettors were tearing up tickets, cursing and yelling at the women who'd had the bad sense to come with them to the track. When the money is gone, anyone within range is a target for the loser's bad judgment. I only passed through the boiler room on my way out to the car.

Rick and I were watching and betting on the races one night, when he pointed out something in the program to me. "Look at this next race. What a laugh. Look at this horse, Coronary Carrie". The cheap claimer had looked terrible in the program, and I can't remember whether he'd ever won a race. Someone must have owned him for a tax loss. Now that Rick pointed it out, I looked up at the tote board, and there was Coronary Carrie at ninety-nine to one. "Who would bet on a horse like that?" Rick asked. Then we heard that famous, "And they're off!". Slicker than shit, Coronary Carrie streaked to the lead. Could this be the same horse that we read about in the program, with times so slow that he'd still be running around the track when the race was over? I thought that the horses were all tattooed so officials could tell them apart. We crumpled up our tickets for that race and threw them on the floor. Men were walking around, stooped over and picking up discarded tickets to see if anyone might have mistakenly thrown away a winner. These men were known as "flippers" but I doubt if any flipper that night found a ticket for Coronary Carrie. Somebody was probably heading for their safety deposit box the next morning, carrying a manila envelope stuffed with cash, but it sure wasn't me. We turned on the radio that night on the way home, and what should we hear but . . . "Zip-a-di-doo-da Zip-a-di—ay. My oh my what a wonderful day". "What the hell kind of a day is this?" Rick asked. "It sure as hell isn't zip-a-di-doo-da." But he never gave up. In spite of choosing a hobby even more discouraging than fishing for carp, he was hooked on the horses and said that, when he died, he wanted to be cremated and have his ashes strewn on the back stretch. And he wanted horse angels to fly him to his rest, hopefully a little faster than Coronary Carrie could run: the real one, that is.

Before I was ever old enough to go to the race track, I was exposed to horses at The Sweet Shop, a place in downtown Rustbelt with a soda fountain. Uncle Julian had promised me a banana split, so I jumped into his 1936 Plymouth. The whole car smelled of the pipe tobacco that nearly covered up his body odor. Even now pipe tobacco is pleasant to me, bringing memories of Uncle Julian and how we kids always gave him a can of Sir Walter Raleigh every Christmas. If we had even more money we'd give him a can of a more aromatic mixture from the Wally Frank's catalog. As we drove toward town, I could picture the big banana split waiting for me, and only for me, not even having to share it with anyone. Living out in the country with our animals and our gardens, we had plenty of food, but treats like a banana split came rarely, if at all. Uncle Julian puffed away on his pipe while he drove along, tramping down hard on the accelerator with his big black "police shoes". They were just old "clod hoppers" to us, but Uncle Julian wore them to work and, for Saturday nights, he'd polish them up for his formal night at the movies. Like live embers from a campfire, sparks flew from his pipe and burned BB sized holes in his woolen pants. One of the fellows I knew told me that he often saw Uncle Julian drinking beer at the Basement Bar, and thought it was disgraceful that the family didn't help him out and buy him some decent clothes, as poor as he seemed to be. Years later, when we went to clean out Uncle Julian's house after he died, we found all of the clothes that we had bought for him. The flannel shirts and pajamas were still in their plastic wrappers, the trousers still had their creases, and a whole lot of sympathetic bar patrons had been buying him beers.

The Sweet Shop was located on one of the main streets, down near the railroad overpass. I'd never been in there before, and was impressed with the big booths and their black seats, and the long marble counter at the soda fountain. There was no one to be seen in the booths, and when Uncle Julian sat me up on one of the high stools in front of the curved necks of the soda dispensers, I was the only one at the counter. A swarthy man in a white shirt that barely covered his abundant crop of curly black chest hair, came out from in back and, walking up to Uncle Julian he shook his hand, asking "What can I do for the kid?" Uncle Bob told him that I'd like a banana split. Shaking his head, the swarthy man said he might have a few bananas but there no ice cream in the store. Soon Uncle Julian and the man, the owner of what I had hoped was an ice cream parlor, left me sitting alone at the counter. They passed by a long row of empty booths, disappearing into the back rooms. I could hear a radio playing, and could make out the excited voice of an announcer as he called the race. Even a little country boy knew that Pucker Up was probably the name of a horse and not a flavor of ice cream. After a time, Uncle Julian came out of the back room and said, "Let's go". He told me that maybe we'd come back again, and the next time Mr. Swarthy just might have ice cream. But if he asked me, I must have turned him down. My first banana split was bought with my own money It didn't taste nearly as good as the one I'd anticipated, years before, at the marble counter of The Sweet Shop.

Religious training started long before formal schooling, and being good Lutherans my folks enrolled me in Sunday School around the age of three. There was a Sunday school class especially for little guys, with even miniature wooden chairs about the right size for a leprechaun. Once when I fell off my chair, Mrs. Erickson plopped me down hard on my seat, like a sudsy shirt back into the wash tub. "I know her," Uncle Julian said, when I described her to him. "She's got a big bay window." He probably knew Mrs. Erickson long before, when they both were young. She was big and round, and always wore black; she must have had a closet full of black dresses, because I never saw her wear anything else. Each Sunday we attended, we were handed a colorful card picturing events from the Bible. God found His way into most of the pictures, of course, and He was usually pictured as a powerful old man hovering above the ground, dressed in a white robe with a long white beard to match, signifying his advanced age. He looked a lot like the Greek and Roman statues, in a way, but had the decency to keep His genitals covered.

I was easily frightened as a kid, so I didn't like the card that showed the disobedient people being bitten by snakes. They had melted down their gold and jewelry to make a golden calf and on the card, even though they were sorry and raised their arms in supplication, the disobedient folks were bitten anyway. Moses was standing above, glowering down at them and holding his engraved rock tablets; and I just knew that he was saying, "I told you so." We had small envelopes for Sunday School, to get us used to the idea of giving money to the church. Usually our folks would send us with a nickel in our envelope; more if you were rich, but maybe only a penny if you weren't. On a corner near the church was a drug store where Pa liked to stop, on the way to church, to pick up the Sunday paper. Larry Angelhoff and Barry Gilligan liked to go there too, after they opened their envelopes, shook out their nickels, and turned in empties when the offering plate was passed. Since soda was still a nickel, they went to the drug store for a candy bar or a bottle of pop after Sunday School. Damn! why didn't I have the guts to defy the grumpy old man in the robe, and spend my nickel for a treat? Besides, there weren't any venomous snakes around Rustbelt.

Although organized religion left me cold, spirituality was another thing altogether. During the period when I tended bar and we tried subsistence living, life was pressing in on me from all sides, and I mentioned to a few people that I wanted to sign up for a monastery: no bills to pay, just tending the garden, walking the grounds, stopping for food and prayers at the proscribed hours. One afternoon when I came in to work at the bar, I found a little eight inch statue of a monk in a cassock. He was placed on the counter behind the bar, and had a note with my name on it pinned to his cassock. With a big smile on his face, and his tonsured head, he looked the image of the peace and contentment I was seeking. When I picked him up to examine the gift, someone yelled, "Push on his head, push on his head!" So I did. His robe parted and his dick popped out, and my trip to the monastery was put on indefinite hold.

Tony was my brother-in-law, my wife's brother, and for the last twelve years of his life, though he lived at home with his dad for part of the year and went to a sheltered workshop there, he stayed with us for the rest of the time. With no sheltered workshop where we were living, he just hung out with us and was a great help on our little farm. Back then, not many folks at the workshop, or at the special school he'd attended before that, had a formal diagnosis; Tony was just considered "retarded".

He loved cars, and could memorize the license plate numbers on them; he knew the names of all the models of all the cars by their shapes. His big hobby was putting together plastic car models, and we always kidded him that he was "gluetiqing" the cars, and was going to pass out some day from the glue fumes. We always knew when he was busy with a model; the whole house smelled like the solvent in his glue.

We called him an instant bullshit detector. Tony could cut through the nonsense in any situation or conversation. When I was first going with his sister I'd come up to visit and was going to stay overnight. Since there were also five boys in the family, the conversation came up at the supper table about where I should sleep. Tony had the solution. "Why doesn't he sleep with Sis? He's her friend," he said. If he didn't like something, Tony went into the bathroom and grumbled. Our daughters reminded him to change his under shorts, and when he forgot to clean his glasses, we'd remind him that the problem wasn't his eyesight, but the dirty glasses. He took great pride in washing the dishes, when it was his turn, but was indignant when reminded about leaving food specks on the plates. Sometimes the kids would put their ear up to the bathroom door to hear the complaints, and laughed when they heard him complaining about the food, wondering "Why don't they get some Hamburger Helper?". We were probably low on money at the time, and the food products advertised on television weren't in our budget.

At one time we had a large garden, and he went out to pick some green beans. Tony wanted to help, but squatting down in the row he just scratched his head, muttering to himself about whether each bean was ready to be picked or not, torturing himself with indecision. My father, up visiting at the time, said that short people were better at weeding and picking anyway, since they didn't have so far to bend over. Tony, a tall man himself, slapped his knee and just laughed and laughed, "That's a good one, Mr. Hallenberg!" Samuel Carter stopped at our house to warm up, on his way back from town; in a period between vehicles, he was on foot. Tony was by himself, and later, when I told Samuel that Tony was "retarded", he said. "There ain't nothin' wrong with that dude. I talked with him for hours." And it was true, Tony was a great talker, knowledgeable in a lot of areas, and with his bullshit detector in place he could always liven up a conversation. His motor control was awkward at times, though, and not thinking I sent him out with a little hand saw to cut out a pesky branch in the driveway. The branch was still there, but he came in the house with a badly bleeding finger. I took him in to the doctor right away; he joked with him, cleaned him up, slapped him on the back and gave him a tetanus shot. I don't think that we ever got a bill.

Tony's nemesis was our pigs. We used to buy them as "feeder pigs" after they were weaned in the spring, and fed them up until cold weather, when they weighed in at over two hundred pounds. Then we butchered them. Tony often fed the pigs, and they knew that he was afraid of them. As soon as he stepped over the electric fence to the pig yard, they'd come up to him and sniff his pants cuffs with their dirty snouts. It drove him wild.

We had plans to build a little mud room off the back door, where we could hang our coats and take off our boots when we came in from the outside. Although it was a good idea, the mud room never got finished. We did pour a concrete slab for it, though, using our little one-third yard cement mixer. and, proud of our days' work, we decided to treat the family to a pizza, and left Tony and the kids while we went into town to pick it up. We had a few beers while waiting for the pizza to bake, returning home in a happy mood, the pizza in the truck. I could see something was wrong as we pulled up the lane, though, as the kids were milling around and Tony was looking at the cement slab and scratching his head. We walked up to the almost dried cement and saw the little spiked footprints of pigs trailing through the cement, with Tony's large footprints in apparent hot pursuit. The electric fence must have gone down, and in a vain attempt to get them back in the pen, the kids and Tony chased them through the cement. The pigs weren't too far away, though, just like a pig to stick around for the next meal. After all the torment, Tony got his revenge at butchering time. He took great delight in eating the pigs, and laughed when we told him that the pork chops came from the pig who always sniffed his leg. When we lived in Michigan, we cut up the pigs on our kitchen table, which was actually a big picnic table we'd moved into the house. I wasn't sure about the cuts, so I had a book open, with a picture illustrating how to cut up the pigs, reading as I cut and sawed. We took the legs to a town about twenty miles away, where they smoked hams. After we moved back, we still raised a few feeder pigs, bringing the "three little pigs" home in the back of a Gremlin, but when they were ready, we just called up a small town butcher shop that sent out a truck, picked up the pigs and called us when they were ready.

Tony died trying to cross the street. He was on the way home from the sheltered workshop when one of his friends called to him from across the street, and he didn't see the delivery truck. Tony never went anywhere without his glasses, but strangely enough, he forgot them that day; they were sitting at home on the dresser. At his wake, an elderly monsignor from town, long retired but still saying mass once a day, stopped by to tell us how lucky Tony was. Though Monsignor had been trying to get in for years, Tony just leaned over and fell right into heaven.

In a lifetime of startling successes and crushing defeats, none of these things seem worth a lot of thought on reaching senior citizen status. Only the sights and sounds remain as real memories, and the accomplishments, or the lack of them, are the shadowy things of nightmares. I read in an article by an American playwright who was dying of cancer, that the thing that stuck in her memory was the smell of flannel pajamas. And our old neighbor and friend Ned Walker said, when he was in the hospital with prostate cancer, that he only wondered whether he'd hurt anybody. The triumphs were nullified by defeats that followed, and the tragedies were softened by the passing of time. One of the greatest memories for me was sitting in my high chair in the kitchen, when we still lived in the city. My mother and Little Grandma were heating peaches in a big stock pot, and they speared the steaming hot peaches with a knife, setting them aside to cool. Then they skinned the peaches, cut them into slices, and placed them on the tray of my highchair. What a treat! They were still warm and sweet when I stuck the slices in my mouth. The same thing happened when they were canning tomatoes. I thought that the entire world existed just to bring me treats.

When we lived in the country and the kids were little, we bought a small metal incubator. We had laying hens and a rooster, so we saved the fertilized eggs and put them into the incubator in the bathroom, where we faithfully turned the eggs every day. The chickens were given to us by a friend when we moved to Michigan, so we had a variety of breeds. The rooster was a Rhode Island Red, and the hens were Barred Rocks, Leghorns, Buff Orpingtons, and a few others. The little chicks hatched, appropriately enough, on Easter Sunday, and it was a thrill to peek through the window of the incubator and see them peck their way out of the shells. They grew up to be the strangest looking chickens you ever saw, with their coats of many-feathered colors. They went under a brooder stove that we set up in the attached garage that turned into the living room, and became the healthiest chickens we had ever raised. I don't believe that any of the little chicks died. Not at all like Mrs. Golden who lived on the road into town. She had what, at one time, was a two story house, but the upper story fell apart and gradually went down until she now lived in a one story bungalow. She raised chickens that were truly "range hens", except that their range was out onto the road. When people drove by, they quite often ran over a hen. If the person had any conscience at all, they would stop and pay her for the loss of an egg producer. I think the old lady raised chickens mostly for their income as road kill. It's hard to say whether she ate them or not after she was paid for the loss.

When Grandpa Hallenberg came over on Sundays to eat dinner, he and Little Grandma spoke in Swedish. They were divorced, and he lived by himself in a tiny house with one bedroom, built by Grandpa and his boys on a lot next door to Uncle Ansgar's. Both of their properties were more like a couple of acres instead of small lots. And there was no drinkable water, only a pitcher pump on the kitchen sink that went to a shallow well of surface water. We had one like that in our barn in Michigan. To sink down a well you use a well point with a copper screen to keep out the debris, and hammer it down with a sledge hammer, adding sections of pipe as you go. I got ours down to about fifteen feet. There was a privy behind Grandpa's house that had morning glory vines climbing up a trellis on the sides, and a few ramshackle outbuildings that Uncle Bob used for a garage when he took the place over after grandpa died.

Grandpa died way too young, and I wish that he would have been around while I was growing up so that I could get his slant on life. The only thing that I remember him saying was, "You kids are soooo intelliyent." He ate his peas with a knife, and Pa said that once he pushed down so hard on the plate that he broke off the blade on the kitchen knife. He was the stuff of legend in the family, and not all of it was complimentary. Grandpa had a habit of stabbing a potato with a knife, and then sticking the whole potato in his mouth. It worked all right most of the time, but at one meal the potato got caught in his throat. He gave a mighty cough to dislodge the potato, and when it came out it flew all the way across the table. He never did own a car, so that when he went shopping, one of the boys would have to take him. Ma told me, when I was older, that she thought he was eccentric. He carried a gunny sack with him when he went shopping, and as he picked things up at the grocery store and elsewhere, he just threw everything into the gunny sack and slung it over his back. It usually worked satisfactorily except for a fishing trip with Pa and his two brothers. There was a lot of preparation for a fishing trip. First they had to collect minnows, soft-shell crabs, and hellgrammites. They also had a lot of beer which grandpa carried in the usual gunny sack slung over his back. But one time grandpa got a cramp in his arm and dropped the sack, breaking every one of the bottles before they could drink their "bottle bass".

I had to be less than five years old when I sat in the tiny, cramped kitchen on Davison Street on mornings when my father didn't have to work. A little Bakelite plastic radio sat on a ledge and we listened to the fifteen minute live shows that came from a radio station in Chicago. It wasn't taped and there was no nine second delay, so whatever happened came over the airwaves. Arkie the Arkansas woodchopper sang his songs while people in the studio tried to make him laugh so he couldn't finish his songs. One of my favorites was a song about the good little boy who always held the lantern while his mother chopped the wood. Then there was Lulu Belle and Skyland Scotty, who sang about how they were "goin' back to where they come from". I had a record of theirs, but loaned it out to a friend and never saw it again. Rex Allen sang songs about cowboys, and he had a deep, rich bass voice when he sang "to de-roolem, to de-rialem, to ride em, to roam". But he left the station to go to Hollywood, where he tried to be another drug store cowboy like Gene Autry or Roy Rogers. He traveled around the country to promote his first movie, and we went to see him in person at the one of the movie theatres down town. In the movie he beat up on the "owl hoots", and when the movie was over, he appeared in person on the stage in his spiffy clean outfit and played a song on the guitar. It seems, in retrospect, that he should have stayed at the radio station. In spite of his booming voice he surprised me by being a small man about my size. America's taste was changing, and movies required something more sophisticated than a fight over the rights to a water hole. Even Roy and Gene were having troubles promoting their movies, so they didn't need a new cowboy. At one time there was Johnny Mack Brown, Lash LaRue, Hopalong Cassidy, and even a black cowboy star whose name I've forgotten.

You'd be wrong if you thought that I didn't have childhood worries. My father sat there in the little kitchen and told me how he had been docked at work. I didn't know what that meant, but it sounded serious. I found out later that he was only late by fifteen minutes, and the foundry took a few bucks out of his paycheck.

No doubt it was necessary to show up for the company picnics, but I can only remember going one time. Once was enough, because my eyes must have been as big as saucers, watching people the likes of which I'd never seen before. Oh sure, we had plenty of eccentric relatives in the family, but there was always a certain reticence and restraint in our comportment. At the picnic wooden tables were set up in a rectangle, and inside there were men in white aprons, handing out bottles of beer as fast as they could. A group of black guys were wandering around and trying to collect a little spare change by singing what I thought was a spiritual. I couldn't understand the words, but it sounded like "do law. do law". A lot of people wandered around staggering drunk, even though it was early in the afternoon. My father stepped up to the booth, and at another man's urging, he drank a beer. I had never seen him drink before, and it was understood in the family that alcohol was something akin to poison. Pa was never violent, but after he had a few more beers a drunk staggered up, and Pa kicked him in the seat of the pants. And, of course, the women in my life . . . Ma and Little Grandma . . . were usually washing dishes, canning food and cooking. But I saw that some women at the picnic took a jollier approach to life. Some of the factory workers and their mates were lolling around on the grass near the beer tent, and one lady was laughing as she took her husband to the car. He was drunk and seemed to be sick. They must not have lived very far from the park, because she was back in a hurry, laughing that she had dropped off her husband (I hoped not in the street somewhere.) She found, in short order, another man to smooch and was just as affectionate as if he were her husband . . . perhaps, even more so. I think that the party was winding down when the big boss came out with the entertainment, a polka band, and he started singing along with the accordion player: "God Bless America.". The big boss led the singing. He had a big round belly poking obscenely out of his short sleeved shirt, where some of the buttons were missing, and he had a bald head with just a little fringe of hair around the ears. He reared back and bawled out the lyrics to the song while somebody poured beer over his head. It seemed to me sacrilegious to sing a patriotic song, drunk and with beer running down your face. It was my first and last foundry picnic.

Our oldest daughter says that when times are bad, she imagines and transports herself to her grandparents' farm, to the view from the bathroom window. The bathroom was on the landing between the first and second floors, and was small, with a steam radiator that kept it warm even in the coldest of winters. She remembers the scene, looking out the window and down to the tarpaper covered chicken houses and the little barn, and out across the fields to the cottonwood trees with their leaves shimmering in the breeze. I like to think about sitting in the kitchen, looking past the apple and pear trees, and remembering when there was still a cow pasture on the east side of the house. The sun would be coming up over Dolander's house on the far side of the field, and bobwhites sang. Ma described all these things to me in letters, after I'd left them behind to go on to school and to the army.

And then I returned to the farm, long after, and went for a walk; my cousin's blond hair was still caught in the barbed wire fence in the back where our hut used to be. Memory sometimes makes things from the past seem a whole lot better than they were at the time. When Ma was close to ninety, I mentioned the chickens that we used to have and reminded her how she used to carry water to the chicken houses in five gallon calf feed buckets. "I hated those birds," she said. What a shock! I just assumed, since she never complained, that she was fond of the egg route and those old laying hens.

When we were little, Ma read to my brother and me before we went to sleep at night. There was a book about King Arthur and his Round Table, but I don't remember hearing about Queen Guinevere and her love life, so I figure that Ma probably thought that it was best to omit that chapter. We had Uncle Arthur's Bedtime Stories, which were religious in nature, and a janitor in one of the chemical plants where I worked told me that it was a Baptist book that he'd had as a kid, growing up in the South, down on the Mississippi Delta. The other books that Ma read from were Grimm's Fairy Tales and Aesop's Fables. But the one story that remained with me was the story about Peter Puckle and the Whippity Elves. Peter Puckle was walking along minding his own business when he passed a hollowed-out tree that was crying, "Let me out. Please let me out." There were little elves entrapped inside a hollow part of the tree behind jail bars made of cobwebs. They seemed so pitiful and sad that Peter Puckle swept aside the cobwebs and let out the elves. Of course, they proved to be not at all the harmless and pitiful things they seemed to be as long as they were contained. They ran through the town, causing mayhem and committing all sorts of felonies. Like most of these stories for children, Peter showed remorse and a great deal of grief, even before he had to put on a show for the judge.

Nobody seems to walk anymore. Even kids in high school drive to school in cars that I still can't afford. There was a guy, I think his nickname was Pooch, who walked all over Rustbelt City's downtown carrying a shoebox. I always wondered what he was carrying in that box. How could you make a living carrying around a shoe box? Now there is nothing left in downtown Rustbelt City except offices for lawyers and title insurance companies. Back when my brother and I walked along the road to school, Ma told us to always walk on the left side of the road or else the angels wouldn't watch over us. We were supposed to keep an eye peeled for the cars coming and get off the road. And, when we lived in the Michigan countryside, my wife and I and all four kids walked, this time down rows of asparagus, cutting the spears and hoping to make our fortune by hard work.

It all started when we bought a pre-smashed pick-up truck, since at that time we couldn't afford anything better. We took Bill Summerall with us to look at a truck that was advertised for sale in the local paper. The truck had been involved in a dispute with a tree, and consequently its front was smashed and one of the headlights hung down like a dislocated eye. Bill's presence should have been a warning, but we bought the truck and drove it away. I used some duct tape on the headlights. One of our neighbors said he always knew that it was us driving by, because the lights shone on top of his pine tress instead of down on the road. But it would do for a farm truck. We hauled manure from a stable to enrich our garden, even though the rear shocks broke off and the truck really sat low under a load. The windshield was cracked, but if you squinted you could see through it, and besides, who needed a windshield on the farm?

We rented some extra land that was planted in asparagus. It looked as if we might be "sitting pretty" for the coming winter, and we would have been if the darn expenses hadn't rolled in. The soil was sandy, perfect for asparagus and a local farmer took care of the field for us with weed killer. When the asparagus was ready, the entire family went to the field to harvest it. We cut the asparagus with knives, and threw the spears into buckets, bushel baskets and finally into the back of the truck. Even the youngest, who was probably two years old at the time, wandered up and down the rows with a little bucket of his own. The sun was bright and the day was hot, so my wife solved the problem by removing her shirt. In fact, we all removed our shirts. I noticed that the rural mailman went past our field more than once. When we finished picking, we crossed the sand road to where there were woods and a branch of the river flowing through. During the happy hippy days someone had built a cabin on the property. No doubt it was after reading Thoreau, but now there was no one living there and the place was abandoned. We took off our clothes and cooled down by swimming in the cold water.

After returning to the farm with a full load of asparagus, there was nothing left to do but drink beer and take the truck to the local cannery. I think that the cannery was paying about fifty cents a pound at the time, so there was no reason to stint on the beer. My wife took off for the cannery while I stayed home with the kids, and, wanting to finish the job, she took the main highway instead of the back roads. Of course, this was the day that the state police came to our county and set up one of their random vehicle check points. They motioned the truck over, and with no escape route in sight, my wife had no choice but to pull into the checking area. No headlights, no brakes, no shocks, no solid windshield and, for us, no luck. Ticket in hand, my wife went on to the cannery, parked at the loading dock, and was promptly backed into by the truck ahead of her. When the other driver got out he approached the truck, looked it over and, scratching his head, asked, "Lady, can you tell where I hit you?" The missus went to court, and all the money from that day's asparagus harvest went to pay the fine; we were still out the money for the beer. Par for the course: a few thorns, a few roses, and a lot of chaos in between.